Tequila Midnight

A Jessica Watts Southwest Suspense Novel

Kathryn Dodson

Renegade Reads

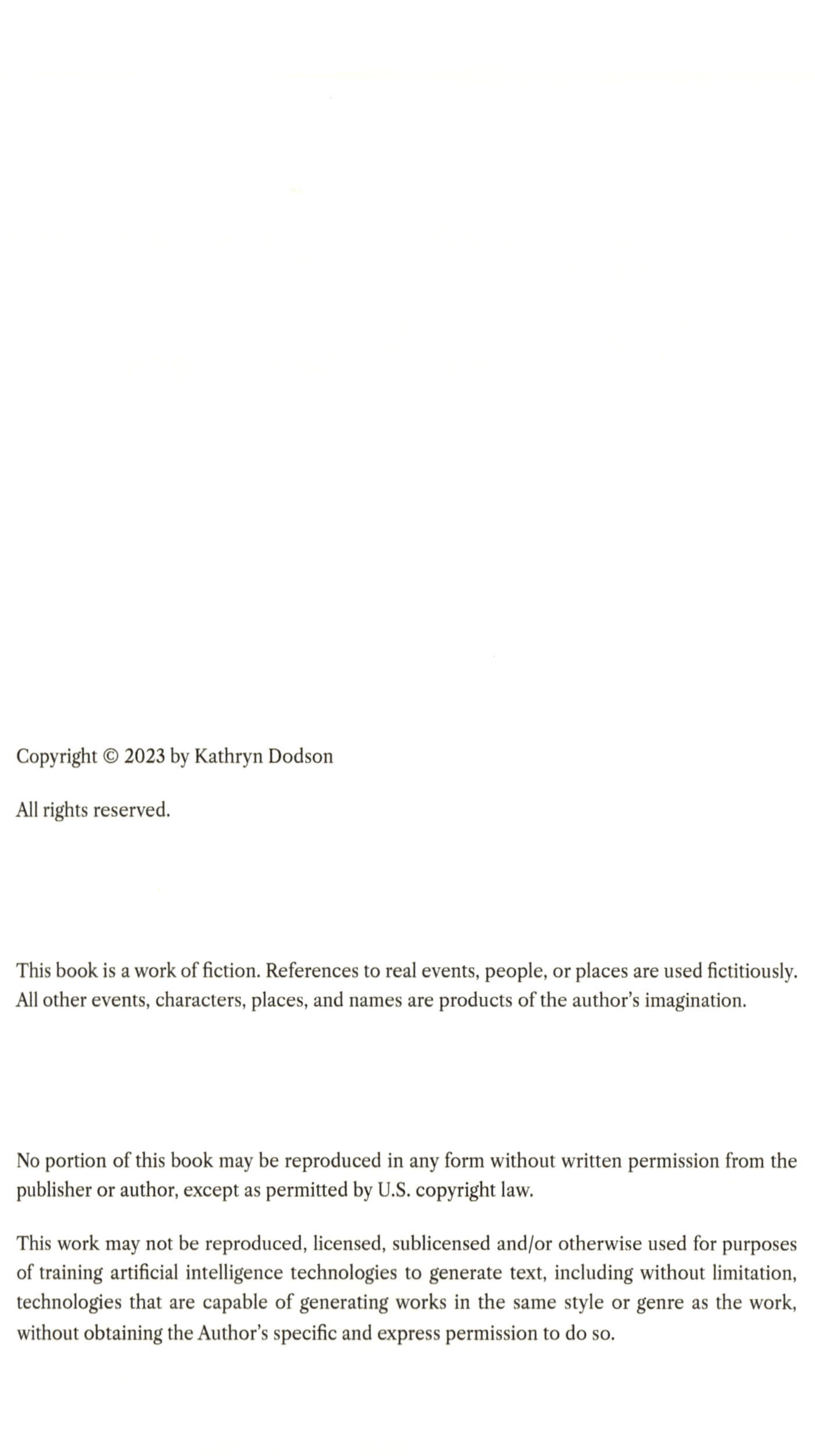

Contents

Chapter 1

J essica crept down a dirt road blackened by a starless night. Thirty miles south of the Texas border, houses made of plywood and corrugated metal lay strewn about the desert like tumbleweeds, and she wandered the tire-rutted path between them.

The crack of gunshot blasted through the night.

She leaped from the road and slid against the nearest house for cover. Doors and windows closed with a thud or a creak. Lights winked out in the nearby homes, then silence surrounded her.

Residual heat from the day's sun still warmed the wall she pressed into, as she hoped to become invisible. The night had grown cool, and she wished she could stay in the relative comfort of the building's heat and protection. But she'd come here to make a delivery for an important client, which might mean figuring out the origin of the gunshot, and where the bullet had gone.

Hopefully, the shots came from some idiot celebrating his kid's birthday or his own manhood. Worst case, one end of the gun belonged to someone in the drug trade, a fairly common occupation on the US/Mexico border.

A hit of danger washed through her, clenching her gut with dread but prickling the skin on her arms with excitement. She shouldn't be here, needed to figure out how her job had gone from fancy industrial real estate deals in executive offices to dropping off paperwork after hours in a part of town so isolated GPS didn't know it existed. She glanced at the manila envelope clenched in her hand. What kind of crap job had Tomás gotten her into?

The envelope must have crumpled when she heard the gunshot. She smoothed it against her thigh as best she could. She had a job to do. In her line of work, not delivering killed careers. She stepped back into the street.

Light shone through a window a couple of blocks away—that had to be her destination. Tomás's guys wouldn't have been frightened by the gunshot. Hell, it had probably been their gun.

She crept forward, taking her time and aiming for quiet. She reached the edge of the property and tucked herself behind the corner of the house to listen, scraping against the rough stucco. It was a solid house for this neighborhood.

Voices drifted toward her, and she froze.

"She'll be here."

Jessica recognized Tomás, sounding lazy in the amped-up night. Earlier in the day, he'd told her he wouldn't be at the drop site. Clearly, he'd lied. She fingered the packet again. She'd watched him sign the piece of paper and slip it into this very envelope before sealing it and handing it to her. Nothing but paper and ink. She'd never transport drugs or anything else that would get her in real trouble. So, why was he here?

"No creo."

Low and raspy, Jessica didn't recognize the second man's voice, but he'd probably spent a lifetime sucking on Marlboros. Whoever he was, he didn't believe she'd show up. He clearly didn't know her—she always finished her jobs. It was the only way to get the next one.

She stepped away from the house, ready to approach the door. After a single step, the sound of a chair scraping across the floor floated through the open window. She paused, breathless, willing herself not to make a sound.

"I'm telling you she'll be here. And I can trust her not to open the envelope. Unlike you guys. Text me when it's over."

Quick footsteps, then a door opened and shut. There must be a back entrance. She heard the roar of an engine, then tires crunching on gravel. Probably Tomás's enormous black Escalade.

What kind of trap had Tomás set for her, and why? She had carefully developed her reputation as a cross-border real estate broker and jack-of-all-trades. She had earned the trust of people in high places on both sides of the border. When they needed a document delivered or money—she preferred not to know as long as it wasn't drugs–Jessica got the call. It could be a real ego stroke. And it could land you in a Mexican shantytown in the middle of the night.

She straightened her shoulders and breathed deeply, if quietly, before stepping forward. She paused just before the window and glanced inside.

A man stared back at her.

The surprise shocked her to her core, but she slipped on her poker face as quickly as possible, squinting to look tough and hoping he hadn't noticed her moment of fear.

"Hola." Jessica nodded at him.

The man didn't say anything but turned and opened the door. A shaft of light spilled through and illuminated the dusty street.

"Pase," smokey voice commanded.

Jessica passed through the door and into a brightly lit room filled with five men, the one at the door and three seated in metal folding chairs under bad paintings of Jesus and Mary. The fifth man reclined in a bulky wooden club chair with dirty orange and green cushions straight out of 1975.

He was probably the ugliest man she'd ever seen. Dark, mottled skin, a nose that had been punched one time too many, thinning hair draped across his dome in strips. Even uglier was the gun resting near his crotch. She almost laughed when she imagined him accidentally shooting himself there. The image kept any fear at bay. Their scare tactics wouldn't work with her. She'd been on her own a long time and had built an impenetrable wall of bravery brick-by-brick. This was the last guy who'd get past it.

"I have a package for you." Jessica tried for a bored tone.

"¿No habla español? The ugly man's eyes peered up at her.

"Poquito. Just a little." Her standard response. She spoke Spanish like a native, but rarely let anyone know, especially on midnight deals that smelled like danger. More than once, those around her had been stupid enough to assume she told them the truth and had casually started spilling secrets, thinking their use of Spanish would protect them.

"Give it to me." He held his hand out.

She paused before handing him the envelope. Usually, she consummated deals in a boardroom or at a country club table. She greased the wheels, made things easier. Bringing one sheet of paper to an unsavory character far on the edge of town frustrated her. She didn't want to build this type of business. Tomás had crossed a line, and he'd hear about it. She handed the man the envelope without saying anything.

"I will have one of my men escort you to your car." The words came out in a snarl, although the man's face didn't change.

"No thank you." She turned to leave, the sooner the better.

"I insist."

She turned back to him, stressing each word. "I said no thank you."

"Paco." He nodded at one of the men along the wall. "Paco will accompany you, Miss Watts. This neighborhood can be very dangerous."

Yeah, thanks to you. But she didn't say anything. She knew who had the gun.

As she exited the building, Paco walked beside and slightly behind her. He didn't say a word in the five minutes it took to get back to her truck. She got in and started the vehicle while he stood just outside the door, staring at her with crossed arms. His position pulled his shirt up enough so she could see the pistol tucked into his waistband. She didn't flinch. Paco could show off, but he was way too far down the org chart to decide who got shot.

She drove away, relieved to be done with assholes with guns for the night. Her fingers turned the stereo up to eleven because blasting AC/DC made her feel like a badass. It made fear impossible.

She was going to kill Tomás. Well, not literally kill, there was enough competition for that on the streets of the Mexican drug war. A typical next generation son of a wealthy Mexican businessman, Tomás wouldn't have sent her into a situation that would lead to bad press, especially since he planned on expanding daddy's empire to both sides of the border. She'd helped him obtain real estate for his nightclubs and mobile communications company in El Paso and Juarez. On her recommendation, he'd joined the El Paso Chamber of Commerce, and Jessica had even set up a few meetings with city officials for him. She'd proven herself useful. He wouldn't want her killed.

By the time she pulled up to the Bridge of the Americas, one of three border crossings between Juarez, Mexico, and El Paso, Texas, her breathing had slowed and her anger had returned to a medium simmer. She'd leave Tomás for another day, but she still needed to work off the rage. She told her phone app to call Angus.

"What's up?" he asked, answering on the third ring.

"Are you smoking? Do you have someone over?" She didn't mean for the questions to come out sharp. Not when she needed a favor. But she knew Angus. He'd been her best friend since elementary school and remained trapped in some kind of post-high school nirvana of shaggy hair, rock and roll, and weed. Although tonight, she needed him to be the responsible one.

"You're a little keyed up. I'm alone and watching a movie. Want to come over?" he asked.

"Nah, I've got to head out tonight. Can you take care of Tela?"

"Yeah." He breathed the word in a sigh of heavy disappointment. "Anything else?"

"Thanks. I owe you." She always owed him. She should have gotten a cat instead of a dog, then she could have one of those multi-day feeders and wouldn't have to rely on anyone. She'd prefer that to begging favors.

"You know, there's a way you can pay me back."

The innuendo sounded sexual, but experience said she'd receive a lecture on good behavior if she bit. "Gotta go. I'm at the border station. Thanks for your help." She ended the call before he could guilt her into going home instead of out. She needed loud music and strong drinks tonight. Vices without bullets.

———

Jessica opened the door to the bar, and the stench of beer, sweat, and Mexican food beckoned and repulsed her. The sound of pool cues hitting balls and David Bowie's "Major Tom" assaulted her ears. She smiled. A dive bar on a Thursday night could soothe the soul like nothing else.

She took her place on the round vinyl and chrome stool but kept her elbows off the sticky bar. A rectangular bar top filled the center of the room, and two bartenders in the middle served stale beer and whatever else customers wanted. She waved two fingers at Scott, her favorite barkeep.

"What'll it be?" he asked.

"A shot of Patron and a double IPA."

"You're here late." He poured the shot and placed it on the bar in front of her.

She slugged it down, enjoying the burn in her throat. "Yeah. I've got some catching up to do. Can I have another, Scotty?"

"Let me get your beer first."

She watched him walk to the other end of the bar. His Wranglers fit perfectly. Of course, she already knew that. She'd taken them off him once.

She surveyed the room. Dudes with long hair played pool. A couple of suits she recognized sat on barstools. A few couples whispered across square tables. Who brought a date to a place like this? She noticed a big guy leaning over the jukebox. Levi's, and they fit better than Scott's Wranglers.

"Here you go," Scott said, setting a frosty pint of amber liquid in front of her. "You still want that second shot?"

"Damn straight. When have you known me to stop at one?"

"Never." Smile lines crinkled toward his shaved head, but his blue eyes held something sad.

"You know I love you, Scotty."

"Honey, you love everyone."

"Every chance I get," Jessica said, downing the second shot. She felt better already.

She'd finished half her beer when the big guy returned from the jukebox. He took a seat directly opposite her across the bar.

He was gorgeous. She took a long sip from the beer to give her mouth something to do besides gape.

He had to be six-five, with messy platinum blond hair and eyes you could drown in. His arms and shoulders were just this side of bodybuilder. A girl could bury herself in that body. Warmed by the alcohol, she took off her leather jacket, staring at the guy the whole time. Scott stepped into her field of vision.

"It looks like your blue eyes are wandering. Can I get you anything?" he asked, one eyebrow raised. He knew her game.

"Yeah, another shot. And send one to him." She nodded across the bar.

Scott gave her a hard look, but one side of his mouth tweaked up in a grin. "Should I warn him about you?"

"He looks like he can handle himself."

As soon as Scott had served the guy, she lifted her shot glass to him. He had the look of a confused puppy, but a guy that hot would have garnered plenty of free drinks. She watched him smell the tequila, never a good idea.

She held her glass aloft, waiting for him to down the shot, but he got off the barstool instead and circled his way to her.

"Scotty, I need some limes." This guy was an amateur.

Scott set down limes and a saltshaker just as the guy arrived. His broad shoulders practically blocked out the sun, or at least the bar light over the pool table, which wavered nicely in her more liquid world. She loved this moment when all the edges softened. Thank god for tequila.

"Hi," the guy said.

"I'm Jessica." She waved her glass in front of him. "Don't tell me you're not a tequila fan."

"I thought I'd come enjoy it with you. You've got limes." He visibly brightened.

"Yeah. We can do this the old-fashioned way." She licked the inside of her forearm and sprinkled salt on the wet patch. Jessica locked eyes with him as she slowly licked the salt from her arm. She had to turn away to find her glass on the bar, and when she turned back, he felt closer. At five-ten, she rarely felt small, but he loomed over her in the sexiest way possible. This kind of danger, she could handle.

She brought the shot glass to her lips and let the liquid slide down her throat, slow and languorous. She swam in his pool blue eyes, savoring the last drop of tequila. Trading the glass for fruit, she brought a lime to her lips. She ran her tongue over it but didn't bite.

"Now it's your turn," she said.

He nodded, not saying anything. She released his eyes and let her own travel down the length of him. His thin T-shirt hinted at hard muscles. Her hands wanted to touch him. Hell, she wanted to press her whole body against his. She let her eyes fall to faded denim. Apparently, he wanted the same. The tequila radiated through her, filling the world with possibility.

She looked back into his eyes. "Ready?"

He nodded again. Not a lot of words with this one.

She reached for his forearm with both hands, turning its pale inside toward her. "May I?" she asked. She understood the importance of consent.

"Please." His voice cracked.

His skin warmed her cold fingers, and she dropped her head, her dark hair falling next to his tan forearm. She reached for it with her tongue, running it along the soft, hot skin. She kissed his arm before lifting her head.

"Salt," she whispered, tasting it on her tongue. She found the saltshaker with one hand and poured a fine layer onto the wet spot she'd left. She released him and handed him his glass.

His cheeks had gone bright red. He lifted his arm and sucked the salt from it as if stealing the remnant of her kiss. Briefly, his hand wrapped around hers, then he took the glass from her. He threw the shot back in a gulp, then reached past her for a lime, wincing as he bit into it.

"Man, I hate that stuff." He ran the back of his hand under his watering eyes.

"Sorry. You should have told me."

"No way. I wouldn't have missed that for the world."

Her smile reached down to her toes. This was going to be everything. Gorgeous guy, up for a little fun, and he wanted her. He made the unpleasantness of her earlier job fade away.

They spoke words she couldn't remember seconds after they hit the air. Her arm drifted to his. He sat on the stool beside hers, facing her so their knees interlocked, long legs touching.

She learned he'd arrived in town a few weeks ago. Maybe he was from Idaho or someplace like that. He came here to work for a cousin's shipping company. It sounded boring. His body spoke louder, warm and close and bulging in all the right places. He wouldn't solve all her problems, but he would definitely solve the ones she had tonight.

By the time she settled the bill with Scott, the guy had his hands at her waist. The minute they were out the door, he pulled her to him and kissed her. It was gentle and sweet and didn't meet any of her needs. She locked her arms around his neck and practically crawled up him, pulling his bottom lip into her mouth, forcing him to acknowledge her desire.

He lifted her, and she wrapped her legs around him. She'd never been with someone so strong, he carried her like she was nothing. Soon, her back pressed against the cold metal of a truck, hopefully his. She wanted him. All of him. As soon as possible. In the cool tequila night, he could fill every need she had.

"Is there someplace we can go?" she asked.

"Yes." The word came out in a breathless growl.

She heard the truck unlock, and he slid her down his body until her feet touched pavement. She crawled into the cab and slid into the passenger seat. A pang of regret slipped through her as they passed her truck, but she shouldn't drive.

The awkward, silent drive only lasted five minutes on empty streets. He pulled into a driveway in front of a squat brick house in a 1950s development full of almost identical homes. Beyond lawn maintenance and the color of the bricks, she couldn't have told them apart. She brought her focus back to the guy. She couldn't remember his name. It didn't matter as much as his body.

"Is this okay?" he asked, the pool blue eyes gone dark in the night.

Jessica placed her hands on either side of the strong jaw and pulled him toward her. Her lips brushed his gently, once, then again. The passion raged back, and they made out like teenagers with five minutes left until curfew.

"Come on," he said, pulling her out of the truck. "We have to be quiet when we go in the house."

Giggling, they tiptoed through the entryway and down a hall until he pulled her into a large room set up like a studio apartment. He made his bed. Jessica never made her bed. The door closed, the lock clicking into place, then he came up behind her, wrapping one arm around her waist to pull her close. His other hand lifted the hair from her neck. He kissed her below her ear, on her collarbone, next to her bra strap. She leaned into him, knowing he would fill every empty spot inside her.

<hr>

Jessica woke to a headache that throbbed in time with her heartbeat. Her eyes itched, and she would have killed someone for a glass of water. The gentle snoring beside her also seemed timed to her pulsing head. She got out of bed and made her way to the kitchenette along one side of the room, fumbled for the faucet, and once she heard water, stuck her head under and drank. She'd seen cats do it better on YouTube.

She found her pants, and with them, her phone. It wasn't quite six o'clock. She had to leave, but, of course, her truck was miles away. She went and sat on the bed beside the beautiful man, wishing she could remember his name.

"Hey, wake up. Good morning."

He grunted but didn't wake. She rubbed her hand along his torso, a heady combination of soft skin and hard muscle. "Hey, wake up."

He rolled onto his back, releasing a wave of inviting heat. "Come back to bed."

"I can't. I've got to go. Work. Can you drive me to my truck?"

"Sure. Just a minute." He groaned again and sat up, giving her a lopsided grin before stretching and exposing every perfect muscle on his chest.

Memories of hands and mouths and teeth on skin reeled through her brain. She fought them off. Her body betrayed her as a shot of electricity ran from swollen lips to breasts and lower. She wanted to climb back on top of him almost as much as she wanted to leave. She jumped up from the bed and looked for the rest of her clothes.

The minute he was dressed, she left the bedroom and headed for the front door. She heard voices in another part of the house and prayed she wouldn't run into anyone.

"Hey, Brett. Is that you?"

Jessica had already opened the door and hurried out. Brett, she assumed, slipped out behind her.

"Sorry, that was my cousin's wife. It's probably best that she doesn't see us leaving."

"Works for me," Jessica said. She climbed into his truck and noticed the garage and Brett's bedroom shared the same location. Great.

They drove through a gray light special to mornings on the west side of El Paso. A stark desert mountain range bisected the city, and while the dawn seared the eastern side of the mountains, the west side remained shaded from the early morning light. On a normal day, Jessica would have enjoyed the cool desert air and black mountains outlined in the bright of the rising sun. Today was not normal. Of course, it wasn't abnormal either.

Sometimes she needed a warm body and the hunger of another person that matched her own. This guy was better than most. He'd fed that hunger again and again until they fell asleep, slick and exhausted in each other's arms.

Unfortunately, now he verged on ruining a good thing by talking. Honestly, did he just thank her for coming over? She sure wasn't going to thank him for filling her up eight ways to Sunday, even though she was damn grateful.

"Can I take you to dinner tonight?" he asked.

"I'm sorry, I've got a standing date with my neighbors on Friday."

He gave her a quizzical glance, but she didn't explain. She didn't want him to fish for a reason to invite himself over. She lived by one and done, or tried to.

"How about this weekend? I've got plenty of time off, and you can show me some of your favorite places in town."

"I'm sorry, I can't."

He actually looked sad. Most guys acted like she'd given them a Christmas present when she didn't want to stick around. "I've got to go out of town this weekend and see my parents." Now why the hell had she said that? That's the last thing she'd ever do.

"I thought you said your parents had died."

Shit. She didn't remember telling him that. "It's just a figure of speech."

"Which part? That they died or that you're going to visit them?"

"They left me when I was sixteen, and I haven't seen them since. So, in a way, it's like they died. And I lied about going to see them. I'm sorry. You seem really nice, and I had a fantastic time last night. I mean really fantastic." She reached over and stroked his denim-covered thigh. "Honestly, I just don't want a relationship."

He stopped talking after that. She thanked him for the ride when he dropped her off at the parking lot. He screeched away like Richard Petty.

She hadn't meant to piss him off. She'd developed phenomenal interpersonal skills as part of her job. Skills that helped her talk about money or international relations, but they abandoned her the second she slept with someone. Her lack of tact around personal relationships was just one reason she never dated people she met through work. Instead, she'd perfected her pick up routine. She could count on one hand the number of guys she still talked to that she'd taken to bed. No strings, no regrets, no future.

The thought stripped away all the satisfaction from the night before. She could still feel him on her body, but the fullness she'd enjoyed had disappeared, leaving a familiar hollow space.

She shook her head as she started the truck. Maybe she was just hungry. She stopped by the Whataburger drive-thru for two breakfast taquitos, then drove the fifteen miles home to the horse farm on the outskirts of town—her getaway where she could leave the city behind. She loved El Paso, but it housed a lot of bad memories.

Each mile she drove ratcheted down the tension of lousy parents, a questionable job, and her own dubious decisions. The last quarter of a mile, the road turned to washer-board dirt, then she entered sixty-four acres of paradise. Railroad tie fencing outlined rows of dark green alfalfa. The road continued toward a terracotta-colored home and barn, with bright white fencing lining the pens and arena.

Jessica didn't follow the road but turned off onto a short drive that ended at a small, rectangular adobe building. Home. And despite what she'd told Brett, she did not need to work today. She couldn't wait to crawl into her unmade bed and fade into nothingness.

She expected to hear Tela at the door scratching and whining. The Catahoula Leopard dog hadn't had a waking moment of stillness since Jessica brought her home four years ago. She swung the door open to find Angus asleep on the couch and Tela staring at her from where she snuggled in the crook of his knees.

"Hey, girl." Jessica rubbed the dog's head and silky ears, one blue eye and one green eye looking into her own with nothing but love shining back. She kissed the dog's forehead, then went to find aspirin and water.

Fortunately, she only had to take three steps to the right to enter the kitchen. The large bottle of Tylenol waited for her on the counter, where she'd left it after the last bender. She stuck a glass under the tap and filled it to the top before downing two pills.

Angus stirred. "You're back."

"Yep. Thanks for taking care of Tela. I didn't see your car outside."

Angus rolled over, dislodging the dog. His dark hair splayed in every direction, permanently in need of a cut. His half-closed, sleepy eyes tried to focus on her as he spoke. "I parked up at the main house. I had to talk to Luz and Sarah about something."

"Hopefully not about me." She tried staring him down, but he didn't seem to notice. Jessica had become adept at avoiding lectures from friends, but she hoped Angus had covered for her.

"Nope. I'm thinking about helping Sarah with that kids' therapy program she wants to start with the horses."

Tela scratched at the bottom of the door and whined. A ball of energy, that dog had two settings: asleep or on the move. The sleep setting had clearly switched off.

"I'll take you for a run in just a minute. Let me shower first," Jessica said to the dog.

"I'll take her," Angus said. "I can let her run up to the big house and get my car. I'll drop her off when I leave."

Every muscle relaxed. Jessica could shower, crawl into bed, and not worry about anything. "Thanks. I owe you big time. Again."

"Don't worry, I'm keeping track. You'll pay me back someday. Are you going to be up at the house for happy hour?"

"I wouldn't miss it." She walked over and planted a kiss on his forehead. "Thanks. You saved me." Then she headed to the tiny bathroom to wash away the fear and grime and sex that had collected in her pores.

"I'm trying to," he said.

Jessica closed the door on his words. She refused to add guilt to the mix.

Chapter 2

T he ringing of the phone pulled Jessica out of a deep sleep. Tela jumped off the bed, shook herself, and howled after the second ring. Jessica shushed the dog and reached for her phone. Tomás.

"Good morning." She tried to make her voice more chipper than sleep filled. It must not have worked.

"Are you feeling okay?"

"Fantastic." She took a long sip from the glass of water on the nightstand. "What kind of shit job did you send me on yesterday? I heard you leave the house."

A heavy sigh came through the line. "Sorry about that. There's someone important who needs a job done. It's delicate, and I think you'd be perfect for it."

"Who is it? You know I won't do anything drug related." She refused to break that one rule, the one her father had ignored. No matter what else happened in her life, she wouldn't repeat his mistake.

"I know. Everything's above board on this one. It's just, well, it's about family. You know how people are here, tough faces, strong arms. If people find out you have family issues, they'll think you're weak."

"You know, solving family issues is not my area of expertise." She let the silence hang in the air. Tomás knew her background. Hell, everyone on both sides of the border knew about the downfall of her DA father caught helping the wrong side in the Mexican drug war. He'd been arrested, prosecuted, and would be on house arrest until he died. Fortunately, her parents had left town in shame shortly after the trial, moving to the middle of nowhere Texas, better known as Fort Davis. Jessica hadn't talked to them since.

"Jessica, you know everyone. I was born and raised in Juarez, and I don't know half the people you do. And you never take sides, so people trust you. Also, you never stop until the job is done. Remember when you drove forty miles through a sandstorm just to show a client a building? This job needs that kind of dedication. You're perfect for it."

"Why doesn't anyone bring me straight up commercial real estate jobs anymore? I miss dealing with some guy back in Indiana who I never have to meet. I'm not sure how my career morphed from selling buildings to delivering documents and making introductions." She stopped the rant. "Bring me a deal that's all numbers, no emotions."

"Next time. This one's going to have a lot of emotions. The people you met last night were his guys."

"Oh, you mean the guy with the gun? He looked like he had the emotional intelligence of a rock." That hadn't been true. He'd seen right through her tough girl act. He'd forced her to have an escort, just so she'd understand he controlled the night.

"I don't think you'll have to see them again. You passed the test."

"Great. What did I win?"

"Quite possibly a whole lot of money."

That stopped her. Money, she could use. Jessica had dreams of buying her own house instead of living off the good intentions of friends. She even had one picked out, an old adobe down by the river with Saltillo tile floors and a huge yard for Tela.

She looked around her rental. She could see all of it from the bed pressed against one end of the rectangular room. The small bathroom to the right had been patched onto the outside of the building like a tumor. The couch sat directly across from the front door. A small table tripled as a place to eat, a desk, and a storage counter for random stuff. The kitchen beside it included a dorm fridge, a sink, and a couple of feet of counter space crowded with a microwave, electric griddle, and coffeemaker. She'd be thirty soon. She yearned to live like a grownup. And she wanted a place of her own that no one could ever take away.

"So, what can you tell me about the job?" she asked.

"Not much," said Tomás. "It's for Ruben Velasco."

"The guy who owns the cement company? I've never done business with him."

"He owns the cement company, two construction companies, is a silent investor in half the industrial parks in Juarez, and owns a couple of hotels, among other things. He's rich." Tomás emphasized the last word.

"You're rich," Jessica said.

"My family's rich, but he's a different kind of wealthy, the kind I want to be. His investments go far beyond Juarez. His construction company has branches in half the cities in Mexico, and he controls almost all the cement in the country."

"Why does he live here?" Jessica thought she knew, and the term family concerned her the way it would have in New York, or Sicily.

"Family. I think his wife is from here."

"Tomás, *la familia* in Mexico doesn't always mean blood relatives."

"I promise, it's about family, the regular kind. The kind that annoys us."

Annoyed, abandoned, it depended on your perspective. "What's next?" she asked.

"He wants to meet you on Monday. He'll pick you up at your place."

"No way in hell. I don't need any job that bad. He can pick me up at the real estate office downtown."

"Fine. Two o'clock?"

"That works. Will you be there?"

"I'll meet you at your office before you go. It's in the Chase Bank building, right? I can't go to Juarez with you. I've, uh, got a meeting at the chamber."

"You're sure this is legit?" she asked. Tomás sounded a little cagey—and way less arrogant than usual.

"It is. And I've given him my word that you'll do a great job and handle this with discretion."

"Yeah, discretion, that's my middle name. See you Monday."

The day's heat retreated with the sun as Jessica walked down the road to the terra cotta house, Tela bouncing in front of her. The dog barked when she neared the parking area, and a four-legged welcoming crew rushed noisily around the corner to greet them. Jessica reached down to scratch the head of a stout Labrador while a Corgi danced at her feet.

When she entered the back patio, she didn't see Luz or Sarah, so she settled into a rocking chair under the twinkle lights. Her best friends, actually some of her only friends, had instituted the weekly ritual. Friday night happy hours on the patio, or inside by the fire on cold winter nights, were always Jessica's favorite part of the week.

She spied a pitcher of Luz's famous margaritas and a vat of guacamole on the table. Jessica had brought chips as usual, and she knew an empty bowl awaited them. She took a moment to sit and relax before offering to help in the kitchen. Her heartbeat slowed and she could breathe a little deeper in this safe space. Nothing bad would happen here.

She gazed at the tempting margaritas but ultimately avoided them. Last night's tequila probably still ran through her veins. She opted for a beer in the cooler beside her instead.

"You're welcome to stay for dinner," Sarah said, walking outside and pulling her long blond hair into a tie. "I'm making three-bean chili."

"That sounds delicious, thanks." Jessica tipped the long-necked bottle of Shiner in Sarah's direction. Every morsel that came out of Sarah's kitchen was delicious. Some foods, like the chili, Jessica had loved since childhood. Her mother and Sarah had competed on the rodeo circuit together when they were young and remained fast friends until her mom left town.

Sarah's partner Luz entered the patio and sat to Jessica's right, still in the work clothes she'd worn to her job managing hundreds of people in the City of El Paso's parks and recreation department. "So, spill it. What did you do last night?" Luz had her bulldog face on, and Jessica knew she'd have to give them a good story.

"Well, after my delivery in Juarez, I stopped by the King on the way home."

Luz rolled her eyes. "How can you stand that disgusting place?"

"Cheap booze."

"Girl, you need to raise your standards."

"That's another reason I love it. No standards." She'd meant it as a joke, but truthfully, no one she knew from work and no one who would have known her parents were likely to show up at King's. She could give in to her baser needs there without worrying about anyone spreading rumors. Or truths.

"I saw Angus's car when I left for work this morning. I take it you met someone?"

"That a problem?" Jessica didn't want to get testy, but she didn't need the third degree. She'd make her own decisions about how she spent her time.

"Aw, was he nice?" Sarah walked over and handed her a plate of empanadas before taking the seat in front of her. The sweetest person Jessica knew, Sarah had asked the question before. She couldn't seem to help wanting Jessica to find that special someone, the way she'd found Luz. That was not why Jessica visited dive bars.

"Sarah, I love you, but I didn't go to the King to find someone to date."

"But a relationship might be good for you."

"Oh, we had a relationship. I think he might have been the best-looking guy I've ever had a relationship with. And it lasted for hours."

"Stop!" Luz threw her hands up, but her lips held a smile. "I don't want to hear any more. Take your depravity somewhere else. Man, I need a drink."

"Well, at least she found someone cute! You should see him again." Sarah's softness balanced Luz perfectly. Sarah asked about relationships, loved horses, and helped anyone who needed it. Luz cared about the facts, the money, and having a good time. A familiar wish that these two had been her parents lodged in her chest.

"Mom, you know I don't do second dates," Jessica whined, teasing Sarah.

"You should try it sometime. It's nice to have someone to come home to." Sarah gave Luz a wink.

Jessica couldn't imagine being in that kind of relationship. Sarah and Luz had been together since before Jessica had known them. Jessica's mom, a former rodeo queen and barrel riding champion, had met Sarah back in the rodeo days. Sarah had been youth champion at seventeen in reining, a discipline where she made quarter horses spin and slide the way they'd never need to chasing actual cows. Jessica didn't inherit her mom's love of rodeo, but her gratitude for the sport introducing her mom to Sarah never ran dry.

Growing up, Jessica's mom had brought her to the farm every weekend for riding lessons with Sarah. The lessons didn't stick, but the friendship did. So much so that when she aged out of the college dorms at the local university, Sarah and Luz offered her a room in their home.

When she'd asked them if she could live in the house on the edge of the property instead, they'd said yes, and even replaced the electrical wiring. Jessica paid the utilities and a paltry rent and showed up on Friday evenings with a bag of tortilla chips and a twelve-pack of beer.

Luz left to change out of her work clothes, and Sarah took the bag of chips and poured them into a bowl. Jessica watched the mountains turn purple and then black as the night darkened. Friday nights on this patio meant friendship and safety, despite the teasing. Luz and Sarah always welcomed her, along with a motley assortment of friends and neighbors.

A couple people stopped by for a beer, the man down the street with an experimental apple farm and a friend of Sarah's who bred racehorses and had taken Jessica hot air ballooning once. Friday nights varied by the people who stopped by, but pretty much everyone wanted booze and company and the chance to relax at the end of the week.

The Friday ritual let Jessica forget about the job that had her crossing the border sometimes several times a day. She found the acting harder than the travel. She convinced everyone she liked them, and they all liked her, or at least the person they met. But she made sure they never knew the real Jessica, the woman who refused to acknowledge the trauma of her parents leaving the same way she refused to acknowledge they still walked the earth just a few hundred miles away. She papered over all of that by doing favors for dangerous people and covering any fear or distaste with alcohol and sex. She wasn't meant for a regular life.

"Hey, everyone," Angus said, arriving from the parking area.

Tela bounded across the patio to greet her favorite dog sitter. Jessica gave him a wave and stayed seated, even though his broad smile and shaggy hair made her want to jump up and give him a hug. He nodded back at her and showed the champagne bottles he held in each hand.

"Welcome," Luz shouted. "What's the celebration?"

"Today, Sarah had her first horse therapy patients, and she let me sit in," Angus said. "You guys should have seen it. First, the cutest little girl ever showed up. She had long golden curls and hid behind her mom until she saw Bosco."

"The pony?" Jessica asked. "He's the best."

"Yeah, she loved that little guy. That kid made my day. Maybe my week," Angus said, an infectious grin plastered on his face. "The girl had anxiety issues, but she petted Bosco's neck and even led him around a little bit."

Sarah laughed. "Thanks for the champagne, and I'm glad you were there. Unfortunately, it didn't go quite so well with the next kid."

"It was a boy with autism, and I don't think he wanted to be near the horses," Angus said. "He and Logan had a stare off. I'm still not sure who won."

"You put him on your prize quarter horse?" Luz gave her partner a questioning look.

"Oh, today was just to meet the horses and see how the kids took to them. First, they'll get to know the animals, groom them, and walk them around the barn. They may never ride, and if they do, that comes much later."

"Thanks for letting me be there. You deserve a toast." Angus raised the bottles.

"Thank you for bringing champagne," Sarah said.

"I'll go get champagne flutes," Luz said. "Jessica, come help me."

Jessica followed her into the house, not sure why she needed help with so few people at happy hour. Not that it mattered, she'd do anything for these two.

"Go get the cake out of the fridge in the garage. I want to celebrate Sarah's new venture. I can't believe I made it this far without her finding it."

Jessica laughed and ran to the fridge, coming back with a white cake with what looked like My Little Pony frosted in blue. "Nice icing," she said to Luz, who'd stacked salad plates, napkins, and forks on the counter.

"It's the best I could do on short notice. Fortunately, Angus called and reminded me before I left work."

They heard the pop of a champagne cork from the patio. "Let's go," Luz said, "Grab what you can."

Jessica hustled out to the patio, managing to carry the cake and two flutes. Someone had turned on music, and the air glowed with the festive twinkle lights.

"Are we seriously going to have cake before dinner?" Sarah asked.

"God, I hope so." Jessica's stomach rumbled in anticipation. "Congratulations."

A couple Luz knew from work arrived, followed quickly by a guy who boarded his horse at the farm, and the small affair evolved into a party. The sugar high and champagne made Jessica giggly, at least until Angus asked about her latest job. Her anger with Tomás for testing her lay just below the surface.

"I'm afraid it's going to be a shit show, although it's supposed to pay well."

"Who's it for?" he asked.

She took advantage of the closeness of others on the patio. "Do any of you know Ruben Velasco?" she asked loudly. The newcomers shook their heads, but Luz and Sarah shared a long, hard look that Jessica couldn't decipher.

"Nope," Angus said.

"Please tell me he's not your next client." Sarah's look of concern told Jessica that she had heard of him. That seemed strange. Sarah spent her days on the farm, as far from international deals as one could get.

"Can't do that," Jessica said. "What do you know about him? All I've learned is that he seems to control the cement industry in Mexico, and even Tomás Garcia calls him rich."

The mood on the patio changed. Luz thanked people for coming, and Sarah practically pulled the glasses from their hands. Angus stayed, but Luz herded everyone else to their cars.

She returned with a stern look, worry just beneath the surface. "Jessica, I think you should stay away from Velasco. He's not a good guy, and I think your dad was involved with him."

"Fuck." She hated any mention of her family. They were gone. She was over it. "Can we please not talk about my parents? Besides, that was fourteen years ago." Fourteen and a half, actually.

"You should know these things. Go talk to Alma, she'll fill you in."

The last thing she wanted to do was talk about her parents with her attorney, Alma Rey, who also happened to be Luz's sister. Appointed as her guardian after her parents left, Alma stayed with Jessica until she turned eighteen and guided many of her school and career moves. But Jessica had found Velasco on her own, met him through her contacts. She'd worked so hard to build a life independent of her parent's mistakes.

"I really don't care who my dad was involved with. This isn't a drug deal. And I'll decide when to talk to my attorney." She took a breath and pulled the anger out of her voice. Luz only wanted to help. "I'm not going to let my dad's shadow dictate who I work with."

The conversation died. A breeze kicked up, stirring the leaves in the trees and sending a chill across her skin. Jessica realized she'd gone a step too far.

"I'm sorry. I had a really late night and think I need some sleep. Thanks for having me over."

Jessica called her dog and trudged down the lonely road to her house. She caught the scent of woodsmoke on the breeze, a homey smell. The scent brought back memories of Christmases and her mom cooking stew on cold nights.

She turned the thoughts off, something she'd mastered a long time ago. In the years since her parents left, she'd learned how to pack the empty places with deals and adventure, danger and sex.

That Ruben Velasco had been involved with her dad became a challenge. She could take the measure of this man and decide if she wanted to work for him. She would control this game. And hopefully make a lot of money in the process.

Chapter 3

On Monday, Jessica met Tomás outside of her office building. The afternoon sun's searing glare brought a sheen of sweat to Tomás's forehead and made Jessica wish she'd worn something other than a black pantsuit. Between her discomfort and thoughts about her dad's connection to Velasco, Jessica half wanted to call off the meeting.

Tomás fidgeted, his eyes shifting up and down the street like he expected a monster, or a gunman, to jump out from behind a car. Unlikely, on this side of the border.

"You've got to treat him with respect," Tomás said. "He's important, and I vouched for you."

"Tomás, I always treat people with respect."

"I know." He peered down the street again. "That's why I recommended you. Here, give me your phone. I have a new phone number, and I'll input it for you."

She handed him her phone. It slipped through his fingers and landed with a smash on the pavement. "No!"

"I'm so sorry." He swooped down to pick it up. As he turned it screen up, she saw the spiderweb cracks glint across the screen. "Let me take care of this. Stop by my office as soon as you're back, and I'll have a new phone for you and a sturdier case. Then you can let me know how the meeting went."

She shook her head. "Must be nice to own a phone store."

"It's a lot more than a phone store. I'll even upgrade the model for you, but I've got to run now."

She said goodbye to his back as he scooted down the block. Tomás had built a reputation on being suave and smooth. Today, she'd seen a different side of him, and it made her wary.

A Cadillac Escalade with privacy windows as black as the paint pulled up beside her. A skinny man with a pencil mustache jumped out of the passenger seat, then opened the back door of the behemoth SUV. He gestured for her to get in.

She rooted her feet to the ground. "Hello, I'm Jessica Watts," she said, sticking out her hand in greeting. She couldn't dictate everything, but she'd damn sure try to set the tone.

"Pedro Esparza. Please, we are to take you to meet Señor Velasco." His English wasn't perfect, but she appreciated the effort. He briefly shook her hand, then gestured toward the open car like Vanna White turning numbers.

The dark interior of the vehicle contrasted sharply with the bright El Paso sun, and it took her eyes a minute to adjust. She had company, the ugly gun guy from the other night. Great. She nodded at him. He nodded back, a creepy smile curling his lips.

They didn't speak as they crossed the border, and the Mexican border guards waved them through without asking for identification. This Velasco guy had some pull.

Jessica kept her eyes glued to the window. She knew the streets of Juarez like she'd been born there, and she wanted to see where they were going. She prayed it wasn't back to the shantytown, not that she could do anything about it. At least Tomás knew where she was and who accompanied her. Hundreds of women had disappeared in this city, and even now, no one knew what had happened to them. Some said it was a serial killer, others the drug war, although the disappearances started well before then.

Fortunately, they pulled up to a modern glass and chrome office building near the country club. Pedro opened her door and escorted her inside. The reflection in the glass showed the guy from the backseat following two steps behind.

As Jessica walked into the four-story atrium that served as a lobby, a wall of ice-cold air slammed into her. Velasco must spend a fortune on air conditioning. Normally, the desert sun would have turned a glass and metal building into an oven in the heat. Still, she could see why he did it. The soaring panes of glass sparkled in the sunlight and caused rays to bounce off the white marble floors. It shimmered like the inside of a glittery snow globe.

Pedro and gun man escorted her to the elevator. As they rose to the fifth-floor penthouse, Jessica steeled herself for the coming encounter. She had to be friendly, professional, unflappable.

The elevator doors opened onto more white marble. In front of her, an older woman in a sharp red suit sat behind a large white desk. Jessica couldn't quite see in the open double doors to her right. Power wafted through the hallway.

The woman stood, raised one haughty eyebrow, and nodded toward the double doors. "Ms. Watts, Mr. Velasco is waiting for you."

Jessica smiled at the woman, although she wanted to roll her eyes at the stiff formality. The receptionist moved toward the doors, her heels clicking on polished rock.

A floor to ceiling window backlit the huge office. Unadorned, glossy wood walls flanked the window, and in the center of the room sat an enormous mahogany desk. As put together as his office, Ruben Velasco rose and beckoned her forward.

Black hair with more than a handful of salt swept away from his head, revealing a sharp widow's peak. His goatee had been trimmed so severely Jessica was surprised she hadn't seen the barber leaving the building. As she reached across the desk to shake his hand, she admired his immaculate, perfectly cut suit and noticed thick gold cuff links the size of nickels.

"Welcome, thank you for coming here today," he said with a smile that didn't approach his eyes.

"It is very nice to meet you."

"Please sit."

Only one chair fronted the desk. As Jessica sat, she looked behind her. Pedro and the gunman stood at attention halfway between her and the door. They had planned the meeting to intimidate her, but why? She wouldn't be here unless Velasco needed her. Maybe he operated this way with everyone.

"How can I help you?" she asked.

Velasco steepled his fingers. "I have a very delicate situation. I have lost my daughter. Doraliz."

What the hell? How strange to refer to someone that way. Perhaps the typical formality of the English language in the mouths of the Juarez elite had resulted in a poor translation. "Lost?"

"Yes. She is twenty-four and very strong-willed, and I do not know if she has run off or if it is a matter of foul play. My men," a rabid sneer crossed his face as he glanced at the two men behind her, "have been unable to find her."

Compassion welled in Jessica at the thought of a woman lost in Juarez. But it quickly waned as she watched the dispassionate man in front of her. He should be terrified. So many women in Juarez had vanished. "Are you afraid she's been disappeared?"

That cracked his slick exterior, but only for a moment. A wrinkled forehead and worried eyes flashed across his face, but he quickly smoothed them away. "I do not think anyone would harm my daughter. The people here, they know my reputation."

Reputations in Juarez were inked in blood, and the word dripped with intimidation. The threat delivered its icy dagger. The city was rough. Beyond rough. For a handful of recent years, Juarez had led the world's per capita murder rate. Blamed on the drug war, few understood exactly who pulled the triggers.

The lack of understanding resulted in constant fear. Someone's tone of voice, a few words seemingly innocuous but laced with deeper meaning, could signal a kidnapping, murder, or disappearance. Jessica managed to avoid the darker side of working in this battlefield by focusing on legitimate business deals. That had become more difficult as the city's reputation faltered.

She dug into his unexplained threat, wondering if he thought he could scare her. "What exactly do people know about you?"

"They know I am a man of my word."

Jessica worked to keep a straight face. Pride and bluster wouldn't help her. It wouldn't help him either. "I'm not sure I'm what you're looking for. I usually handle real estate transactions and documents." She stared deep into his eyes, challenging him to be honest with her or cut her loose.

Instead, she watched his face crumble into despair. He'd used his pride as a shield to conceal his fear. A shock of recognition rolled through her. He thought he could control things by hiding behind tough emotions. Jessica had learned early how others could disappear. Her parents' departure had carved a chasm in her heart. That kind of pain could take your breath away. It took years to build a wall tough enough to withstand that type of hurt.

"Please," he said, his voice a ragged whisper. "The police have found nothing. My men, nothing. I must find her."

His pain ensnared Jessica. What if she'd had a parent who had cared enough about her to want her the way she imagined Ruben Velasco wanted his daughter? She closed her eyes on the thought. That wasn't her life. But maybe she could make a difference in someone else's. She tilted her head in affirmation. "What can you tell me about her disappearance?"

He opened a drawer and pulled out a white padded envelope. Here, I have a list of her friends. She left our home two weeks ago and told my wife she was going shopping with her friend Paula Romero. We have spoken with Paula, and she knew nothing about these plans. We do not believe Doraliz has crossed the border, and she hasn't been on any flights out of Juarez."

"Have you checked her credit and ATM cards? What about her phone?"

"There has been no spending on her cards. We recovered her phone. It was left in a dressing room at the Chatelet Boutique. She tried on one dress the morning she disappeared. No one has seen her since."

"Did she buy the dress?" Jessica had never been in the boutique, but she'd heard of it. Like a Ferrari dealership, why bother going in if you couldn't afford the prices?

"No."

The silence drew out. Finally, Jessica spoke. "I assume you have followed up on any leads. How do you think I can help you? I'm not a detective."

"You are friends with Tomás. So is Doraliz. I am hoping that since you are younger and move in circles that my daughter might inhabit, you may be able to find more information from her friends than we have. If you find her, or if you learn information that will help me find her and bring her home . . ." He dropped his head into his hands.

Silence pressed in from all sides. It pushed at the tough, transaction-focused woman she spent her life trying to be and dug into a softer part of her that wanted to help someone.

"I don't usually take on work like this, and I'm still not sure I'm the right person for the job." Why hadn't he hired a private investigator?

He looked up, and she peered into that soft place where his pain matched her own. It made him more human. A tear rolled down his cheek, and he brushed it away. "I understand. My people and the police will continue to look for her. But anything you learn might help."

She nodded. She could try.

He nodded as well, transforming almost instantly into the cold businessman she'd met when she walked into the sterile room. "You will have five thousand dollars a week for your expenses. If you help me find her in thirty days, I will pay you thirty-thousand dollars more."

Jessica looked out the window behind him. The amount of money impressed her and would go a long way toward her dream house, but she was more curious about his rapid transformation. Could her own father hide his pain so adeptly? Did he ever struggle with losing her? Probably not. That had been his choice. A sob lurched her away from her memories.

"I am a father." A world of hurt rang through Velasco's words. "I need to know that my daughter is safe. You have connections, especially with the younger generation. I hope you will be able to learn something that my men," he stopped to glance at the men behind her again, "cannot. Please, Ms. Watts, I need your help."

"Okay. I'll try."

The trip back across the border was silent. Stepping out of the Escalade and back onto her own turf made the whole experience seem like an ugly dream. Except for the envelope in her hand, the one Sr. Velasco had pulled from his desk before she left. It had some heft to it.

She retrieved her truck from the valet and headed to the drive-thru of her favorite taco shop. She opened the envelope in the anonymous line. It held a report in Spanish with facts about the missing woman, a leather-bound address book, and in a smaller envelope, a stack of one-hundred-dollar bills. Fifty of them.

Had she known the envelope's contents, she would never have walked around downtown El Paso with all that cash. Velasco really needed to be less dramatic. After the woman in the drive-thru handed Jessica a bag of tacos, she parked behind the restaurant and put together a plan.

The report included the names of Doraliz Velasco's friends. Many matched the entries in the address book. Jessica recognized a dozen people. Doraliz was a few years younger than she, but the young elite in Juarez partied in pretty tight circles.

She called one of the names, Federico. His dad owned a commercial real estate company, and they'd collaborated on a couple of deals. In minutes, she had an invitation to a party the following night. Hopefully, Doraliz's friends would be helpful.

Jessica deposited the money in her bank before heading to Tomás's office. She thought about moving some directly to her savings account as she pictured the house by the river. Instead, she put it all into checking. Who knew what the expenses on this case would be?

"Hola, Jessica," Tomás's secretary, Soledad, chirped as Jessica opened the door.

"Hi. How's that new husband of yours?" Jessica asked. She'd become close with Soledad over the many deals she and Tomás had done together. Even though she couldn't be more than twenty-three, Soledad's friendliness and reliability made her a pleasure to work with. Jessica probably wouldn't have put up with Tomás's arrogance if Soledad hadn't been there to handle all the back-end work.

A huge grin spread across the young woman's face. "Jessica, we have to get you married. It is so nice to have someone to come home to every night." She waggled her eyebrows.

"I know you're Catholic and all, but you don't actually have to be married to enjoy the fun part of marriage."

She shook her head. "You have such a bad attitude about men. Go on in," she nodded toward Tomás's door. "He's waiting for you."

Unlike Ruben Velasco's spare office, Tomás had fancy electronics on every available surface. Dual monitors graced two adjustable onyx desks. A rack sporting five different sets of headphones hung within arm's reach, and Tomás sat in a giant gaming chair that fully cupped his body. The office equipment contrasted with his swept-back, gelled hair and perfectly cut suit. She imagined he geeked out in here every time the office door closed.

"Jessica, here's your new phone." He handed her the latest model iPhone.

"Um, this is way nicer than the phone you dropped. I can just get the screen replaced."

"Don't be ridiculous. For me, this is just inventory. Soledad picked out a couple of cases. I'd recommend the silicone one, less slippery." He set two cases in front of her.

Jessica immediately reached for the navy silicone case. Soledad knew her tastes. "Thanks, I appreciate it."

"So, I assume you took the job with Velasco?"

"Yes. How well do you know Doraliz?"

Tomás sat back in his chair, pensive. It took him a moment to respond. "Well, I guess I've known her since she was born. You know how it is in Juarez, certain families are pretty tight. But she's ten years younger than me."

"Yes, I know how the wealthy families stick together in Juarez. Tight is an understatement. What do you think happened to her?"

"Doraliz has always been a little feisty, so at first, I thought maybe she'd just taken a little vacation to get away from her parents. But it's been too long now. I'm worried about her. Everyone is."

Jessica heard true concern in his voice. What could have happened to this girl and how on earth was she supposed to find her? "Her dad seems to think I could get something out of her friends that his men couldn't, but it seems like you could have done that."

"You're a lot closer to her in age. Also, honestly, a lot of those kids don't like me." He shifted in his chair, somehow aging in the process. "It's more important that they respect me."

"If you've got any leads for me, I'd love to hear them."

"You'll be good at this, just start looking around. Why don't you check in with me every few days? Perhaps I can help. After all, it's really important that you find her."

Jessica wondered about the emotions that ran just below Tomás's smooth exterior. He stood, effectively ending their meeting.

So many threads ran through this missing woman's story. Hopefully, the party would bring some clarity to who she was and where she'd gone.

Chapter 4

Jessica should have washed her truck. She swung into a circular drive the next evening and coasted into a fairyland. Spotlights turned the dark night bright and lit lush grass and weeping willows. Spray from numerous fountains captured the light, and rainbows flashed in each tiny droplet.

The mansion hosting the party abutted the Campestre Country Club, the most exclusive neighborhood in Juarez. An enormous two-story stucco home with a red tile roof and two large turrets perched at the apex of the drive. Ornate concrete and iron scrollwork surrounded every balcony and window, giving the house a wedding cake feel.

A valet opened the door of her grimy truck, careful to keep any distaste off his face. His stony look cracked when she stepped out of the vehicle. She took the stunned gaze as a sign she looked a lot better than the truck. Hell, she knew she did. She'd traded in black jeans for a spaghetti-strapped scarlet silk dress that pulled and draped in all the right places. Strappy sandals, makeup, and soft, silky hair thanks to a conditioning pack she'd used completed the look. Party girl had replaced tough girl and professional girl. It amazed her what clothes and a little warpaint could do.

She sauntered into a foyer with a patterned marble floor and impressive chandelier. A great room shimmered in front of her. Women in brightly colored dresses were scattered across the vast room like candy. Thighs and busts popped out everywhere, making her mid-thigh shift look matronly. The men wore colored denim and button downs, the fad of the moment. Everyone had shiny hair, glossy eyes, and a drink in their hand.

She spied Federico near the glass doors that opened onto a patio and pool. He raised a drink to her, and she made her way across the room. He kissed her cheek and wrapped a hand around her waist.

"It's lovely to see you. Thank you for inviting me." She tried to sparkle.

"Anytime. I'm glad you could come. How's the real estate business? I haven't seen you in a few months."

"It seems a little slow. How about with you?" The small talk led to her asking about his family, and they continued the long, slow dance that accompanied introductions in Mexico. The US custom of a quick hello before jumping into the meat of a conversation was considered rude. Federico introduced her to the two men who flanked him as the banter continued.

Finally, a pause in the conversation allowed her to turn her attention back to Federico. "I could really use a drink."

"I apologize. I am being a terrible host. Come with me." He led her to a bar in the corner. An icy silver bucket contained a selection of hard seltzers and bottled mixed drinks. Budweisers filled another.

"What's the age when men in Mexico stop drinking crappy American beer?" she teased.

"Thirty. I've got two years to go."

"You know," she ran a hand through his prematurely graying hair, "you could make the switch early. No one would know." She hoped the intimate gesture would keep him off guard. She had work to do tonight.

He laughed and walked behind the bar. "If I remember correctly, you're a tequila girl."

"Good memory."

He pulled a black bottle encrusted with tiny skulls from under the bar, then poured a generous serving of dark amber liquid into a highball glass. "Ice?"

"No, thank you. And thank you very much." She lifted the glass and poured a few drops onto her tongue. Smokey oak and hints of vanilla exploded in her mouth, undercut by a smooth tequila burn. This was not shot glass tequila. "Incredible."

"I thought you would like it. Let me introduce you to some people."

She filtered in and out of various groups, trying to understand how they fit together, deliberately not asking about Doraliz. Not yet. She occasionally returned to the bar to refill her glass from the bottle Federico had left on the countertop.

The women were beautiful, perfected in a way that made her think of surgery and heavy makeup. In their teens and twenties, they wouldn't have needed any of that, but the standards of beauty in Juarez reached unfathomable heights. The men ran the gamut from gorgeous to self-assured, each of them groomed to become the city's elite. Something about the night made her think of *The Great Gatsby*, maybe the shining eyes and occasionally clenched jaws.

She met quite a few people from Doraliz's leather address book. She circled back around to these once everyone seemed lubricated with drink or whatever else they might have imbibed.

"May I?" Jessica asked, pointing to an empty spot on a sofa next to a woman with raven-black hair and a sparkling black dress that plunged almost to her waist.

"Please," the woman said.

Her glittery eyeshadow matched her dress, but her wide brown eyes held more sophistication than the clothing suggested. She moved her knees aside to allow Jessica room on the cushion next to her.

"Paula, right?" Jessica asked. "We met earlier."

"Yes. What brings you to this side of the border? You're from El Paso, I assume?"

"I'm a friend of Federico's. I do a lot of work over here. Real estate." Jessica took a long sip of courage. "I haven't made it to a party in a while and was hoping to run into Doraliz Velasco. Do you know her?" Of course she knew her, she'd been in the book.

Something in the woman's eyes snapped shut. Her plump lips became a fraction more severe. "How do you know Doraliz?"

"I met her at the Gala Diseño." Jessica had done her homework. The society page of various magazines and journals documented Juarez's elite, and she'd seen photos of Doraliz at the design event a few months ago. Jessica had attended as well, although she hadn't met Doraliz.

"I do know her," Paula said. "But she won't be here tonight. Please excuse me."

Jessica had no better luck with the next person, a man this time. According to the society pages, he had dated Doraliz for a while. Nothing. He didn't know where she was and stiffened as he changed the subject.

As the night wore on, Jessica replaced tequila with water. She needed to be sharp for the questioning, not to mention the drive home. No one seemed to notice. She'd been drunk enough times to fake it easily.

Finally, she found a woman, younger than most. Plump, happy, drunk, and somewhat coherent. Exactly what Jessica needed.

"Hi, I'm Jessica." She approached the woman who searched for something in the bar's wine cooler bin.

"I'm Claudia. I think they're out of peach."

Jessica looked into the icy water. "Let me see." She walked behind the bar. A counter-height refrigerator opened to reveal a variety of drinks. "Is this what you're looking for?" Jessica handed her an icy can.

"Oh, yes! Thank you, you saved me. I thought I would have to drink the lime one."

"I can't imagine anything worse. Glad I could help." It took everything Jessica had not to roll her eyes.

"I'm Claudia," the woman said again, clinking her drink against Jessica's glass.

"I'm Jessica. I don't think we've met before. Hey, do you know Doraliz Velasco? I haven't seen her in a while, and I hoped she'd be here."

"Doraliz is my friend," Claudia said, a little too loud for comfort. "She's my friend, but I haven't seen her."

"I haven't either," Jessica said, lowering her voice and hoping Claudia would mirror her. "Do you know where she's been?"

"I don't know where she is. I miss her." Claudia stumbled toward a group of three women nearby whom Jessica hadn't met. "Hey, do you know where Doraliz is? I miss her." She practically screamed the words.

For a second, Jessica wished Claudia back. Far drunker than she'd realized, the girl might cause problems in the already wary crowd. Still,

Jessica followed her over, hoping to learn something. Instead, Doraliz's ex-boyfriend came over and took Claudia by the arm.

"You're wasted. Let me take care of you." He pulled her away. Claudia stumbled after him, still asking about Doraliz.

"I guess she had a little too much to drink," Jessica said to the remaining women. "Who's she talking about?"

Just then, Federico came over and took her glass. "Let me get you a refill."

"Thanks," she said, then turned back to the women.

"It must have been Doraliz Velasco. I'm surprised she's not here," said a blond in a green spandex jumpsuit.

"Yeah, I haven't seen her in a few weeks. She's probably in Europe or something," another one said.

"Here you go," Federico said, appearing at her elbow again. "Come with me. I'd like to introduce you to a friend of mine. He's got a parcel of land in south Juarez that he may sell soon. It would be perfect for development."

Jessica followed him, happy to have tequila in her glass again. She took a long sip, then coughed. "This is different."

"Yes. Since you're a tequila aficionado, I thought you'd enjoy trying a Clase Azul Extra."

"Isn't that like a two-thousand-dollar bottle of tequila?" She took another sip.

"Almost. Do you like it?"

"Um." She sipped it again. "I think I like the other one better. This tastes a little rough around the edges."

"Jessica, I'm disappointed in you. I'll have to take you tequila tasting. Maybe you can take a trip to Jalisco with me. Drinking tequila in the fields where the agaves grow is extraordinary."

"I'd like that, and I think this is growing on me. It must have been switching from one to another that tricked my taste buds." Despite its harsh taste, the tequila worked its magic, making her feel warm and floaty. Federico led her onto the pool deck and toward two men backlit by the blue water.

Federico introduced her to them and started talking about the parcel of land. Jessica found it hard to focus on anything but the ripples in the pool. She turned back to the men and couldn't remember their names. She had to start getting more sleep.

She closed her eyes for a moment, and when she opened them, she stood in a white walled hallway with Federico and Doraliz's ex-boyfriend. She had no idea how she'd gotten there. Suddenly, a burst of pain hit her face, followed by a flash of white-hot light. Then nothing.

Chapter 5

She woke too groggy to open her eyes. How much had she had to drink? Her head had never hurt like this. Hell, her whole body hurt. Instead of a soft pillow, her cheek rested on a cold, slick floor.

A chill flooded through her when she realized there was nothing but her flimsy silk dress between her and whatever floor she'd ended up on. She might have to start going to AA after this one.

She tried to sit up, but the pain that sliced through her head kept her trapped. She pulled her arms forward, or tried to, but something bound her wrists behind her. What the holy hell? She forced her legs under her and sat up, the effort making her nauseous.

Whatever binding held her wrists was loose enough to wriggle out of. She got one wrist free, then brought the other one forward. She touched the man's belt wrapped around it. Then she scanned her body. She hadn't had sex. Thank god for small favors.

She felt her way around the dark room, and her hands found the cold porcelain of a toilet. She used it to haul herself up, then promptly threw up into it. Aspirin. If she didn't stop this headache, she'd never be able to get out.

She made her way to the sink in the dark and rinsed out her mouth, then splashed water on her face. Shit! Pain bloomed again. Her hand found the light switch on the wall.

Holy crap. No wonder her head hurt. Her right eye was purple and swollen shut, and the remnants of a bloody nose traced down her face.

Those fucking punks. Her face hurt less now that she could see what had happened. She hadn't been punched in the face since high school when Mandy Shuster made up a song about her dad being a criminal.

She ran up to Mandy and pushed her. Mandy returned the favor with a left hook to the eye.

Her mind swam back from the memory. The bigger problem revealed itself with drunken clarity. She could see she'd been punched and knew she'd been cuffed, kind of, and left to rot on a bathroom floor. Hopefully, she was still in the party house and hadn't been moved somewhere else. Her cloudy mind took stock of the facts but didn't really seem to care.

She cleaned the blood off her face, leaving brown smudges on a cream-colored hand towel. Her mind planned ways to get back at Federico and the other guy, Doraliz's ex, but even in her fog she knew now wasn't the time. She'd received their warning about investigating Doraliz. She needed to get home and regroup.

She opened the door to the bathroom as quietly as she could. Nothing stirred. She could see into the front entryway, and the gray light of early morning lit the marble. Relief washed through her as she recognized the house. She took her sandals off and hooked them over one finger before she padded down the hallway. Glancing into the great room, she saw the aftermath of the party. Empty glasses, a pink stain on a white rug. She thought about stealing the expensive bottle of tequila beckoning her from the bar but thought better of it and opened the front door instead.

Her dusty white truck shared company on the circular drive with a Porsche Boxster and a Land Rover. The keys were in it. She reached over to unlock the glove box and found her wallet, money, and passport card intact. She started the engine and headed back to El Paso, her head pulsing with pain and worried thoughts.

Angus's Ford Escort waited in front of her house. She opened the door as quietly as she could. Tela looked up from the bed, with Angus gently snoring beside her. He'd earned a place on the bed, hell, he spent more time at the house than she did lately.

She wanted to shower the grimy night away, but her head pounded, and it just seemed like too much effort. She found her Tylenol instead, took four, and left her dress on the floor as she slipped into bed next to Angus.

"Hey," he said, groggily throwing an arm over her.

"Hey. Thanks for taking care of Tela. Go back to sleep."

Of course, he didn't. Instead, he rolled over, rose on his elbows, and looked at her.

"Oh god, what happened to you?"

"Someone slipped something into my drink, then punched me."

"Did you call the cops?" Angus sat up and gently pulled her hair back from her face to study the wound.

"I was in Juarez." No one called the cops in Juarez, at least no one who needed help.

"Let me take you to the hospital or the emergency clinic." Panic rose in his voice.

"No, Angus, I'm fine. I just need to sleep."

"You're not fine!" he practically yelled. "You can't do this job anymore. What if they had killed you? Women disappear in Juarez all the time."

"They weren't going to kill me. They were just a couple of rich punks. It makes me even more curious about what happened to Doraliz, with friends like that."

Angus crawled out of bed and Jessica laid her head back on the pillow, waiting for the Tylenol to kick in. She closed her eyes and listened to the clatter of kibble dropping into Tela's metal bowl.

She tried to sort through the competing thoughts that swirled through her. She wanted to get back at those degenerates, but even more, she wondered what they were hiding. She remembered the drunk girl who seemed to be the only one who cared about what had happened to Doraliz. Hopefully, she hadn't met a similar fate.

Jessica couldn't imagine Federico hurting anyone, but he had let her be hurt. The name of Doraliz's boyfriend floated just outside her grasp. Claudia. No, that was the drunk girl.

Could Federico and his friends have disappeared women? She'd almost nodded off when the thought invaded. They were too young to be responsible for the early disappearances. Women had been vanishing on the border since before they were born. But who knows what young men with too much money did for fun. No. She'd known Federico for years. Her brain hurt too much for this.

The bed sagged with Angus's weight. He covered her swollen eye with something that sent a flash of cold shooting across her face.

"Ow! Fuck that hurts!" Jessica tried to sit up, pain searing through her eye socket.

"Let me do this. It's ice." Angus sounded on the verge of tears.

Jessica opened her good eye. "I'm sorry, Ang. I wasn't expecting it." She relaxed into the pillow. "Try again."

She bit her lip to bear the pain. His touch was gentle, and once the ice started cooling the bruise, the pain lessened. "Thanks. It feels really good now."

"I worry about you all the time." She could hear the tears in his voice. She kept her eyes closed.

"I've been getting in trouble since elementary school. You know that." Jessica kept her voice light, but guilt mixed with the sudden awareness that she had been lucky. Maybe the drugs had infuriated her instead of warning her of danger. She didn't want a job where she woke tied up on bathroom floors. Why couldn't she ever have a soft place to land?

She reached for Angus. "Come here, please."

"I've got to take care of your eye."

"Just hold me." She hated the desperation in her voice.

He lay down beside her, moving gently. He kept the ice on her face but managed to stretch his lean body along hers. Warm comfort flooded her, a triumph over fear, danger, and death. As long as she could feel him, she was alive.

She wrapped her fingers around the nape of his neck, pulling him forward until their lips met. The hunger in her grew. She needed his weight, the touch of his skin, the act of giving and taking, as proof of life.

"Jessica, stop. We can't do this. You're hurt." He breathed the words into her.

"I need you. I need to feel alive." The tears that escaped her eyes cooled her skin before disappearing into the pillow. He kissed her, slow and carefully. Angus, the one she relied on to help her feel better when people said things about her dad, the one who cared for Tela as much as she did, the one who fixed her when she hurt. She sank into him again, relying on him to fill the empty spaces.

He kissed her with tenderness, then with more urgency as his body grew hotter. He managed to gently hold the ice pack to her eye while his lips explored her neck and breast. His free hand stroked her sides and belly and thighs, each silky pass of his palm leaving a warm trail of healing in its wake.

By the time he shifted onto her, she trembled with desire. Sex was beautiful with him. Slow, hot, with none of the acrobatics and show of the guys she picked up in bars. She'd have to quit this someday. She couldn't need anything this much and not end up disappointed.

But today, she let herself have him. More careful than he'd ever been, his gentleness touched a bruised place inside her. He soothed it and healed it until she sparkled with life and let everything go. Then she slept.

Jessica woke to a patch of afternoon sun warming her bed. A dull ringing in her ears and an inability to open her left eye remained, but her mind had cleared. She reached for the hurt eye and touched a cool gel pack.

"Angus?"

"Right here."

She turned her head and saw him next to her, reading a novel. Tela rose from her spot between them and licked Jessica's face.

"Good girl." She petted the dog. "How do I look?"

The dog cocked her head and whined. Angus spoke. "Your eye is dark purple now instead of red, especially underneath it, but the swelling has gone down a lot."

"Thanks for taking care of me."

"Always. Can I get you anything?"

"I'm starving. Any chance you want to go get me gorditas from the Little Diner?"

"Can we have a serious talk about your job first?"

Shit. She knew this would happen. But she owed it to him. Her brain must have considered the Doraliz issue as she slept, because she knew what she had to do. She took a sip from the full glass of water beside the bed.

"I have to find her, Angus. She may be in trouble."

"Why are you the person who needs to find her? You're not a cop or an investigator. You sell Mexican buildings to American companies so they can take advantage of cheap labor. And you have a side hustle delivering documents and checks and other things people trust you with. That's very different from finding a person."

"I got close yesterday. This woman may be in trouble, and she's got a family who's worried about her. That really means something to me. Besides, those guys have something to hide, and I don't want to leave her with people who may hurt her. Or maybe they don't want to hurt her, they just don't want me looking into this."

"Then don't look into it. It can't be worth the money. I'll give you money."

"Angus, you don't have any money. You work in a record store."

"I own a record store."

"You can hardly afford to pay yourself. And besides, I like my job. It's exciting."

"Last night was way too exciting. I can't watch you do this to yourself." His emotion pulsed through the room.

"I didn't ask you to." She saw her words hurt him. She might as well have punched him in the eye. But she had to. She'd done it for years: tried to get him to care a little less, to find someone else, but Angus was loyal as a dog. He deserved the whole marriage and family bundle she'd never offer him. They'd had that tired, ragged argument so many times. He told her he wasn't waiting for her, but he was always there to pick up the pieces.

Angus groaned and threw his book on the floor. "You are impossible."

"She needs to be found. I promise, no more parties."

"How about no more Mexico?"

"Let me see what I can find out from here. It's not like I can go out looking like this."

"One more thing." He leaned toward her, his face serious. And very sexy. "I want to stay here with you, at least for a few days. If these guys get mad again, I don't want you here alone."

"Fine." Despite her constant desire to handle things on her own, his offer brought a sense of relief, and safety. She had one condition. "But only if you don't tell Luz and Sarah what happened."

"Who do you think I got the gel pack from? It's not like you'd have something like that lying around."

"Damn it, Angus."

"Chill. I told them you had too much tequila and slipped and knocked your head on the bar."

"You're kidding. And they believed it?"

"Have you met you? Anyone would believe it." He swept his thumb under her injured eye so softly it felt like silk on suede. "I'm staying for a week. Then we'll talk. No arguments." His thumb lowered to her lips and pressed against them, stopping the coming protest.

She nodded. One week. She could handle that.

Chapter 6

The minute Angus left for work on Monday morning, Jessica dialed Federico's office. His secretary asked her to wait, then returned to the phone and said he was unavailable. The long pause told Jessica he was in the office but didn't want to talk to her.

She tried his cell phone, and it went to voice mail. Her anger grew. She would make him answer for this. She called the secretary back.

"Please tell Federico that if he won't talk to me right now, I'll come to the office and make sure everyone sees my black eye and knows where it came from. Tell him he has sixty seconds to take my call." She'd do it too. It wouldn't ruin his career or anything, but having a professional, American woman blame you for her black eye would spread fire-hot gossip among his colleagues. He'd have trouble overcoming the rumors.

Federico came on the line. "What do you want?" His voice sounded stiff, and angry.

"What the fuck, Federico! Do you want to explain what the hell happened to me at that party and why?" She spat the words at him.

"Do you want to explain why you used me to invite you to a party where you started an inquisition about Doraliz Velasco?"

She had used him, but that alone shouldn't have gotten her drugged, punched, and thrown in a bathroom. "Sure, I'll tell you that. Her father hired me to find her. He's worried about his daughter, and after what you did to me, I understand his concern."

"I would never hurt Doraliz." He sounded sincere, shocked even.

"You had no trouble letting me get hurt. Maybe you didn't land the blows, but you watched it happen. Did her boyfriend get angry at her for dumping him or something? You can't tell me he wouldn't hurt someone. He slugged me just for asking about Doraliz."

"You're getting involved in something you know nothing about. Doraliz isn't like the rest of us. You need to leave this alone."

"What do you mean Doraliz isn't like the rest of you?" From what Jessica knew of Doraliz, she was young, rich, Mexican. She'd thought of her exactly as she'd thought of the others. She also noticed his interesting use of the present tense, as if he knew Doraliz was alive.

"Jessica, take my advice and stick to real estate. There's nothing for you to find in this search. And if you think we're dangerous, then you don't know her father at all. Don't call again." The line went dead.

Jessica stared at the phone in her hand. Last night, she'd have bet the boyfriend had lost control and hurt Doraliz. Speaking with Federico confused things. He almost made it sound like he wanted to protect Doraliz. But why?

Doraliz and her friends seemed to have perfect lives. They didn't have to worry about money. The men usually went into the family business and the women became socialites, married, and had kids. It wasn't a life Jessica would have chosen, but it definitely had its advantages. The money and status alone had to be better than always scrounging for the next job.

Jessica needed to learn more about Doraliz. She probably should have started with that, but what the hell did she know about finding people? She propped up the pillows in bed and got out her laptop, searching for anything she could find about Doraliz Velasco.

Doraliz had attended Loretto Academy from kindergarten through high school. Jessica knew the Catholic girl's school, a beautiful mass of stucco buildings perched on a hilltop in El Paso. Many rich Juarenses sent their kids to private schools in El Paso. The tradition had existed for generations.

After graduating, Doraliz left the area to attend Harvard, where she received a bachelor's and a master's degree in women, gender, and sexuality. Smart girl. Maybe Jessica had been a little quick to lump her in with the typical Juarez elite. She'd been in Boston for six years, a huge distance in time and place from the border. She'd only been back eighteen months before she disappeared.

Back in Juarez, Doraliz had become a spokesperson for her father's companies. What would cause someone to come back here, to transition from academia to being a shill for cement and construction materials? It seemed like a long fall.

Jessica dove into the woman's social media pages. Scrolling back through Doraliz's Instagram posts, the disconnect became real. Photos of nightlife in Juarez, many with Paula, the sparkly girl who hadn't wanted to talk to Jessica at the party. Those photos Jessica expected. The ones shot in the streets of the Juarez colonias, slums basically, like the one Jessica had visited on the edge of town, surprised her. A white-haired beggar with no teeth and outstretched palm, children selling gum in traffic, a pregnant woman with a dirty face sweating in the harsh sun, depicted a far less glamorous side of Juarez.

The interspersed photos, shots of beautiful people at fancy parties mixed with those depicting poverty and a lack of hope, jolted Jessica's sensibilities. They continued like that, wealthy versus impoverishment, happy and shiny followed by a child with a runny nose half covered in flies. It had to be deliberate. Did someone not like the message? Or perhaps Doraliz couldn't take it anymore. The photos made Jessica sick to her stomach, and not just the ones of poverty.

Eventually, Jessica scrolled back far enough to find Boston, the green and gray of grass and river instead of the beige and brown of the desert. The photos of people in Boston showed happy, healthy college kids in dorm rooms, on bikes, drinking beer. And protests.

That surprised Jessica. Doraliz had attended her fair share of protests. In Washington, D.C., New York City, Portland, Seattle. Another interesting facet to add to the woman.

Doraliz also documented vacations. She seemed to prefer the tropics. The location data listed Mexican beaches, Belize, Costa Rica, Honduras, and at least half a dozen trips to Caribbean islands. These photos came in three varieties, those featuring bikinis and swim trunks, a gallery's worth of colorful cocktails, and scuba. Jessica recognized

Doraliz's long wavy hair and hazel eyes from behind a mask and snorkel, then climbing onto a boat with a tank on her back, and a series of underwater shots. You couldn't have paid Jessica to jump in the ocean with all that gear. It didn't seem natural for someone from the desert to pick scuba diving as their hobby, but Doraliz had.

Jessica had seen a few photos of Doraliz with the boyfriend who'd likely given Jessica a black eye. She also found several photos of Doraliz with Tomás. He'd told her he knew Doraliz, but these photos suggested he knew her quite well, despite their ten-year age difference. The further back Jessica went, the more photos she found of Tomás. In one, on a beach, he stood behind her, hugging her. In a selfie, she kissed his cheek. Why hadn't he told her the truth about their relationship?

She thought about calling him, but if he'd wanted her to know the truth, he'd have told her. She kept combing through the information. She could always confront Tomás in the future.

Doraliz had two friends she tagged the most on social media. One was Paula. The other, Lauren Feldman, still lived in Boston. Jessica easily found her address. She looked up the professors in the Women and Gender Studies Department, wondering if any among the stern faces would help.

By the time Angus returned, Jessica had learned everything the internet had to offer on Doraliz. She'd even read a summary of her master's thesis, ironically, on the disappearance of women in Juarez. Perhaps that's where the connection lay. If Doraliz had continued her research here, she might have gotten a little too close to the answers. Too many people had too much to hide in the Mexican city. One more woman, even a prominent one, was a single grain of sand in the desert of hundreds of women who had disappeared in the city.

Angus checked on her eye and asked about her day. She wavered between pampered and annoyed, but she enjoyed having someone to talk to besides the dog. He must have sensed not to stay too long, because he'd only been back for about fifteen minutes before he took the dog out.

"Hey, let's go to dinner," Angus said when he'd returned from his run with Tela. "There's a black Ford Explorer parked at the junction with the main road. It was there this morning, and it hadn't moved when I came home."

"And?" Jessica asked.

"I want you to take your truck. I'll follow in my car."

"Because?" she asked, trying to figure out his odd concern.

"I think maybe they're watching you."

She looked at him and rolled her eyes. "I doubt it. Who would be following me?" She didn't mention her call to Federico.

"Just do it, Jessica. Please."

"Okay, okay. Let me see if I can cover this bruise with makeup." She went into the bathroom and pulled out every tube and pot of concealer and foundation she owned. The swelling had receded, and the edges of the bruise had tinges of green, but the dark purple showed through layers of makeup. She'd buy something heavier while they were out.

She added sunglasses to her outfit to hide her eye and block the evening sun. As she rolled down the gravel drive, she looked for the Explorer. It sat right where Angus said, about fifty yards from where she turned off the gravel road and onto pavement. How had he even noticed it? She'd have thought it was a farm vehicle, except it was a little too shiny and didn't have a truck bed. She turned onto the paved road and continued, checking her review mirror. It didn't seem to follow. She didn't see Angus behind her either. Fuck. She couldn't worry about every little thing.

They'd decided on her favorite pizza restaurant in town. She'd picked it in part because of its proximity to a drugstore where she could find something to cover the bruise. She parked at the restaurant and walked to CVS. Five minutes later, she returned, a bag of potions in her hand. A black SUV idled near her truck.

She stood in the parking lot, deciding whether to retreat into the store, sidle over to the pizza place, or walk right past them to her truck.

Screw it. After all she'd been through in her life, she wouldn't let some jackass in a big car scare her. She walked past the SUV peering inside to see the driver. Dark windows blocked her view, and when she glimpsed in through the windshield, she couldn't identify the baseball capped man shrinking into the shadowy interior. The vehicle continued down the lane as soon as she'd passed.

She put her cosmetics in the car and went into the restaurant. A few minutes later, Angus joined her at the table.

"They followed you," he said.

"I know. Don't get your panties in a wad, but I saw them in the parking lot."

"Jessica, you have to take this seriously!" He grabbed the edges of the table, and Jessica wasn't sure what he'd do next.

"I am taking it seriously, but I am not going to let them intimidate me."

"Well, let me tell you, they are intimidating the hell out of me!"

"I can tell." She doubted she could have picked a worse thing to say. Angus never got upset, but now his cheeks turned bright red, and he continued to grasp the table as if it might save him from drowning, or from attacking her stupidity.

He seemed at a loss for words, so she tried a different tack. "Look, would it make you happy if I left town for a few days?"

"What do you mean?"

"Well, I've been learning a lot about Doraliz. She was actually pretty interesting. She graduated from Harvard, and I thought I'd go see if her friends up there are a little more helpful than the ones in Juarez."

"Jessica. Let me say this again, hopefully in a way you'll understand. There. Are. People. Following. You. I don't think they'll stop at the city limits."

"What if you help me sneak out of town?"

Angus looked thoughtful for a moment and even released the table. "How?"

Although Jessica had made the trip up on the fly to calm Angus down, now that she'd brought it up, it seemed like a great idea. "What if you snuck me out in your car? They won't even know I've left the house."

"We don't even know who they are, although they seem plenty dangerous."

"That sounds like a great reason for me to leave El Paso." She worked her phone, looking for flights. "I can get on a flight to Boston three days from now at six in the morning and come back a few days later for about five hundred bucks."

"Where are you going to get that kind of cash?"

"I've got five thousand dollars from Daddy Velasco burning a hole in my pocket. This seems like the perfect thing to spend it on. Maybe I'll even ask for a raise."

"Except that those may be his guys out there."

She had thought about that. She didn't think Federico or anyone of that generation would have her so obviously followed. It seemed like more of an old school trick. "Maybe, but with your help, I can shake them. You'd have to stay at the house and look after Tela."

Angus sighed, deep and heavy like she'd hoisted the weight of the world, or at least of all her problems, onto him. "I'll do it, but only because I think you'll be safer there than here. But you have to stay in a nice hotel. No going cheap, no Airbnb where you'd be on your own."

"Scout's honor." She lifted two fingers.

"You were never a scout. And your honor is definitely questionable."

"That's for sure. But I do want to find this woman." The photos of Doraliz at protests and diving into blue water flipped through her mind. A vibrant woman with a family who cared about her had vanished. For once, Jessica could do something good with her talent. "I think there's some honor in that."

Chapter 7

Four-thirty in the morning came way too early. Jessica grabbed her bag while Angus started the car. She crawled into the back seat of the Ford Escort and drew her knees up into the world's most uncomfortable position, but it allowed Angus to close the door.

"Did you see them?" she asked when she felt the car make the turn from gravel to pavement.

"It's too dark. I can't tell if they're there."

A few minutes later, Angus let her know they were on the highway. She started to sit up.

"Stay down!" Angus yelled. "They might be following us."

"One knee is squishing my left breast, and I think my elbow is threatening my asshole. I can't stay like this forever."

"You can stay down for thirty more minutes. I'll drive fast."

She grumbled but had to admit she'd lucked out in her getaway driver. They'd had fun the past few days, or at least she had. She pretended to be annoyed each time he called to check up on her during the day, but she secretly loved it. He stocked the fridge, made coffee in the morning, and brought her delicious meals at night. It was almost worth the punch in the face.

She'd meant to kick him out of her bed but hadn't. It was comforting making love to the same person every night, and not waking with the urge to escape. And she slept like she'd been drugged. The biggest problem was that she could get used to having him around, and that was not who she wanted to be.

She tucked that problem away. She'd promised him a week. That promise she'd keep, along with the one to herself to make sure he left after seven days.

She'd learned young how love could mean giving all of yourself to one person, even if it destroyed someone else. That's what her mom had done. Jessica would never create a situation where she'd ruin other people just to stay with a man. And she'd never let herself get hurt like that again.

She tried to turn away from the ugly memory of her mother's abandonment, how easily she'd chosen to follow her husband to Fort Davis instead of staying with her sixteen-year-old daughter. Stuck in the car, unable to see forward or back, the thoughts threatened to bury her.

"Where are we?" she asked, struggling to escape from the claustrophobic beliefs.

"Close. Five more minutes."

Jessica closed her eyes and started counting the seconds, willing time to pass. When they arrived at the airport, she'd wedged herself in so tight Angus practically had to use a crowbar to pull her from the car.

"Thanks," she said, giving him a kiss on the cheek.

He pulled her back and kissed her fully on the lips. She softened into the kiss.

"Be careful," he said when they came up for air.

Jessica headed straight for the gate. None of the early morning travelers seemed to follow her, or care about her at all. She ordered a coffee and found a seat where she could survey the passengers. Nothing seemed amiss, just a bunch of sleepy travelers waiting on a plane to take them somewhere else.

After they'd boarded, she relaxed and looked through the notes and photos of Doraliz Velasco's life at Harvard. She didn't know how she'd have done this job pre-social media. She wondered how much of this information Ruben Velasco and his thugs had researched. Had they looked as far back as Boston? Surely, they had, unless they didn't believe she'd made it out of Juarez.

———

The next morning, she made her way to a brick building on Chauncy Street, the home of Lauren Feldman. As she passed through the iron gates and crossed a brick-paved courtyard, she stepped into the colonial America of elementary school history books. Green trees shaded greener grass and it all looked so proper, a different time and place than the deserts of home.

She pulled on the front door of the apartment building. Locked. After a few minutes, a young man rushed out. She smiled at him, and he pushed the door wider so she could enter. Sarah had always told her she had her mom's friendly eyes. Her dad had given her and her mother matching pendants one Christmas, aquamarine to match their eyes, he'd said. She'd thrown the pendant into the Rio Grande in a fit of rage but still used her eyes to her advantage. They stood out against her mahogany hair and black eyebrows. Something about them helped people in her job trust her, the same way they beckoned people to stop her on the street and ask for directions. Today, they'd probably given her access to the building without a second glance.

She found the door to Lauren's unit and knocked. She waited, then knocked again. Nothing. She debated leaving a note, but after what had happened at the Juarez party, perhaps it was best if people didn't know she had questions about Doraliz.

Returning to the crisp morning air, Jessica used her phone to figure out how to get to the Schlesinger Library. Allegedly, the missing woman's thesis would be housed there. She walked across a green lawn, caught in a kaleidoscope of red brick, bright foliage, and white painted window sashes. It was beautiful, but the multi-story buildings, saturated colors, and crammed streets hemmed her in. The sky crouched small above her, instead of expanding like a dome until it reached the mountains or a far horizon. She wondered whether the sophistication of the area had attracted Doraliz, or if she also missed the freedom of home.

Eventually, Jessica found the library and went to the desk for help. A young woman who must have been a student looked something up on the computer and wrote down the section and directions. Jessica quickly found the tome and opened it at a long wooden table that reminded her of an older, richer version of the library at her college, the University of Texas at El Paso.

Even the title, *Femicide in Ciudad Juarez: Gender, Power, and Murder in a Mexican City*, seemed to put Doraliz in danger. Jessica thumbed through the book, stopping to read pages far drier than the title suggested. The hundreds of women murdered or missing horrified her. She'd heard of them over the years but had become inoculated to the crimes. Here, in a library far from home, a mass of silenced women assaulted her.

She wished she'd never opened the book, never learned the word *narcofosa*, mass graves attributed to organized crime. She wanted to unlearn the two types of murders, intimate ones perpetrated by someone close to the victim, and systemic sexual murders resulting in tortured bodies abandoned in the desert. The *maquilas*, foreign companies that industrialized northern Mexico lured women from throughout the country, gave them mobility and independence, and left them vulnerable. These women became an affront to the power and aggression of machismo, and despite international attention, investigations went nowhere. The names of women who'd disappeared and nameless bodies discovered in the desert created negative space, suffocating black holes where lives used to exist.

As she neared the end, Jessica realized that while Doraliz had written of the patriarchy, gendered roles, and the feeble rights of women, specific people were absent. The system hurt the women, not individuals. Their names were unknown, the crimes went unsolved, and the aggression and hyper-masculinity of machismo carried on.

While Doraliz hadn't named names, her dissertation cast a bright light on the troubles in her hometown. Had this caused her disappearance, or was it something more intimate? A family member, a friend. Or maybe just a desire to leave the ugliness behind. After reaching the last page, Jessica wanted to leave it behind, and she'd only skimmed the dissertation, not given birth to it.

She turned back to the beginning and read the acknowledgments. A single line graced the top of the page: *To my major professor and mentor, Dr. Phyllis Gold, thank you for the strength and guidance to bare my soul.*

The absence of the Velasco name, the parents who'd funded every word, spoke volumes. Jessica closed the book.

The murders in Juarez clearly haunted Doraliz. In her search for theories in the hellscape of home, she had avoided the men most often blamed. Her written words revealed systemic, not personal, issues. To bare your soul was personal.

She looked up Professor Gold on her phone and located her office. The woman at the library desk gave her directions.

Jessica tramped across the verdant lawn toward Professor Gold's office. Lawns meant status in the desert, and waste. Water was precious. Here, they symbolized wealth in a different way. If you could afford the space for a lawn in such a dense community, you must hold wealth and power. The role of power in Doraliz's study must have infiltrated her thoughts. After all, it was just grass.

Jessica found the door adorned with the brass nameplate Phyllis A. Gold, Ph.D. She knocked.

"Come in."

Jessica opened the door to find a tiny woman with spiky gray hair buried behind a paper-laden desk. "Dr. Gold, I'm Jessica Watts. Do you have a minute?"

"Sure, come in. You're not a student of mine, are you?"

"No." Jessica sat and tried for her warmest smile. She didn't think Professor Gold would punch her in the face, but so far, people seemed reticent to share information about Doraliz. "I've come here from El Paso, Texas. I've been hired to find an ex-student of yours, Doraliz Velasco. Did you know she was missing?"

The shock on the professor's face answered the question. She sat up straight, seeming to grow in size and authority. "What? When did this happen?"

"She's been gone just over two weeks." Jessica watched the professor turn thoughtful, then resolute.

"Well, that's interesting." The woman sighed, but her face remained emotionless.

"Interesting? Aren't you worried about her? I just looked through her thesis. You know what can happen to women in Juarez." How could interesting possibly be the right word to describe the disappearance of a twenty-four-year-old woman?

"Well, yes, I am worried. But Doraliz is a resourceful woman. Why are you here?" The professor's gaze was no longer friendly.

"Her family hired me to find her."

"Also interesting. You look a little young to be a PI."

"I help with things on the border. Deals and things." Why was it so hard to explain her profession? She thought of herself as a fixer. If you needed real estate, she found it for you. If someone needed documents delivered, she'd make it happen. Whatever you needed, she'd be there.

"You help with things. So, you help find the young women who are disappearing?" The professor seemed more interested now.

"No. Only this time. I help with buildings, and money transfers, documents." Not exactly the important stuff.

"Oh. I see. You help the rich people, like the Velascos." The interest on the professor's face faded.

"Yes. They are very worried about their daughter." Indignation laced Jessica's voice. Who was this woman who seemed worried about Doraliz one moment and uncaring the next?

"You know, Doraliz's theories about power and money were fascinating," the professor said. "Even the wealthy can be caged by society."

Was this supposed to be a hint? "You think Doraliz was caged? Do you think she's in trouble?" Jessica needed frankness, not word games.

"Mexico is not exactly a bastion for women's rights. No place is."

"You're right about that." Jessica needed to move the conversation toward specifics. "Do you think Doraliz would come back here if she was in trouble?"

"Well, if she did, I certainly wouldn't tell you about it."

Great. Jessica tried a different tack. "If she was so concerned about the women in Juarez, why didn't she try to help them? She went to all kinds of different protests in the United States, environmental, women's rights, police brutality. But in the year and half she was back in Juarez, she worked for her dad as a spokesperson. I'm not aware of anything she did to act on the ideals in her thesis."

The professor steepled her fingers under her chin. "Tell me, how powerful is Doraliz's father?"

Jessica remembered how Tomás had categorized Ruben Velasco. "Even the rich and powerful in Juarez consider him an echelon above them."

"How many of those upper echelons have blood on their hands? How would you fight that from the inside?"

"I don't know. I haven't thought about that. But I am really worried about her." Jessica wondered if the shadow of her bruise showed through her makeup.

The professor softened. "I honestly don't know where Doraliz is. I haven't heard from her in months. Doraliz's passions ran deep, but she had a hard time being herself in that family and living within the codes of the Mexican elite. Sometimes, family is just not worth it."

"You don't have to tell me that." They sat together in the truth of that moment. Jessica wondered about the professor's story.

Finally, Professor Gold spoke. "The blessing of adulthood is that we choose our own family. I think you should leave Doraliz alone."

"What if she's hurt?"

"What if she isn't?"

They stared each other down, Jessica thinking about the loneliness of the world and the questions impossible to answer. If Doraliz was alive, she was alone. Jessica knew the state well. She could be alone because she made a choice, or because someone made it for her.

Had Jessica had a choice? She could have gone with her parents and left everything she knew. High school, friends, her future. Or her mom could have stayed so she wouldn't be alone. Her mom chose to leave.

Doraliz. She was here to find Doraliz, not parse her own past. "Thanks for your help. If you think of anything else, let me know. I need to find out what happened to her. This is personal for me." Jessica took out a business card and stretched it toward the professor.

"You don't need to find her," the woman said. "But you're clearly tied up in this. You may want to ask yourself why. If something bad has happened to Doraliz, and I pray it hasn't, then we are likely too late. If she chose a different path, you should honor that." She took Jessica's card and put it directly into the trashcan. "Please leave. I won't be contacting you." The woman crossed her arms. Her stare had gone cold.

Jessica left the office. While her picture of Doraliz became clearer with every visit, she'd hit another dead end about her location. She returned to the apartment building, hoping Lauren Feldman would be home.

Someone let her in, again. The security in this place sucked. She rapped on Lauren's door.

"Coming," a voice said from inside. A few seconds later, a woman with a mass of dark blond hair opened the door. She startled when she saw Jessica and half closed the door. "Who are you?"

"I'm Jessica Watts. Are you Lauren Feldman?"

"Yes," the woman answered, wary and questioning.

"You're friends with Doraliz Velasco, and unfortunately, she's gone missing. I've been hired to find her. Have you seen her in the last few weeks?" Jessica tried to summon her inner detective but didn't know if the direct approach would work.

"Huh. Good. I have no idea where she is."

"Good? You think it's good that she's missing?" Maybe Lauren's friendship status had changed. But she wasn't angry. Perhaps she knew something.

"Like I said, I don't know where she is." The woman closed the door.

"Are you hiding her?"

The door cracked open. "Are you kidding? She'd never come here. This is the first place people like you would look. Please leave." The door closed again.

At least people here were nice enough to say please when they kicked her out. She tried one more time. "Are you sure you can't help me find her?"

"Leave now or I'm calling the police."

Jessica followed directions. In a way, the trip had been a bust. But it didn't feel that way. For the first time, it seemed like maybe Doraliz had escaped rather than been taken. But that left two big questions: why and where.

Jessica wandered back to the hotel, unsure of her next move. She tried to imagine the streets as Doraliz had seen them, but it didn't help. The surprise on the women's faces meant Doraliz wasn't in Boston.

In the room, Jessica splayed across the hotel bed. White bed linens, anonymous prints, she could have been anywhere in the country. When she traveled for work, every American hotel room looked pretty much like this one.

Her conversation with Doraliz's professor haunted her, especially the part about the rich being caged. Jessica had the opposite problem. Her parents had left without teaching her to fly. But she'd figured it out on her own, and that's how she worked best.

Doraliz seemed to have the opposite dilemma. A smart girl, she'd returned to her parents' cage in Juarez. It didn't make any sense. With her education, surely, she could have gotten a job almost anywhere. Did she return to Juarez to follow up on her thesis? Did that get her in trouble? Perhaps the cage was made of money and, despite her education, she didn't have the know-how to live on her own.

Jessica called Sr. Velasco and left a message with his secretary that she'd like to talk to him and his wife. He called back immediately.

"Have you found my daughter?"

Shit. She should have made that clear to the secretary. "No sir. Not yet. But I have learned a lot more about her. I would like to speak with you and your wife about Doraliz. I think it will help me locate her. Do you have time to meet on Monday?"

"My wife is very upset about Doraliz. I think it would hurt her more to speak with you. Perhaps you can just talk to me."

Jessica sighed. "If you want me to find her, I need information."

"Fine. I will send a vehicle for you. I'll have my secretary call you with the time."

He hung up before Jessica had the chance to tell him she'd drive herself. Cage indeed. Daddy had control issues.

Chapter 8

"You're back!" Angus opened the door wide. "You should have called me. I'd have picked you up at the airport." He walked toward her with open arms.

Jessica put a hand on his chest to stop him from embracing her. The trip and constant deliberation about Doraliz had exhausted her. She needed space. Plus, Angus's week was about up. He'd want to stay, and she just couldn't have that. "I made it back fine on my own."

"You know I like helping you."

"I know. And you've helped me a lot. I owe you." That she meant. The debt went back decades, and she'd never be able to repay it.

"You don't owe me. This isn't a transactional relationship." Frustration filled his voice.

"I know." She stepped in and hugged him hard. Someday he'd realize she'd never be enough for him.

"You're ready for me to leave, aren't you?"

"You know how I am. You're the best guy in the world, but I'm better off alone."

"Why do you believe that? And don't tell me about your parents, I've heard that sad story a million times. You're a grown woman now. Don't let the scars they left make your decisions for you." He almost whispered the last words and tried to take her hands as she backed away.

She snapped her hands from his, his soft words hitting like a gut punch. She could never become the woman he needed. "Why the hell do you keep hanging around when I've told you over and over again that I'm not the one? There are a million girls out there better for you than me. Go find someone who will love you the way you want. And where's my dog?"

"Tela's at the big house with the other dogs."

Jessica could tell her verbal punch had landed by the sadness in his eyes. She rolled her bag into the house and started unpacking. Each movement jerked with frustration. He always pushed too far. It would be so easy to give in, but she'd promised herself to never hurt him the way her parents hurt her. Better a few little cuts along the way than a future amputation. She couldn't imagine her world without him, but she needed him at a safe distance.

"Jessica, look at me."

She turned to him, hands on hips, prepared to block whatever emotion came her way.

"I want you. I've always wanted you. You know that."

"But that's your problem, because you know I don't want anyone." She willed the tears in her eyes to stay put. She hated wounding him, and she'd done it too many times. He had to go live his own life.

She left the clothes half unpacked on the sofa. "I'm going to get Tela." It hurt too much to stay in her small house, watching their few days of pretend domestic bliss disintegrate. If she were a different person, she'd choose him. But that wasn't the life she'd been dealt.

———

This time when Ruben Velasco's secretary escorted her into his office, the two thugs she'd met before were already seated along the wall. Surprisingly, Sr. Velasco nodded at them to leave before inviting her to sit in the lone chair in front of his desk.

"Thank you for coming. I wish you had let my driver pick you up. It can be dangerous for a woman to drive alone in Juarez."

"Thank you for the offer. It wasn't possible today," she said. Even though she drove in Juarez all the time for her job. Even though he probably knew she hadn't run any errands since he likely had other thugs follow her.

"What have you learned of my daughter?"

"I've talked to some people who knew her, and I hoped you and your wife would answer a few questions."

"You are scheduled to speak with my wife after we talk. What questions do you have of me?"

"I assume you are aware of your daughter's thesis research on the murders of women in Juarez. Did she continue this research after she returned home?"

"Everyone in this city is concerned about the missing women. I believe she completed her research when she received her degree. When she returned home, I hired her to help with one of my companies. She is a spokesperson for Cemexico."

"Do you believe she ran away?"

A flush of anger crossed his face. He tried to smooth it, but two deep lines creased his forehead. "If I were certain, I would not have hired you."

Jessica waited him out. Maybe she could get the truth out of him now that he seemed flustered.

"My daughter is a very smart woman. Perhaps it was difficult for her after being in such an esteemed academic center. You know, I went to Harvard as well."

Jessica raised her eyebrows. Surely, he wouldn't turn this conversation toward himself. He must have seen her surprise.

"But that is not why you are here. Have you spoken with her friends?"

"Some of them. They aren't eager to share information." The chill of waking up on a cold bathroom floor filled her spine with ice.

"Yes. I have had the same response. I cannot tell if they are hiding information about Doraliz. Perhaps she needed a break from this city, but it is time for her to come home now. Her place is in this family."

Images of gilded bars sprouted around Jessica. While imaginary, their heft seemed real. "Señor Velasco, I don't think I'm the right person for this case. Your daughter is an adult, and if she chose a different life, that is her decision." Jessica knew from experience that choice, when it came to family, rarely felt like an option.

"You have agreed to this job. You have taken my money. I expect you to learn everything you can about my daughter's disappearance and report back to me." Any hint of frustration had gone. Stone-faced and cold-voiced, he stared into her as if his look alone would erase her words.

"You need to hire a professional." How the hell had she gotten into this mess? She'd built her career around buildings and documents, things without emotions, for a reason. Family would never be her area of expertise.

His neck reddened. His hands clasped together so tightly it looked painful. He appeared ready to erupt.

Eventually, he took a long breath, the volcano turning to ice. "You are my last resort. I have hired others, worked with the police, used my own men. As a young woman, you may understand her and her friends better than those who have tried to find her so far."

His voice filled the room. Then he paused, seeming to fight his own emotions. He took a long shuddering breath, gaining control, and returned his attention to Jessica. "You will do this job. You will gain the trust of her friends and talk to them. I hired you based on your reputation. You make your living off my people like a parasite. If you want to continue your esteemed career, you will do as I ask."

His accusation stole the oxygen from her lungs. How dare he threaten her career? Jessica had to escape the poisonous room. Velasco's chilling formality, interrupted by flashes of anger, made her question his sanity. The thought that he could have killed his daughter flashed through her head. She'd fallen deep into the belly of a dangerous world.

He must have noticed his effect on her because he relaxed and almost sounded sorry. "We protect our own in this city. If you do not have the competence to complete my request, I will have to inform my friends of your," he seemed to search for the word, "inadequacy. I promise, you do not want this. Now, you said you had questions for me."

She held her breath, struggling to identify her next move. Velasco certainly had the contacts to ruin her career. But could she work for someone who threatened her? Part of her wanted to run for the door, but rash action would be stupid. She'd take the next step and regroup later.

She took a breath and dove back into interview mode. "Doraliz traveled a lot. What were some of her favorite places?"

"I made sure she was well traveled. Europe, the Middle East, South America. She is very sophisticated, my daughter. Perhaps she has returned to Spain or Italy."

Jessica stared at him. Nothing she'd learned about Doraliz made her think Spain or Italy. He spoke about the daughter he wanted, not the one he had.

"Try again with her friends. Tomás told me people trust you. They may not want to talk at first, but you can gain their trust and find her for me. If you have any additional questions, let me know. I believe it is time for you to see my wife. She is waiting for you in the conference room."

"Thank you for your time." Jessica couldn't wait to escape the room, despite having gained so little information. She doubted she had anything more to learn from him, seeing how little he knew his own daughter.

"You must understand that Doraliz is my only child, and this has been extremely hard for my wife. Please treat her with care." He opened his desk and took out a manila envelope, which he handed Jessica when he stood to say goodbye.

Jessica could tell from its weight it contained another payment. The woman who carried her wallet and phone in pockets now needed a tote to cart around this man's dirty money. Still, she took the envelope. She didn't want the work, but she had to find a way to quit that wouldn't jeopardize her career.

The secretary led her down the hall to a conference room with a table for eight. A woman wearing a white turtleneck, fur-collared vest, and slim white pants sat at the table. Smooth ash-blond hair curved artfully around razor-sharp cheekbones cut across drawn cheeks. Her hand clasped a pack of cigarettes. A book of matches lay on the table, yet the room smelled of Chanel, not smoke.

The woman looked Jessica up and down with pure, unadulterated judgment. Jessica checked her clothing for a stain. She wore her everyday professional uniform: black boots, black slacks, a silk shell top, teal today, and a black jacket. Not high fashion, but she considered it classy. Doraliz's mother looked like she'd just smelled a wet dog.

"Hi, I'm Jessica Watts. I'm here to talk about your daughter."

The mask of superiority dissolved and grief emerged. Dark brows framed troubled eyes gone wet, and the artificially plump lips thinned into a grimace. The woman turned the pack of cigarettes over, flat side, tall side. Flat side, tall side.

Jessica lowered herself onto a hard chair at a table so large it made intimacy impossible. The room stilled except for the cigarettes softly slapping the wood.

"Señora Velasco, thank you for seeing me. Do you have any idea what happened to Doraliz?"

The woman shook her head. When she set down the cigarettes and raised a hand to wipe away a silent tear, Jessica noticed a tremor. "I hope you can find my daughter." The reedy voice had a pleading tone.

Thoughts of abandoning the job vanished. Sra. Velasco's heartbreak struck at Jessica's core. This woman loved her daughter. "I hope I can too. Any information you can give me would help."

The woman nodded.

"Are there places she might have gone? People she might have wanted to see?"

"I don't know." The woman looked down at her hands. "I have no idea what happened to her. She had just come home after so many years away."

"Doraliz seems like a smart young woman. Maybe she just needed to get away for a while. Do you think that could have happened?"

A sigh shuddered through the woman's entire body. "I hope you are right. Perhaps she just needed to get away." Sra. Velasco leaned toward Jessica and fixed her with a hazel stare. "She was always very intelligent, but so rebellious and fierce in her beliefs. I tried to help her learn to function in a world with rules, but she hated being confined. I think it would have been better if she hadn't gone so far away to school."

"To Harvard?" How could a mother not want that kind of success for her daughter?

"Yes. They had a lot of influence on her there. They took her to march in the streets and filled her head with ideas."

Lady, that's what college is for. Jessica stopped herself from saying the words. She chose different ones instead, keeping the frustration from her voice. "You mean ideas like trying to understand why the authorities have been unable to solve the disappearance of hundreds of women here in Juarez?"

"Those questions bring nothing but trouble. We should not talk of that." The woman's eyes bored into Jessica.

"But the disappearances were the subject of Doraliz's research. Do you think this is related to her disappearance?" Why couldn't these people talk about the subject that had driven their daughter's intellectual life?

Sra. Velasco's eyes widened with black fear. "No! It is not possible. She did that research when she was far away. It stopped there. She wouldn't have continued that here. It is dangerous. And besides, here in Juarez, the people know who my husband is. No one crosses Ruben Velasco. No one would dare hurt Doraliz." She crossed her arms.

"Then please help me. I can't find her if everyone refuses to tell me where she might be. Where would you go if you were Doraliz? Do you think she's in Mexico? Did she take her passport?" Why couldn't anyone just tell her where they thought Doraliz had gone? She kept her gaze on Sra. Velasco, hoping to break through.

"I have her passport. She left it in her room." The woman grew still and circled her index finger around the room. She leaned closer and whispered, "Doraliz loved to scuba dive."

Following her lead, Jessica leaned forward and spoke softly. "I've seen photos of her with dive equipment. What were her favorite places? Cancún? Cozumel?"

Sra. Velasco cocked her head for a moment, seeming to think. "The beaches in Mexico are like our backyard," she whispered. "It's impossible to visit there without seeing people you know. Doraliz, she loved Central America. She used to go to the big islands off the east coast of Costa Rica and El Salvador."

"Costa Ri—"

The woman put a finger to her lips and shook her head, her eyes warily scanning the room. Her hand still shook. The room had ears, a fresh circle of hell.

"Is there anything else you can tell me? Did she take her scuba equipment?" Jessica whispered.

"She did not take anything. Everything of hers is here."

"I don't understand." Jessica tried to keep her voice low, but frustration made it difficult. People just didn't disappear. Except for women. In Juarez.

Sra. Velasco shook her head, whether in shared exasperation or sadness, Jessica couldn't tell. But then she leaned forward, almost touching her head to Jessica's. "She couldn't have flown unless she has fake identification. Maybe she could sneak across a border, then get to an island." The woman's voice was so low Jessica strained to catch the words.

"Anything else?" Jessica asked. "Is there a particular place, a person she might know?"

Sra. Velasco shook her head, then sat up straight, the icy veneer returning to her face. "Thank you for speaking with me," she said, her voice slightly louder than necessary. "If I can be of assistance again, please let me know."

Sra. Velasco rose. She paused as she walked by Jessica. A wiry hand reached out to grab her wrist with ferocity. "Please bring my daughter home." Her other hand swiped the matches off the table. "For you," she said, pressing them into Jessica's hand and abandoning the cigarettes on the table.

Jessica jumped up and followed her out the door. She wouldn't spend one more second in this building than necessary. In the parking lot, she hugged the envelope of money to her chest and dug her truck keys out of her pocket. A bit of her power returned as she unlocked the truck, got in, and steered onto the crowded streets of Juarez.

She had been controlled and manipulated in that office building. Driving her own truck away from it, putting distance between the controlling father and bizarre mother, returned her to herself. Family sucked.

Doraliz's family might be even more screwed up than hers. She'd actually had a pretty good family life as a kid. But things had gone south about the time she hit her teenage years. Even before he'd been arrested and tried, her father had changed. He worked later at night and on weekends and seemed perpetually tense. Of course, she hadn't known there was a good reason for that. Instead, just as hormones turned her into a whiny, angsty version of herself, her dad had transformed into a total dick.

Jessica bet Doraliz's dad wrote the book on that. He commanded, threatened, exploited. She hated working for him and couldn't imagine being related to him. And the icy mom. Once, Jessica had loved her mom with every thought and drop of blood she had.

Those days were long gone. She'd traded pink dresses and tiaras for black jeans and tequila long ago. The jeans and matching eyeliner came the day her mother left. The tequila came a little later. She'd spent a lot of nights drinking at the clubs in Juarez after high school. Everyone did. It helped her escape from the responsibility of being on her own.

The Velascos gained points for funding their kid's education. Jessica's parents had been gone for almost two years when she started at UTEP, taking a job at Starbucks to help pay her way. Jealousy toward Doraliz came easily, but in the end, Jessica probably had the better deal. Her parents' leaving had forced her to grow up early. It had been terrible, and she wouldn't wish that kind of fuckery on anyone, but she'd come out the other end just fine.

Doraliz hadn't been so lucky. She'd either been kidnapped or murdered or had chosen to escape. After a week on the case, Jessica leaned toward escape. The cold calculation she'd seen on Ruben Velasco's face sent a chill through her. Yes, family sucked, but Jessica far preferred hers to the Velascos.

Worry about Doraliz nagged at Jessica as she drove through increasingly uninhabited desert. She'd taken the back road home. It meant about thirty more miles of driving on the Mexican side of the border, but the El Paso bridges could have waits of an hour or more, plus she'd end up closer to home. Also, the New Mexico desert crossing north of El Paso would put quick miles between herself and the Velascos.

The road skirted the Juarez mountains that snuggled up against the western border of the city. The drive took her first south, then west until the city thinned out. Eventually, she hit the junction that headed north to the border crossing in Santa Teresa, New Mexico.

A single gas station sat on one corner of the crossroads. From there, lonely desert stretched before her for miles until she reached the border. The truck had plenty of gas, and she wanted to be home. She needed a shower and maybe a good fuck to cleanse her of the disturbing meetings.

The long straight desert road and desire to put space between herself and Velasco had her pushing the truck's maximum speed. She only slowed when she spotted the dirty green SUV on the side of the road. A Juarez cop?

Damn it. A light spun atop the green truck as it gained on her. She pulled to the side of the road and prepared for a shakedown. She'd been pulled over by Juarez cops more times than she could count on one hand. Thanks to them, she never carried more than a dollar or two of cash in the main pocket of her wallet. To ensure they'd see the lack of funds, she'd hand them her entire wallet with her license tucked behind clear plastic.

She prepared to implement her whole act. First, she'd slip on the fake engagement ring she kept in her car's console. Mexican authorities, and the ones who pulled her over were always men, showed far less interest in her when they thought she had a man behind her. Next, she'd pretend she didn't speak Spanish and couldn't understand what the officer said.

Finally, she'd wear him out with lots of difficult questions in English. Sometimes she performed in a Southern accent just to have a little fun.

She slid the ring on her finger as the truck pulled up behind and slightly beside her. Three boys jumped down from the truck and approached. Boys, not men. They couldn't be more than eighteen years old. And they had machine guns slung across their chests. Fuck this day.

They peered into both sides of her truck, and one of the boys rapped on her window. She rolled it down. They wore camouflage pants, T-shirts, and dirty black baseball caps with the star of the Federales. The Mexican federal police. They'd never stopped her before. She'd seen them on the streets, and they were regular fixtures at the Juarez airport and sometimes at the border crossings. Not good.

"Hola. Bajese del vehiculo, por favor."

There was no way in hell she was getting out of her truck. A ton of steel with a motor and wheels surrounded her, and she wouldn't give up that safety for anything. "I'm sorry, I don't understand. Do you speak English?"

"Get out of the truck," the man-boy said in heavily accented English.

"Why?"

"You need to get out of the truck."

"Why do I need to get out of the truck?"

"We search the vehicle."

"Why do you need to search the vehicle? You can see into the truck bed, and it's completely empty. You can also see in the windows. I don't have anything in the truck. There's no need to search it." She spoke quickly, perhaps to confuse him, perhaps because the guns scared her.

"Por favor. Get out. Now." He adjusted his gun strap.

"Do you need to see my wallet?"

"No. Get out of the truck."

She looked him in the eyes, hoping for sympathy. "I will not get out of the truck."

He turned to the other boy behind him and discussed her. They couldn't seem to figure out what to do. She had never been this vulnerable, or this scared.

The guy looking in her passenger side window rapped on the door with his gun, frightening the shit out of her. "Abre la puerta."

She would never open the door to a gun. Should she try to outrun them now? She'd have to start the truck, which would give them warning, but she could hit the gas hard, duck down, and hope the back of the truck and her seat protected her. If they didn't shoot out a tire, or shoot her, she should be able to outrun them. At least until she got to the border. There'd be lots more guns there. But there would also be more people and they'd probably be less likely to kill her, or whatever these guys really wanted.

The guy rapped on her window again with the gun. If he hit it any harder, he might break it. Shit. The envelope full of money sat in plain view. Her stomach sank as the bad situation got worse.

Gun hit glass again. She looked at the driver's side window where the other two boys focused on their threatening colleague. "Hey, would you ask him to stop doing that?"

"Please, get out of the vehicle."

She could keep the conversation going with the first guy until they gave up, but she didn't know how to deal with the gun banger. She willed herself to stay calm. It was the only thing that would save her.

The guy on the passenger side of the car missed her window and his gun banged against her truck.

"Hey!" That fucker probably dented her door.

The guy on the passenger side started yelling at his colleagues to pull her out of the truck. A chill iced through her as she heard him say they had guns, and they should use them. Her hand moved to the ignition and hovered there in terror. If she started the engine, the man-boy on the passenger side would try to shoot her. If she didn't, he seemed unstable enough to shoot her anyway.

The boys yelled at each other and then those on her side of the truck pointed down the road. Jessica glanced in the rearview mirror and saw a black SUV speeding toward them. It stopped in the middle of the road next to the two trucks. Ruben Velasco's ugly bodyguard got out of the backseat and motioned the boys back toward their truck. She couldn't hear their conversation, but in two minutes, the green truck backed away, did a U-turn, and drove in the opposite direction.

Velasco's man walked to her rolled down window.

"You are free to go now. Next time, you should ride with us. It is very dangerous for you out here. I will follow you to the border to make sure you get back to your country safely."

Jessica started the truck with shaking hands. The immediate danger was gone, but she had never felt less safe.

Chapter 9

Jessica pulled into her driveway and peeled her hands off the steering wheel. They ached from the death grip she'd held since the gunmen had pulled her over. When she stepped out of the truck, she almost collapsed. Her legs swayed but held her steady.

The second she'd closed and locked the front door behind her, she dropped to the floor. Tela's body wiggled, and her tongue darted across Jessica's cheeks. Nothing compared to dog love when you needed a boost.

After a shower where she unsuccessfully tried to wash the grit and fear away, she took Tela for a walk. Warm sunshine and fresh air would help her breathe again. She continued past the drive to Luz and Sarah's house, despite Tela's pull on the leash. Usually, she'd take her to play with the other dogs, but today Jessica desired something more physical. She looked behind her, trying to see if Velasco's men followed her. The road was empty.

At some point, she started running. Tela looked confused, then bounced along beside her. Because of Jessica's vehement opposition to all exercise, the dog probably hadn't seen her run before. She ran faster. The jar of each step, the burn in her lungs, made her feel alive. At least until her wracking breaths forced her to stop, doubled over by the side of the road. Dry desert air filled her lungs as she gulped for breath while the dog licked sweat from her face. Each searing inhalation proved she'd survived.

She walked home, letting the sweat dry. The sun of a cloudless day baked her skin. She felt nothing but love for the dog trotting beside her, yet the emptiness of her life opened like a vast ocean. She had to push it away, fill herself with something, anything, so she didn't disappear.

At home, she showered again. She deftly applied makeup, rimming her blue eyes with kohl so they'd be noticed across a room. A low-cut blouse showed plenty of cleavage, but she accented it with a pendant that nestled between her breasts, beckoning a stare.

She called an Uber and fed Tela. The driver took her to a bar she'd driven by before but never visited. She didn't want to see anyone she knew tonight.

She entered the old adobe building, fresh with white paint but still carrying the layer of dust that covered everything in the desert. The long, dark room had a low ceiling. She hadn't realized the place was a restaurant as well as a bar. To get a drink, she had to walk past rows of tables, one where a father fed refried beans to a toddler and another with an older couple sitting side-by-side while they dined on enchiladas.

She completed her awkward march to the back of the room, a single woman dressed for a party who'd ended up in a dusty Texas bar instead. The middle-aged bartender watched, arms crossed, as she approached.

"I'll have a Pacifico and a shot of tequila."

"What kind of tequila?" He pulled a dripping bottle of beer out of an icy tank.

"Doesn't matter." The tequila had a job to do, it didn't need to taste good.

The bartender set a shot glass on the table, then filled it from an amber bottle. Jessica snatched the drink from the bar, hungry for its release. The burn that seared down her throat confirmed the brew's low origins, but it filled her belly with fire. It was good to be filled with something.

Unfortunately, it would take more than a shot of tequila to conjure enough people to make this bar interesting. An old cowboy, tiny and wrinkled and hunched over what looked like a glass of iced tea, perched at the end of the counter. It was only five in the afternoon, but she couldn't wait, she craved people. Besides, the restaurant would probably fill before the bar, and watching her get drunk and hit on guys wasn't exactly family entertainment.

She ordered another shot and pulled up the Uber app on her phone. Four minutes. Perfect. She finished her drinks, made a quick pit stop, and walked out of the bar just as the driver pulled up. She wanted a sure thing, so she had him take her downtown. The office types would have gotten off work and the bars should be full. She risked running into someone she knew, but desire was the only thing keeping her from slipping into desolation. Risk be damned.

The driver dropped her off at the main plaza downtown. Here, she had choices. She could go to the fancy hotel with the enormous Tiffany dome centered above the round bar. One of her favorite dive bars was a few blocks away, but that seemed far on legs worn out by her run. Instead, she turned right down a pedestrian walk and found a place that styled itself after a French brasserie.

She opened the door to cool air conditioning and the clink of many glasses. Suits filled the room. Women in bright blouses and men in every shade of navy, gray, and black talked and tossed back drinks. She'd find what she needed here. The buzz of anticipation electrified her.

Jessica took the lone empty seat at the bar. She asked for a beer and a tequila, and when the bartender delivered those, she asked for a glass of water. The day had left her parched. Plus, she had to pace herself.

She downed the first shot and finally felt her blood slow in her veins. The urgency to do something, anything to fill the clawing need inside her subsided. "Need," she said aloud. Need, not fear.

Possibilities surrounded her. She ordered another tequila, a better one this time, to sip while she sized up the crowd and looked for a target.

It didn't take long. She eyed a guy down the bar. Decent looking, he had dark blond hair and sleepy blue eyes. When a spot opened up next to her, he made his way over.

"Can I buy you a drink?"

Well, he wasn't original, but she didn't give a shit. "I'll have another." She held up her shot glass and noticed it was still half full. She drained the glass and let the liquid settle in her mouth for a moment, somehow numbing and brightening it at the same time. A happy smile curled her lips, and she looked into his eyes.

"So, do you work around here?" he asked.

"Nope." Why waste time with small talk?

The bartender stopped by, and the guy turned away from her to order the tequila and an IPA for himself. She noticed him slip a wedding ring off his finger and drop it in his suit pocket. Perfect. He was just her type, broken and out for sex. Emptiness grew into desire.

The drinks came, and she laid a hand on his thigh as she sipped. He looked surprised for a second, then hungry. He spun her barstool toward him and locked his knees together with her own. She liked a man who took control. One she didn't have to convince.

The tequila helped him become more handsome, sharpened the edges of his jaw from the office softness they'd acquired. She told him to take his tie off and noticed how he rolled it neatly and put it in the same pocket as the ring. He unbuttoned the top button of his shirt.

She unbuttoned the next one. "There, that's better. Work is over. It's time to loosen up." She let her hand drop back to his thigh, further up this time. She gave it a squeeze while she took a long draw from her beer, savoring it.

"I'm visiting from Illinois. We have a factory in Juarez."

"That's great. You should try this tequila, it's añejo. Smoky." She handed him the half full shot glass. He slammed it back the way she expected.

"Yeah, that's great." His eyes watered. But he held up two fingers to the bartender.

All the bullshit from the day receded. She narrowed her focus to the man in front of her and the incoming tide of small dangers made her ripe with desire. He talked about himself, and she nodded, not listening to the words. She looked at the mouth that would soon kiss hers, savored the warmth of his hands on her thighs. The fingers slowly inching their way up her legs held her interest. The conversation didn't.

"Hey, I'm going to the bathroom." She stood, and the alcohol swirled through her brain.

She used the toilet, then splashed a little water on her face at the sink. Alcohol and desire lit her on fire, and she needed to cool off. Well, she really needed him to fuck her, but they hadn't worked out those logistics yet. She opened the door, and he was there.

He locked the door behind them, then grabbed her, kissing her harshly, one hand behind her neck, the other grabbing her ass. In seconds, he was hard against her. She wanted this so much, yearned for him to fill her, to use her body until there was nothing left but release. Her hands reached for him, stroked him, and the heat ran up her until she couldn't wait any longer. She unbuckled his belt, his pants, slid his boxers down. His lust for her stood at attention, waiting for her touch.

His big paws scraped at her jeans, trying to get into them. She helped, first pulling a condom from her back pocket, then slipping the jeans off her hips. She bent over to push them past her knees. While there, she gave his cock a kiss wet with desire. His groan echoed between her thighs.

When she rose to kiss his lips, he spun her around so she faced the mirror. She reached back to him, handing him the condom. He tore the package open and put it on. Then his attention returned to her. One of his hands roamed up the front of her shirt and cupped a breast, the other felt her, slipped a finger inside.

"Oh god, you're ready," he said.

She wished he wouldn't talk and closed her eyes as he bent her over and shoved himself inside, filling her. He grabbed her hips and pulled her hard into him again and again, each time scraping that core of pain that never really went away, until everything blurred and released.

Finally, the incessant ache of nothing receded. The rush of control, of getting exactly what she wanted, what she deserved, brought her fully back into the world.

"Do you want to go get dinner or anything?" he asked while he washed his hands.

"No thanks." After he left, she locked the door again. She didn't look at herself in the mirror while she washed up and straightened her clothes. She glanced at her watch. Six-thirty, hardly even dinnertime. Maybe she'd have another drink before going home, although she'd gotten what she came for. She opened the door.

There, staring at her with arms crossed and a peeved look, stood her attorney, Alma Rey. Alma, Luz's sister, had been the most consistent person in her life since her parents left. Jessica went to her for advice, and not just about law or money. The look on Alma's face told Jessica she had seen the guy leave, but Jessica played innocent anyway.

"Good to see you, Alma. Do you need to use the restroom?"

"You couldn't pay me to go in there right now." Alma's hands moved to her hips. "What are you doing? No, don't answer that. I know exactly what you were doing. I saw him go in there with you. I heard you."

"Sorry." Fuck.

"Come with me." Alma grabbed her arm and practically dragged her out of the bar. She didn't let go as she pulled Jessica down the street and across the plaza.

"Stop, Alma. I can walk without you hauling me. Where are we going, anyway?"

"I'm taking you home."

"I can get a car."

"I'm not letting you out of my sight." Alma took off in the direction of her office building, still towing Jessica behind.

The white Lexus waited at the valet station. Jessica slumped inside. She mentally crossed downtown bars off her list. Alma didn't say a word as she slid into the front seat. As they drove out of downtown, Alma turned the radio on, then off, adjusted her seat, and reset the rearview mirror. But she didn't say a word.

The eerie quiet didn't last. About halfway home Alma stopped fidgeting and started talking. "How could you do that? Did you know that guy?"

"Well, biblically, I knew him."

Alma slapped her forehead. "Stop. Just stop." She only lasted a few seconds before the next question came. "Why?"

"Maybe I have daddy issues." She shouldn't push Alma this way, but it beat talking about her feelings. That's what Alma wanted, and Jessica would not oblige.

They drove in silence the rest of the way home. The black SUV waited, as usual, near the turn to the gravel road. She couldn't see the occupants watching them, but unease crawled across her skin and lifted the hairs on her arms. She hated that they had saved her, hated that she needed saving.

When Alma pulled up in front of her house, Jessica reached for the car door handle.

"Wait," Alma said. "Today made me feel like I failed you."

Jessica looked into Alma's dark eyes. Melancholy replaced the kindness she'd always seen there. Jessica had done that to her. "That wasn't about you. It had nothing to do with you."

"Then what is it about?"

"I had an extremely hard day, and I'm working a really shitty job right now. That, what you saw, was about blowing off some tension."

Alma shook her head. "There are a hundred safer ways to blow off tension. I'll get you a gym membership."

Jessica just wanted to get inside. As soon as the lecture finished, she could see her dog, take some aspirin, and climb into bed. Not that it was near bedtime. She just needed this day to end.

"Jessica, you know I'm an attorney who works immigration cases. I see too much. It's dangerous out there. You can't trust people you don't know with your body. And you shouldn't want to."

"Well, I do want to. It's my body, and I prefer anonymous sex. I'm an adult now." Her anger arrived in a short, sharp breath. "I've been an adult for a long time."

"I know you are completely self-sufficient. You've been that way since you were sixteen. But it doesn't mean you can't have a real relationship. You don't let anyone get close to you."

"Trust me, it's better this way. I get what I need, then it's done. No entanglements."

"That sounds so lonely."

Alma's words echoed in the hollow space in Jessica's gut. How could it be empty so soon? "I'm doing just fine."

"You're drunk, and I just caught you having sex in a bathroom with a guy you don't know. That's not fine."

"Thanks for the judgment."

"I'm not trying to judge you." Alma's sigh seemed to echo through both of them. "You went through a lot of stuff you shouldn't have had to go through. But you're not the only person to live through some tough breaks. Don't let it color the rest of your life. There's so much good in the world. There are people you can rely on, build a life with. Please don't let the past ruin your future."

"I'm not like you. I don't want the happy marriage and needy kids. I want a life that's hard and fast and sharp. That's what brings me alive."

"That's how you protect yourself. It's not how you live." A lone tear leaked from Alma's eyes and rolled down her cheek.

The walls of the luxury car pressed in on Jessica, and the air grew stale and hard to breathe. This was why she hated close relationships. She would always disappoint the people who loved her. "I'm not the person you think I am. I'm not good like you."

Alma's chin wobbled as she reached out to stroke Jessica's cheek. "I'm sorry you hurt so much. I wish I knew how to help you."

Oh, Christ. Tears came to Jessica's eyes and threatened to spill. "I appreciate everything you've done for me, and I don't want to hurt you, but I need to live my own life."

Alma nodded. "Okay. Can we talk again? Maybe tomorrow?"

"Sure. You know where to find me." She'd have chewed her arm off to get out of the car and leave this conversation behind. A future conversation, one she could try to avoid, seemed a fair trade. "Thanks for driving me home. And I'm sorry."

She walked into the house, locked the door, then threw herself onto the bed. Tears poured into the pillow, and Tela scrambled all over her, trying to lick them away. The black hole she'd tried so hard to fill emptied and grew, swallowing her in its darkness.

Chapter 10

When Jessica woke at midnight, she downed two Tylenol PMs with a glass of water. She refused to deal with her drunken emotions and the shame that accompanied the look on Alma's face. The shame she'd avoided in the bathroom mirror at the bar. She returned to bed, hugging Tela as tight as she'd allow.

At eight in the morning, she fed the dog and let her out for a few minutes before reaching for more Tylenol and crawling back into bed. At eleven, she couldn't sleep anymore, so she broke out her fancy bottle of bourbon. The one she'd bought herself after she closed her first big real estate deal in Juarez. Each glass nudged the self-destruct dial higher, but she convinced herself she didn't care.

That was the problem with being human. Humans cared. She sat on the sofa, bourbon in hand, willing herself back into the darkness. Maybe Doraliz had it right. Perhaps escape trumped living a life that didn't fit. Jessica had rarely ventured beyond the people and places she knew, but Doraliz had seen the world.

Jessica's last vacation happened at fourteen. Back then, she'd wanted to stay on the California beach forever, away from the rental home filled with her parents' constant tension. Since then, she'd traveled to office parks and generic hotels for work, one city interchangeable with the next. The luxury of an exotic vacation hadn't even been a dream.

What Jessica wouldn't give to be on a Central American beach right now, as if switching from bourbon to rum would make her problems magically disappear. Is that what Doraliz had done? Would it work?

Jessica pulled out her laptop and studied Costa Rica and El Salvador. Sra. Velasco had said her daughter loved the Caribbean and had mentioned El Salvador, but the country didn't have an east coast. Honduras lay between it and the Caribbean Sea. Islands dotted the coast of Honduras, and a string of islands stretched north into Belize and the Yucatan Peninsula of Mexico.

Jessica nursed her bourbon, then switched to water. At the time, she'd been certain Doraliz's mother had dropped hints to help Jessica find her daughter. But she'd also seemed terrified someone would overhear them. Had the woman instead purposely led her away from her daughter, or had she used the misdirection to prompt Jessica to figure it out instead of revealing her guess in a room filled with ears?

Jessica brought up Doraliz's social media feed and found the scuba photos. Cozumel, Ambergris Caye, the Blue Hole, Roatán. Each word rolled off her tongue with the promise of an exotic life filled with palm trees and blue water. A new desire tugged at her. The desire to leave behind her mess of a life and escape to someplace beautiful, or better, to try again and do it right this time. Jessica closed the laptop.

The lure of picking a place where she could get lost fired her imagination. It would need to be large enough so a new face wouldn't stand out. A place with lots of tourists where education and the ability to converse in multiple languages could be traded for currency. She could swap sand and cactus for beach and palms, switch dry desert air for humid ocean breezes, exchange the scars of murdered women for oil-slick tourists, trade family for peace. Why shouldn't she go? She wasn't sure whether Doraliz's dreams or her own filled her head.

By late afternoon, Jessica had narrowed her search to two places, Ambergris Caye off the coast of Belize, and Roatán, the big island off Honduras. Both islands met her criteria, large enough to get lost in and touristy enough to provide work opportunities. Doraliz might strike out for a new locale, but to Jessica, starting over someplace familiar seemed easier.

She assumed Doraliz would have to work. Even if she'd squirreled away money, to stay gone, she'd have to support herself at some point. Plus, Doraliz had visited both places multiple times. She could have established connections, reached out, planned.

She might as well flip a coin as to which island to visit first. She grabbed her bag and dug around for a quarter. Her fingers touched something unfamiliar. She pulled out the matchbook Doraliz's mother had given her as they left the meeting. Bingo. The Iguana Restaurant, Ambergris Caye, Belize.

Jessica researched flights, still uncertain whether she wanted to find Doraliz or escape her own mistakes. Several airlines flew to Belize City from Houston. From there, she could take a boat or small plane to San Pedro on Ambergris Caye. She could also fly from Belize City to the Roatán airport.

She hadn't heard of Tropic Air, the airline that flew to the islands. When she looked at the website, photos showed airplanes with front propellers and few seats. Lawn darts. She closed her eyes and hit purchase. She needed a break from her life maybe as much as Doraliz, especially after the last twenty-four hours.

Besides, Ruben Velasco's cash begged to be spent. She'd worked hard to save money in the past in hopes she could someday purchase her own home. She wanted someplace stable that no one could take away. But the filthy money she'd taken from Velasco had already cost her more than its value.

She didn't know if she'd find Doraliz on one of the islands, or any-where. She didn't even know if Doraliz lived or lay buried somewhere in the desert with thousands of other women. But the list of reasons and excuses pushing her to Central America grew long, and she had no reason to stay in El Paso.

Eventually, she showered. Friday had rolled around again, and happy hour at the big house called. Tonight would be a trial, literally. Alma hadn't called all day, despite threatening to when she dropped Jessica off. When your landlord and your attorney were sisters, they became impossible to avoid.

The story of Jessica and the guy at the bar had likely been shared, and she needed to face whatever lectures and disappointment resulted from her action. Tela started bouncing the moment Jessica grabbed her shoes. She'd have to talk to Angus about taking care of the dog when she went to Central America. She almost pulled out her phone to call him. He would understand, even if he didn't like it. He always understood.

She closed her eyes and could almost feel his embrace, see the happiness in his smile. She'd always thought that if she'd had a normal life, they'd have ended up together. They still kind of had. She couldn't remember meeting him, but it must have been in kindergarten or first grade. He'd always been there. Jessica slipped the phone into her pocket. He'd probably be at happy hour tonight. The others would lecture her, but he'd forgive her because he knew her best. He understood she couldn't control the forces buffeting her life, she just had to ride them to the best of her abilities.

Jessica trudged toward the inquisition at the end of the long drive to Luz and Sarah's house. Tonight's hours would not be happy. Tela bounded ahead, excited to play with her dog friends, leaving Jessica completely alone. She used the time to ready her arguments, slowing her steps to give herself a few more minutes.

Sure enough, Alma's white Lexus sat in the drive, as did Angus's Escort. At least no other cars had arrived. Hopefully, she could get this over quickly. She wished she'd taken a shot of anything before walking over, but after the bourbon, she'd decided to get her shit together, and at the very least, not drink alone.

"Hey guys," Jessica said, walking onto the patio. She headed straight for the metal basin filled with ice and water where she deposited eleven of the twelve beers she'd brought. She opened the remaining bottle and took a long swig.

Someone had pulled the chairs into a tighter circle than usual. She took the lone vacant seat, with Angus, Alma, Luz, and Sarah gazing at her expectantly.

"So, I guess we're going to talk," Jessica said. They'd staged an intervention, and she'd willingly arrived at the slaughter.

Sarah started. "We're cooking steaks on the grill, along with potatoes, corn, and a salad. You're looking skinny."

The caretaker in Sarah stalked the circle. Her words told Jessica she'd be her ally, at least a little. Jessica appreciated the gesture but knew it wouldn't be enough. Sarah lived her life through positive encouragement, but that didn't mean Jessica hadn't disappointed her. It only meant Sarah wouldn't give up, or at least hadn't so far.

Jessica wasn't sure about the others. She had never figured out whether Luz or her younger sister Alma was the most aggressive. Tonight, Luz won. "We're here to help you. But you need to admit you need help."

"You know, I can get up and walk away."

"But you won't, because we love you." Alma pinned her with wide brown eyes.

"Honey, what happened before Alma found you at the bar?" Sarah's sweet intention meant to give her an out. She could talk about her hard life, make them feel sorry for her. Then they'd go easy on her. Fuck easy.

"I am working for an abominable a-hole, and yesterday I had a terrible visit with him and his wife. They've hired me to find their daughter, but they aren't exactly forthcoming with information to help me locate her. I don't even know if she's dead or alive. After that horrible meeting, I drove home through Santa Teresa, got pulled over by the federales, better known as sixteen-year-olds with automatic weapons." The sound of gun hitting glass ricocheted through her mind and reignited the fear that partnered with the certainty of death.

"I had five thousand dollars on the seat beside me, but I survived that episode because the jerk I'm working for has goons following me. They pulled up and in sixty seconds, the federales let me go." Jessica looked around the circle at eyes gone wide with shock and distress. Now they understood. "After that, I needed a little stress relief, so I went to a bar, drank too much, and picked up a guy. That is how I relieve stress. It's not like any of you thought I was a virgin."

"Who are you working for?" Alma asked.

"Ruben Velasco."

A chill ran through the air at his name. Alma jerked back. Luz shook her head, then dropped it into her hands, and Sarah made an unidentifiable guttural noise. Only Angus seemed unconcerned at the name, although his smile was absent, and his eyes narrowed in anger.

"What?" Jessica asked.

"We told you to stay away from him." Frustration laced Luz's voice. "You asked about him at happy hour, and we told you he was a bad guy. You have to quit this job. It's leading you down a dark path."

"Your father was involved with Velasco." Alma had put on her lawyer voice.

"What does *involved* mean?" Jessica asked.

Alma looked to Luz before she answered, and Jessica caught Luz's nod. "Your dad, very ineptly, tried to delete some files that prosecutors had gathered in a case against someone in Ruben Velasco's organization."

"You've got to be fucking kidding me." It surprised Jessica that Velasco hadn't used this against her. People had tried to manipulate her in the past by bringing up her father's crimes. Perhaps Velasco realized it wouldn't have worked. She'd never knowingly follow in her father's footsteps. "So, Velasco was involved in the drug case that got him arrested?"

"Yes," Alma admitted. "Your dad took the fall, but there were other people in the district attorney's office with dirtier hands. He rolled because of a sense of duty. He led the El Paso office and tried to protect his people. The others resigned under threat of termination and prosecution. The powers that be needed to contain the amount of damage done to the organization. It was easier to blame everything on one man."

"But he was guilty." Jessica would not allow them to let him off easy.

"He was guilty," Alma confirmed. "And he was prosecuted and is paying for his crime."

"That one anyway." Jessica would not cry. She'd spent her life dealing with the mess her parents had made. The abyss inside her returned, threatening to drag her into the darkness.

"Why did he leave?" She hadn't meant to ask the question or hadn't meant to ask it of these women who couldn't know the answer. In that moment, she'd have given anything to ask her dad. But that would mean talking to him.

"That decision tortured your parents." Alma's voice quieted. "Shame drove some of it, but also fear. He was the eye of the storm, a storm that threatened a lot of powerful people. He feared for you, for your mom. Just because there had been a trial didn't mean it was over. If the case had gone further, it would have exposed some very bad people. Including Velasco."

Sarah's voice broke through the night, teetering on the edge of sobbing. "They worried someone would come after him, after them. They were afraid you weren't safe with them."

"Was I safe on my own? I was sixteen!"

"You were as safe as we could make you," Alma said. "I moved in with you. Do you remember Jaime Castro who moved in next door? He's a cop, a friend of your dad's, and of mine."

"And we made sure one of us visited you every day." This time Luz spoke. It was true. Luz would stop by after work with some errand, or to drop off something she thought Jessica might need. Sarah brought her home-cooked meals and asked about her homework. Alma and Luz's mother would come by with dishes of homemade Mexican food and would have dinner with Jessica. Alma stayed with her at night, although between law school and a job, Jessica didn't see her much. When she did, Alma constantly discussed her future. It could have been worse.

"You do remember that you refused to go with them," Luz said, a hint of anger in her voice. "You said you couldn't leave high school in the middle of your junior year. Your mom pleaded with you to go with them."

"Why did she choose him over me?" Fourteen years of hurt came through in her voice. She couldn't keep the wayward tears from spilling down her face, but she would not break. Not then, not now, not ever.

No one answered for a moment. Jessica gazed at the faces of her friends and saw shame and regret. Except for Angus. A single tear traced its way down his cheek. She'd never seen him so sad.

Finally, Sarah spoke. "I think she thought going with him was temporary. She'd get him set up and then come back and stay with you. Then he tried to kill himself. He thought it would remove the danger to the two of you. She wouldn't leave him after that. And by then, you didn't want her."

A sob escaped Jessica's lips. It was just a symptom of processing new information. She hadn't caused this. "Why do I feel like everyone thinks this is my fault?"

"It's not your fault. No one thinks that. You were dealt a really shitty hand," Luz said. "So, what are you going to do with it?"

"I've done something with it. I've built a life."

"It's a shell of a life." Sarah's words cut the deepest. She'd always seen the emptiness in Jessica.

"I don't know how to make it more than that." Jessica's words came out so quietly she almost didn't hear them herself.

Alma scooted forward in her chair and leaned so she could rest a hand on Jessica's knee. "Why don't you start by trying to repair your relationship with your parents? Read their letters instead of throwing them away unopened. Go see them."

"No." Jessica sat back and crossed her arms. She would not cross that line.

"At the very least, stop working with Velasco. Please. That could hurt you more than anything," Alma said.

"If you didn't drink so much you might understand that." Luz threw the final punch.

After that, the night settled, and the talk and emotions eventually blew away on the breeze. Angus offered to help Sarah with dinner, and the sisters wandered off, leaving Jessica on the patio. She got one more beer and listened to the cricket serenade. The desert at night always smelled faintly of smoke, mesquite or piñon.

Far away, in another part of this same desert, her parents breathed the air, listened to the night. They usually arrived as a burden of guilt or anger, but tonight they just shared the space without making any demands.

She ate with others, made small talk. Listened to Angus talk about his record store which shared space with a popular bicycle shop, an odd coupling that brought a little more business to each. He'd expanded into headphones and other devices. Jessica knew the store barely survived. Angus had enough money to make it another year, and he wasn't the type to plan things out for five years or ten.

She wished she could be like him. He had faith everything would work out, and for him it always had. She wished she could so easily believe in the future, but for her things always verged on falling apart. She had contingencies, savings, lots of useful relationships so that when one door closed another would open. Or she could slip out a window.

"Hey, guys. I'm tired, so I'm going to turn in." Jessica whistled for Tela and the dog came running. The night held the tiniest sliver of a moon, and she appreciated the darkness on her walk home. Dressed in black against a black night, she'd be difficult to spot.

She'd almost reached the front door when she heard a car travel down the drive behind her. It would be either Alma or Angus, and they'd likely stop to talk. She let Tela in the door and waited. Angus.

"Hey, can I come in for a few minutes?" he asked, all sleepy eyes and shaggy smile. Only a hint of sadness remained.

"Come on in." Her smile met his. She couldn't say no, he never did. Besides, he was as much home as she allowed herself.

"Bourbon?" she asked, spying the open bottle on the table.

"Beer, if you've got one."

"Always." She took two bottles out of the fridge and sat beside him on the couch.

"So, it's pretty weird that your dad worked with Velasco," Angus said.

"Yeah. I wish I'd known how deeply involved they were before I started the job. I've always tried to stay away from anything my dad touched."

"You know, you can walk away from this job."

She'd told herself that about five hundred times today. But now she had something to follow up on, a place Doraliz might be. A vision of a different life. "I kind of want to find her. I mean, if I can. If she's still alive."

"And if it gets you killed?"

She heard the pain in his voice, needed to move him beyond it. "It won't. I think she's alive, and I have an idea where she might be."

"Why do you care so much about this girl?"

"Because she's a smart woman with really shitty parents. I understand that, and I want to know she's okay."

"Damn. She's like you."

"Yeah."

Angus turned toward her and took her chin in one hand, turning her to face him. He looked at her for a long moment, and something fierce and protective lit his eyes. "Do you think you'll find a part of yourself if you find her?"

"I'm not looking for me. I'm right here." The conversation had turned in a direction she didn't expect.

"I think you look for a piece of yourself in every guy you fuck and every distasteful person who pays you for a job."

"Hey, knock it off. What the hell are you doing? You're the one person I can trust." She jerked away from him. The little support she had threatened to crumble away. Alma would never unsee what had happened in the bar, and now Angus challenged her. Crappy day turned to crappier night.

"Jessica, I love you. I've always loved you, and I know you don't want to hear that. But you're taking such gigantic risks right now. How many will it take until one doesn't work out? What am I supposed to do if you die?" The last words barely made it out.

She watched him struggle to maintain control. She was poison, always had been. "I didn't ask for your help. I've tried to discourage you."

"You ask for my help almost every day!"

She closed her eyes, the truth too painful to see. She never wanted to rely on anyone, but she did rely on Angus, and not just to feed Tela when she came home late. She relied on him to put her back together when she broke. And she would never quit breaking.

"You're right," she said, eyes still closed. "I didn't mean to drag you into my messed-up life, but I did. Angus, you've got to stay away from me." She opened her eyes.

"I'm not going to stay away from you. Stop looking for yourself every-where else. You're here." He placed her hand on his chest, right above his heart. "Right here."

She tried to pull her hand away, but he wouldn't let her. "Angus, I'm broken. You know that. Run away."

He smiled at that, big and broad. "And I'm not whole without you. I've been following you around since kindergarten. Give me a chance. If you need someone to hold you, let it be me. If you need someone to fuck your brains out in a bathroom, give me a try. I promise I'll be more fun than anyone you pick up in a bar."

"Oh, god. Please don't be jealous. It's not about fun."

"Believe me, I don't have to be fun. You think I can't get so mad I want to punch a wall or screw someone until my mind goes numb?" His sandpaper voice raked over her. He pulled her onto his lap.

She twisted until she faced him, her anger meeting his. "You think you want me because you think I'm someone who can be saved. I can't be. How many fucking times have I told you to go find a normal girl?" She wanted to hit him, to bite him, to make him see how ugly she could be. She dug her fingernails into his arms and straddled him.

"As many times as I've told you I don't want a normal girl." He grabbed her hips and pulled her closer.

She stared into his eyes. Rage and need battled in her. "I am broken. I can break you."

"I know. You break me every time you show up wasted. Every time you fuck someone you don't know. Every time you do something you hate as a cover for how much you hate yourself. You break me and break me and break me. And I am still here."

She didn't know why that made her mad. It made her want to hurt him and give in to him at the same time. She leaned forward and kissed him, then took his bottom lip in her teeth and bit. She tasted blood.

He surged forward, lifting her off the couch and taking her to the bed. Their sex had always been good. Sweet and fun. Tonight, they ripped clothes from each other, clawed and bit. The world hurt, and they found their place in the pain.

The release, when it came, was savage. And then she was spent, her long body on top of his, the anger gone. And he kissed her with all the tenderness in the world.

He rolled her over and kissed her eyelids, ears, and shoulders. He stroked her skin and kissed her belly, each kiss a salve to where the anger had burned, until she filled with light and love and comfort.

She kissed him back, on the shoulder, tentative at first. Growing bolder, she thought of each kiss as a star that would bring him light. She giggled with the kisses, then laughed. He grunted, trying to stifle his own laugh. She took his face in her hands and kissed him with laughter and no intention to hurt.

And after the laughter came the passion. At some point the giggles stopped, and they stared at the truth in each other, curious. Eyes locked, they explored each other in new ways. And when they finally saw into the depths of each other's souls, they closed their eyes and learned new truths.

When she finally shut her eyes to sleep, she wrapped herself up in his arms, connected to every part of him.

———

Jessica woke in Angus's arms, not uncomfortable to be there. She wondered if last night had changed her. She didn't think so.

As long as she'd known him, she'd thought of Angus as someone who hadn't lived through real problems. He had been safe because she thought he wasn't deep. Not very nice of her, but still, a truth.

Last night had changed that. She understood the pain he carried, the pain she caused. Now, she wouldn't be able to toy with him the way she had, and she didn't know how that would work. She was still the same person, had the same needs. Could he really be enough?

The week they'd spent together when she'd been injured had been fun, better than living alone. That she could probably do, although they'd need a bigger place. He lived in an apartment, and she wanted to own where she lived, had been saving for that piece of security for years. She pictured the serenity of the house by the river.

Her mind danced around domestic, pretend scenarios. Eventually, she had to address whether she could change enough not to hurt him. She could probably play house, the way her parents had, but she'd screw up one day. That didn't bode well for Angus. But last night their words and bodies had made a promise to each other, and she'd try to keep up her end, at least as long as she could.

Maybe she would talk to him about moving in together after she got back from Central America. Her mind jumped from hard decisions about building a future to the easier task of finding a missing woman.

Doraliz must have gone to Central America, that's where the clues pointed. Surely her friends' reactions meant they'd covered for her, not killed her. And her father. No matter how mad he might have been about her thesis or anything else, he wouldn't have hired Jessica if he knew where she was. The mother had dropped hints, given her the matches. If Jessica couldn't find her there, she vowed to give up.

Although Ruben Velasco had told her she couldn't give up. That frightening thought might be worth a conversation with Alma. She also needed to talk to Alma about the house she wanted to buy.

She turned her body around and faced Angus. He barely opened one eye and squeezed her tighter to his chest.

"It's time to get up. There's lots of stuff I want to do today."

"Too early," he said and closed his eyes tight.

Jessica kissed him, then gave his lip the softest of nips, just enough to remind him of last night. She watched his face expand into a smile, and happiness bloomed in her chest. She didn't push it away or start thinking about all the ways she would let him down. This time, she just kissed him again.

Chapter 11

Monday morning, Jessica drove to downtown El Paso to meet Alma at her office. A neat stack of files sat to one side of a large oak desk, and light spilled from a plate glass window that looked out over the downtowns of El Paso and Ciudad Juarez. The office even smelled good, flowery like jasmine or orange blossoms, just like Alma. The space physically embodied her lawyer.

The sadness Jessica had noticed in Alma's eyes after the bar incident had disappeared. Today, her posture, the set of her jaw, and the depths of her brown eyes radiated professionalism.

Jessica wondered where to start a conversation that blurred her business and personal life. "I know you suggested I stop working for Velasco, and I really wish I had known about his deep association with my dad before he hired me, but I feel a connection to his daughter. I need to know if she's okay, and I have an idea about how to find her. I'd like to try one more location, and if she's not there, I'll give up."

Alma looked out the window toward Juarez. "Where do you think she might be?"

"I think she might be off the coast of Belize or Honduras. She loved to scuba dive, and I think her mom gave me a hint in that direction. But if she's not there, then I really have no idea. Of course, that brings up another problem."

"What's that?"

"Ruben Velasco seems to think I will work for him as long as he tells me to. If I don't find Doraliz, I'm not sure how to get out of this job."

"Well, it's not like you have a contract with him. At least I assume you don't."

"No. We met in his office, and he's been paying me cash for the job."

Alma snorted. "He's handing you cash, and you have a verbal agreement. As your attorney, I advise you to give the money back, all of it, today. Messenger it to him with a letter that says that you've been unsuccessful, and you have no prospect of future success."

"But I want to find Doraliz. And the last time I tried to quit, he wouldn't let me. He told me he'd ruin my career if I didn't finish the job."

"Well, that might be a blessing in disguise." Alma folded her arms across her chest, her gaze cutting into Jessica.

"What are you talking about? I've worked hard to make connections and build a successful career. I can't let it go now, especially when the second thing I want to talk to you about is buying a house."

"Sometimes you make my head hurt," Alma said, this time spinning her entire chair to gaze out the window. She was quiet for a minute, but Jessica could see she had on her thinking face. "But it's not because you want to buy your own house. I think that part is wonderful."

"Thanks. Maybe I'm growing up."

"Maybe," Alma said, facing her again. "I still advise you to cut ties with Velasco. We need to talk about your job. It was fine when you focused on real estate, working with US companies to find space in Mexico. But since then, you've expanded into areas that make me uncomfortable."

Jessica started to protest, but Alma held her hands up to ask for more time. "You're delivering documents and who knows what else without any protection. I've done similar things, but I've got a law firm behind me. We make sure everything we do is legitimate before we take a job, and we don't deliver things in sealed envelopes when we don't know what the contents are. You're taking too many risks. Just like your dad did."

"I'm not doing anything illegal!"

"How do you know?"

It was a good question. One she couldn't answer. "It's what I know how to do. And it's how I pay the rent." Jessica's shoulders sank. The fancy office and sharply dressed attorney left her defeated. Jessica had scrabbled to put together a career that barely made ends meet. She wanted a more comfortable life, but no straight path led to that goal.

"Do you know how many ways there are to pay the rent?" Alma asked as if reading her mind. "More than I can count. You are smart. You could be an attorney, or work for the world trade center or chamber of commerce. You could choose a career that actually helped people who needed it, instead of working for people who use you as a pawn."

"Ouch." Jessica shouldn't have come here. She was an adult now with no real reason to discuss everything with Alma anymore. This habit needed to die, now. She could figure it out on her own, just like she did everything else.

Alma must have seen her shuttered her emotions. "Please, don't close me out. I want to help you. I want you to have everything you deserve in life. Let's start with the house. You have plenty for a down payment, depending on the neighborhood you choose. But I worry about your ability to get a mortgage. Banks want to see a steady income with a company name on the checks. Real estate and your other jobs don't give you that."

"Great. So, there's no real way forward." Why had she bothered working so hard? She'd worked her way through school, figured out a career. None of it mattered if she couldn't earn the things she wanted, the security she craved with every cell inside her.

"There are a hundred ways forward. That's what I'm trying to tell you. You've got skills and relationships from which you can build a career. There are plenty of companies that would love to have you as an employee. I can vouch for you. And if you ever want a career in law, come see me."

Jessica stood. She'd spent her life trying to do the opposite of her father. "One Watts did this city enough damage as an attorney."

"You are not your father!"

Jessica had never heard Alma yell before. She wanted to return a flip response, but Alma had shocked her so badly she couldn't say anything. She sat back down.

"Your father was a good attorney, and he wasn't stupid. But he got tied in with some bad people on both sides of the border. I think when he deleted the documents, he did it because he didn't believe he had a choice. That's what these guys do. They convince you that you have to do what they say, or the consequences will be insurmountable."

Like when Ruben Velasco said he'd ruin her career. A sigh escaped. She didn't want to turn away from the line of work she'd spent years building, but that choice might be out of her hands.

"Let me help you," Alma pleaded.

Jessica studied the attorney. She'd always admired her work with immigrant women, those who most needed help. It reminded her of Sarah's work with the disabled. There was honor in that kind of career. Jessica could relate to it, but mostly because she understood how badly help could be needed.

Perhaps that explained her fixation on Doraliz. If Doraliz needed help, whether to escape from someone evil or to escape from her family, Jessica could relate. She wanted to help. It might make up for some of the bad in Jessica's world.

"Can we talk about Velasco?" Jessica asked.

Jessica could see the disappointment in Alma's eyes when she realized she wouldn't walk away from the job. She became a lawyer again, resigned to Jessica's choices instead of passionately discussing new ways forward. "Sure. And we should talk about Tomás Garcia."

"Why Tomás?"

"One of my colleagues asked if you worked with him. It came out of the blue. Isn't he the one who set up the Velasco job?"

"Yes, but I've worked with Tomás for years. He's never been a problem. However, I think Velasco is having me followed." Jessica explained the truck stationed near her home. The one Angus thought Velasco had sent to track her. The truck made her feel vulnerable at night. Except now she had Angus.

"I don't think there's anything you can do," Alma said. "We could try to file a restraining order for stalking, but they haven't threatened you, so a judge probably wouldn't grant it."

"And Velasco might not appreciate my going to the cops."

"Yes. Jessica. He is a very dangerous man. Please reconsider your deal with him. I can try to get you out of this if you'll stop working for him."

"Just one more trip. I promise."

She left Alma's office with her gut in turmoil. She should walk away, but something in her couldn't give up yet. Tomás had said he'd recommended her for the job because she'd do anything to finish a job. If only he'd known how right he was.

She turned the corner into the lobby and ran smack into Tomás. Shock ran through her as if he'd read her thoughts and then appeared.

"What are you doing here?" she asked.

"I'm visiting my attorney. You?"

"Same." She tried to move around him, but he blocked her way.

"How is the search for Doraliz going? I thought you were going to keep me updated on that."

"Well, I've been busy."

"I'd like to hear about it. The families in Juarez are worried about her. I'm worried about her. Let me take you to lunch and you can tell me what you've found. Perhaps I can help." His request seemed kind enough, but she'd seen the photos of him and Doraliz. He had a relationship with her and wouldn't admit it. That made him suspect.

"I thought you had a meeting with your attorney?"

"Oh, he'll see me anytime. My account keeps him and his wife in Porsches."

She cringed at his arrogance. "I can't. I've got someplace to be. See you later." She practically shoved her way past him.

"I'll call you later," he said as she pressed the button for the elevator. "I still want an update."

She sunk into the elevator wall as the doors closed. She'd half thought he would follow her. His showing up unexpectedly and demanding information worried her. He might be more tied into this case than she'd imagined. More likely, her stress had blown the run-in out of proportion. It's not like he could have known when she'd planned to visit Alma.

Jessica stopped by Angus's record shop on the way home. As with Alma, she expected him to try to talk her out of hunting for Doraliz. The store seemed like safe ground, a place she could ignore the passionate Angus who'd bared his heart for her and let her rend it. Her skin prickled at the memory. His vulnerability terrified her. No one should trust her like that. She'd trusted that way once, and it had shattered her.

She parked between Starbucks and Angus's shop. Music floated out the open door as she walked around the building. She pictured Angus on his old acoustic guitar, summoning the coffee drinkers like a siren. Entering the shop, she found him sitting on a barstool, his tousled hair falling over his face as he bent over the honey-colored instrument. When he looked up, his smile grabbed her heart. That anyone could be so happy to see her seemed a miracle.

He set the guitar down and she walked into his arms, knowing she'd arrived to break his heart. She hid in his kiss, in the caress of his touch, needing to keep her heart out of sight and enjoy this scrap of love that felt like home. Home didn't last. She lifted her lips from his.

"Somehow, I don't think you're here for a new cd, but I'm happy to show you my private collection if you'd like to follow me back to my office." His fingers slid just inside the waist of her jeans.

"You are the worst proprietor ever. What if you lost a sale?" She said it with a smile on her face but stepped away from him.

"I'm willing to take that chance."

"Actually, I'm here to ask for a favor." The energy in the room shifted as if he knew she would disappoint him. Or maybe she just projected that emotion. "I need you to sneak me to the airport again."

"I thought you were giving up on the missing girl." His careful words didn't completely hide his frustration.

"I need to try and find her. Besides, it's a job." It was more than that, but too difficult to explain.

"I thought we were trying to build something here."

It hurt to hear the roughness in his voice. Once again, she'd wounded the best person she knew. "I know. I want to. I just need to finish this. I think I know where she is."

"And that is more important than us?"

"It's not like that." But it was, and he knew it.

"I'm not going to help you self-destruct again."

"I'm not going to self-destruct. My goal is to find a missing woman. I just don't want those guys to follow me to the airport. They don't even try to hide anymore." She pointed to the black SUV in the Starbucks parking lot.

And as she knew he would, as he always did, he acquiesced. She'd manipulated him so he would take her to the airport. Once again, she had proved her kinship with her parents. Or her own brand of it.

Chapter 12

Two days later, Jessica left for Belize. Even if she didn't find Doraliz, and she probably wouldn't, she'd get a tropical vacation out of the trip. Early afternoon had arrived when the captain announced the descent to the Phillip S.W. Goldson International Airport in Belize City.

The beige and ecru city she'd flown out of had been replaced by a lush, green jungle. It looked as if someone had recently hacked the runway from the encroaching trees and vines with machetes. When she disembarked, the thick humid air hit her like a wall.

She taxied to the crowded town center of Belize City, then boarded a ferry to Ambergris Caye. She'd forgotten how boats made her queasy and gripped the railing tight as they left the dock. Ninety minutes of traveling over water in every shade of New Mexico turquoise and she stepped onto silky beach sand.

Open air palapas housing bars and restaurants shared space with concrete buildings painted every color imaginable. She trudged down the street, tired and grimy from travel, with sweat steaming through her black jeans and pooling in her boots. The hotel she'd booked had bright white walls with scarlet trim and a beckoning blue pool. She couldn't believe she'd gotten the room for only fifty dollars a night.

A friendly woman checked her in and confirmed the room had air conditioning. El Paso could be over one hundred degrees during the summer, but this wet heat burrowed through her pores and sapped her energy.

With a smile and perky black corkscrew curls that defied the humidity, the woman handed Jessica a key, an actual door key, not a key card. "Have a wonderful stay."

"Thank you." Jessica reached for the key, then paused. "Hey, a friend of mine is working her way down Latin America on a bucket list trip. The last time I heard from her, she was headed here. Her name is Dora. Have you seen her?" Jessica handed the woman a photo of Doraliz.

The woman studied the photo, then handed it back. "She doesn't look familiar, but you should check back between five and six when Mike is here. He owns the hotel and knows everyone in town."

"Thanks, I'll do that."

She unlocked a ground floor room of the two-story cement building. Cool white tile floors and stark white concrete walls greeted her. She turned the air conditioning unit on high, pulled off her boots, and set her bare feet on the refreshing tile. Next, she peeled off her damp clothes and stood naked under the A/C until the sweat dried on her body and her skin prickled with chill. The cold relief brought her more energy than a gallon of coffee. After a quick shower and switching jeans for an ancient pair of khaki shorts, sunscreen, and a tank top, she hit the town.

Jessica wandered the cobbled streets until they opened onto the beach. At the end of a wooden pier, she found the Iguana Restaurant, a palapa that sold conch fritters and piña coladas. The logo matched the one on Sra. Velasco's book of matches. To celebrate the discovery and landing in a tropical location, she pulled herself onto a rough wooden barstool. A slim, dark-skinned bartender with mile-high hair flirted gently with the customers and carried on five conversations at once.

Jessica surveyed the tables crammed into the small restaurant. A trio of middle-aged American men told fish stories, a family at a table nearby spoke what sounded like Italian, and an extremely sunburned British couple nursed drinks and argued quietly about whether to go snorkeling or sunbathing the next day. From the way it sounded, the couple should each do their own thing, but she wouldn't butt in.

When the bartender spoke to the two waitresses, he used a patois Jessica couldn't understand. He approached her and asked for her order with a faint British accent, reminding Jessica that Belize had been British Honduras before gaining independence.

She watched him blend her drink, anticipating the icy liquid slipping down her throat. It seemed to take forever for him to fill the plastic cup and garnish it with a hunk of fresh pineapple, the same fruit he'd used to make the drink.

"Thank you," she said as she lifted the glass to her lips. Her greedy sip shot a dagger through her forehead. "Ouch. Ice cream headache."

The bartender laughed. "It's a danger. Are you here for a holiday?"

"Sort of. I'm hoping to catch up with a friend of mine. She would have come a few weeks ago, maybe gotten a job. Any ideas where I might look?"

"It's not easy for foreigners to get jobs here. Sometimes the expats hire them, but they're not supposed to."

"I see." Jessica looked up at him, noticing the sharpened eyes and stern voice. He probably had to deal with a never-ending stream of foreigners willing to trade labor for a stint in paradise.

Despite the piña colada's fresh coconut and pineapple chunklettes, the cloying sweetness clung to Jessica in the heat. She downed it quickly, risking the headache, then followed it with a Belikin beer, which the bartender promised her the locals drank. The ice-cold bottle and slightly malty flavor tasted like heaven.

A breeze sauntered in from the ocean. That and the icy beer worked better than any massage at relaxing her from the long day. She decided to try again with the bartender, very obviously pulling a twenty from her wallet and dropping it into the coconut shell with the word *tips* etched into it. "So, say my friend wanted to find an expat to hire her on for a bit, where should I check?"

He gave her a long look. "A couple of the pizza places are owned by foreigners, along with a few bars and many of the hotels."

"Thanks," she said as a short man in a white apron came out of the back carrying a plate overflowing with rice, salad, and golden balls of fried goodness. The fluffy batter on the conch contrasted with the chewy texture. Mostly it tasted of the sea, flavored with salt and iron and ocean breezes.

Jessica had a light sheen of sweat again, but each time the breeze came through, it scurried across her damp skin and cooled it. She had another beer and sat on the barstool, breathing in the salt air and letting it pull the tension from her body. Full, and satisfied that she'd reached her destination, she wanted to stay on the barstool forever. But she had a job to do.

When she paid up, she showed the bartender a photo of Doraliz from her Instagram account.

"She looks a little familiar," he said, "but we have a lot of people in and out of here."

Jessica wandered through streets sporting more golf carts than actual cars. She stopped in markets, bars, and a couple of dive shops, always pulling out the photo of Doraliz and asking if anyone had seen her. No positive responses.

She stopped off for another Belikin at a beachside bar. Choosing a picnic table, she kicked off her flipflops and dug her toes in the sand. Something about the cold beer and warm breeze made her wish she could stay forever. She wished Angus sat beside her.

He would love it here. He had defined laid back since childhood, and this island was exactly his speed. She imagined him sipping a drink, shirtless and shoeless on the sand. She took a photo of her beer, catching a bit of wooden table and umbrella to frame the powdery sand and azure sea beyond.

Before hitting send on the text, she thought about including a caption. Her fingers wanted to type *love you*, but her brain told her *wish you were here* was enough. She ended up sending the photo without words.

When he'd taken her to the airport, he seemed resigned, but a new sadness underlaid this. She hoped she hadn't gone too far this time.

The sun had started its descent. A shaft of sunlight lit the beach through a gap in the buildings behind her. The warmth of the sun on her back, the coolness of the sand when she dug her feet down to the damp, and the view conspired to alter her thoughts about her search.

Why wouldn't Doraliz prefer this to the harshness of the desert? Why wouldn't she?

Maybe life didn't have to be hard. But she had to make a living, had to protect herself from the things that could go wrong, had to struggle. Didn't she?

As the last of the sun faded, she rose and stepped into the water. The last time she'd waded in the ocean, she'd been with her parents in California. There, the cold Pacific had tumbled her in its aggressive waves. Here, wavelets welcomed her forward into cool water. Tiny fish played around her feet.

Maybe she could change. Maybe that's what Doraliz had done. She'd love to be like Alma and spend her days helping the people who needed it. She'd love to vacation on sparkling Caribbean beaches with Angus.

No. She left the water. Life had shown her things didn't work out that way. Maybe she needed to take more vacations, and if Angus wanted to come along, well, great. Born to the hardscrabble desert, she had learned to make her way there. She hadn't come here for fantasies of an easier life. She'd come here to find a missing woman.

That no one seemed to know Doraliz reopened fears the woman had been taken, not escaped. Jessica didn't fully understand why, but she needed to follow Doraliz's story to the end. It probably had something to do with their closeness in age and the fact that they'd both been born to crappy parents. Whatever it was, she owed Doraliz something, some kind of closure.

Jessica left the beach and headed back to the hotel. She stopped by the office to see if Mike had arrived, but it turned out she'd missed him completely. He wouldn't be back until the following day. Fine.

She found a place for dinner at the harbor between Ambergris Caye and the mainland. She ordered ceviche and another Belikin at the bar, more to ask about Doraliz than due to hunger.

No one had seen Doraliz. Jessica hadn't thought it would be easy. At least it wouldn't take her long to canvas the small atoll. A few days and she'd know.

After dinner, she found a beachside palapa with a reggae band. She ordered a beer, figuring she'd give the search for Doraliz a rest and enjoy the night. The crowd vacillated between drinking and dancing, glistening skin ranging from black to tan to bright sunburned red.

She'd normally have loved the place, but tonight it made her lonely. Perhaps the travel had worn her out. She could turn in early tonight and begin the search again in the morning.

The mattress ended up being a thin piece of foam on a wooden platform, and Jessica woke sore and deeply tired. Her body clamored for coffee, so she headed for a place she'd seen advertising breakfast.

The teal building had a deck that opened onto the beach. The island teemed with places begging you to bury your toes in the sand and cast your worries into the ocean. She sat in a plastic chair and ordered coffee from a smiling woman with Mayan features who couldn't have been more than sixteen years old.

She tried to decipher the chalkboard menu where scrawled breakfast specialties covered every inch of black in a pastel rainbow of colors. She decided on Mayan eggs with something called fry jack. When her order arrived, the plate overflowed with a huge serving of eggs scrambled with ham and vegetables, a side of black refried beans, and two enormous slabs of fried dough. It was enough food to feed everyone at Friday night happy hour.

While home seemed very far away, the feeling of working hard and never having anything to account for it stayed close. She needed to find Doraliz.

When she paid her bill, she asked the server if she'd seen her friend.

"I think she works at the pizza place," the woman said, all friendly smile and innocence. Finally, a lead.

When Jessica left the restaurant, she'd assumed, from what the woman said, that the island only had one pizza restaurant. In fact, it had four, and they were all closed until later in the day. One, in a resort on the northern end of the island, would be difficult to reach. The hotel offered two rickety bicycles for rent, but Jessica hadn't ridden a bike in years and didn't want to start on unpaved streets filled with pedestrians, golf carts, and cars. She didn't need a trip to the hospital, if one even existed on the island.

She could rent a golf cart for twenty-five dollars for the day, but she preferred to save money and time and start with the pizza restaurants still in town. She showed Doraliz's photo around nearby shops to see if anyone had seen her.

At a juice and cold drinks stand, really just a cut-out window in the side of a pink wooden house, someone said Doraliz used to stop by for juice. Watermelon was her favorite. Jessica ordered a watermelon juice.

The frosty drink tasted like paradise, smooth and only slightly sweet. A block and a half away, Privateer Pizza beckoned. Jessica peeked into the closed restaurant. Wooden tables and chairs filled most of the space, but a long cement bar took up the back wall, with liquor on one side and a pizza oven on the other. Unlike many of the colorful buildings she'd passed, this one glowed white with fresh paint decorated with accents of green and red like the Italian flag. The sign on the door said it would open at eleven. Two hours away.

She wandered back to the beach. Vendors approached her, one after the other. Would she like a tour of the island? A snorkeling trip? A drink from a glass jar of who knows what alcohol with a tiny dead white snake curled at the bottom? Would she like to learn to scuba dive? No to all, especially the diving. And maybe the snake hooch.

The thought of choosing to swim in water infested by sharks and other predators held no appeal for a desert dweller. The only time she'd been on a boat before this trip, she'd floated on a calm, flat reservoir in the middle of New Mexico. She'd been grossly seasick then, so there was no way she'd hold it together floating in a choppy ocean. She appreciated that other people, like Doraliz, wanted to explore the depths of the ocean, but she'd stick to the warm, safe beach and a cold Belikin.

She wandered back into town at ten forty-five and arrived five minutes before the pizza joint opened. Except it didn't open until eleven-fifteen. She knew from standing in front of the plate glass windows for twenty minutes that the staff had arrived. Two women set up tables while a stocky man did prep work near the pizza oven. They all studiously ignored her.

She had planned on getting straight to the questions. However, with the staff not super friendly, she decided to order something, despite not having recovered from breakfast. A small woman with sharp features brought Jessica a menu.

The only things on the menu were pizza and chicken wings, neither of which Jessica could stomach in the growing heat and after a huge breakfast. She ordered a Coke instead. When the woman brought her drink, Jessica scrolled to the photo of Doraliz.

"I'm trying to find my friend. She's traveling through Latin America, and I thought she'd be here by now. Have you seen her?" She pushed her phone toward the woman.

The server's eyebrows raised in surprise, but then she gave Jessica a suspicious glare. "I don't know who that is."

Jessica didn't believe her, but the woman stared her down until a group of sunburned tourists shuffled through the door in search of lunch. While the woman took drink orders, Jessica made her way to the back of the room to talk to the guy manning the pizza oven.

"Hey, I'm looking for a friend of mine. Have you seen her?" She thrust the photo forward.

The guy glanced up and shook his head. "No hablo ingles."

"Bien, hablo español," she replied, letting him know she spoke Spanish. Meanwhile, she knew the official language of Belize was English. The guy just shook his head.

"Can I help you?" Jessica's server stood beside her, arms crossed and legs wide. Jessica recognized the hostile stance.

"No. I'm good."

"Are you ready to order food?" Unspoken but clearly implied was "if not, get out of here."

"Thanks for the hospitality," Jessica said.

She struck out at the remaining pizza places. She even got a taxi to take her to the resort at the top of the island. While no one there knew

Doraliz, Jessica stayed awhile, soaking up sunshine and drinking Cuba Libres at the beach bar.

She made it back to her hotel at five o'clock sharp and found the elusive Mike at the reception desk. He stood at least six foot six and spoke with a Texas twang.

"Nice to meet you," he said. "I hear you've been looking for me."

"Yes. That's a Texas accent. Where are you from?"

"I'm from Beaumont, but I've been down here about fifteen years."

"Wow, I'm from El Paso. What's it like to live here? It seems like paradise."

"Some days it is. It definitely beats the hell out of Beaumont. Same humidity, but with an ocean breeze. And an ocean. Plus, it doesn't smell like an oilfield."

"Yeah, I get it. El Paso has all the beach in the world, but no water."

"I drove through El Paso once. That's pretty stark country."

"It can be." The purple mountains at sunset, the tennis ball yellow of a prickly pear flower, and the way the landscape tinged green after a rain flitted through her head. She thought she caught the aroma of woodsmoke pulling her home.

"Have you enjoyed your stay?" he asked.

"I have. It's wonderful here. I've been looking for a friend who was supposed to pass through here on her travels. Her name is Dora. Have you seen her?" She showed him the photo of Doraliz.

Mike rubbed his chin in thought. "I think that's Sebastian's girl. She's a lot more dolled up in this photo than when I've seen her. People tend to go native once they get here."

"That's fantastic. Who is Sebastian, and where do you think I can find her?"

"That's going to be an issue. Sebastian owned Privateer Pizza, but he sold it and moved to Roatán."

"Really? Why?"

"Some folks who come down here are never satisfied, no matter where they land. If they spend more than a few years in one place, their feet start itching for someplace new. That's Sebastian for you. That guy is from Ireland, but he's lived in Thailand, the United States, Panama, Belize, and now Honduras. Who knows where he'll go next?"

"And you think Doraliz, Dora, was with him?"

"I'm pretty sure that's her. I don't know if she stayed with him. He changes women as often as he changes locations, but I think he had just met her. Anyway, he told me he already had another pizza place down on Roatán."

"Thanks for the information. I think I'm going to try to catch up with her."

"Happy I could help. You can catch a flight from Belize City to Roatán. It's not cheap, but unless you've got a yacht or want to spend days on a bus, it's your best bet."

Chapter 13

J essica took the first ferry back to the mainland the following day. She'd booked a Tropical Air flight to Roatán. The luck of finding news of Doraliz and landing a ticket on the plane quickened her step. She had four days left before her scheduled return to the United States, and for the first time, she believed she'd find the missing woman.

Jessica climbed into the rickety twelve-seater plane with eleven other passengers. Thankfully, she didn't have to take a window seat. The only thing worse than being on a boat in the water would be flying a tiny plane over it.

She sat next to a man from Dallas, which she learned because he incessantly talked about himself. Once Jessica had established that he hadn't been to Belize or Roatán before, and thus wouldn't have run across Doraliz, she quit listening to him. Instead, she stared out the front of the plane, looking at pale blue sky, instead of the iridescent water below.

As if attached by a string, the propeller plane stayed close to the earth. The engine's loud rumble should have made talking impossible, not that her row mate noticed. The low altitude enabled her to track the Central American coast southward. She braved a look across the chest of the still talking man beside her and glimpsed the blue sea dotted with verdant islands. Sometimes a fringe of white sand separated the jungle from the ocean, other times the trees seemed to wade into the water. Sunlight glinted off liquid beneath green leaves, making it difficult to tell where the ocean ended and the land began.

She leaned toward the window, amazed by the constantly changing color of the sea which hued from the deepest sapphire to the lightest aquamarine depending on the depth of the water. Sometimes the change happened within a few feet as reefs rose to break the water's surface, the ocean floor falling a few yards later into an abyss too deep to fathom.

She saw the island of Roatán as they approached. Unlike the flat and sandy atoll of Ambergris, Roatán had a spine of green mountain running from its tip to its tail. It wasn't a large mountain, like her El Paso peaks that tried to split the sky, but it gave the island two definite sides. Long, skinny, and lush, and even from the air not nearly as developed as Ambergris, Roatán seemed like a wilder kind of paradise.

The airport, if one could call it that, was a single strip of pavement laid right along the sea. Back in Juarez, Jessica had helped American companies rent buildings in Juarez many times the size of the tiny airport.

The plane angled down sharply, like an insect landing on skin, and Jessica couldn't push down the fear they'd tip off the end of the short runway and into the ocean. But one good bounce and the plane slowed, her seatmate still droning on beside her.

One of the first passengers off the plane, she shouldered her backpack and walked through the small airport. Somewhat used to humidity, she found it easier to breathe the thick air. She bypassed the men offering taxi rides and headed toward town.

Jessica's research had found half a dozen pizza restaurants on Roatán. Two cruise ship docks had entire inauthentic 'local' villages complete with pizza shops. She doubted Doraliz would be at either of these. Given what Mike had told her about Sebastian opening a pizza restaurant on the island, she didn't think it would be at one of the major resorts, so she crossed two more off her list.

This left the Pizza House at Coxen Hole, the town with the airstrip, and Papa's Pizza, on the other side of the island in a town called the West End. She had already mapped out the location of the Pizza House, just a mile and a half away, and she figured she'd walk.

It excited her to stroll into a new place with an agenda. Maybe she could become an investigator, although whether she would help or hurt Doraliz if she found her was still a little fuzzy. She entered the nearly empty restaurant without asking for a menu. Instead, she headed straight to the bar. She asked for a beer to make up for the steamy walk from the airport. A friendly man with impressive dreadlocks and a wide smile served her. As soon as he set down the frothy liquid, she asked if he'd seen Doraliz. He hadn't, so she downed the brew and got directions to West End, where she had a room reservation and hopefully a missing woman to find.

She caught a minibus across the hills to her hotel. Where the lodge on Ambergris had been a two-story cement building devoid of all but a few palms, the glazed wood Wade Inn sat nestled in a jungle of trees across the street from the water. She checked into an air-conditioned room with a large bed sporting a colorful serape-inspired blanket.

She only stayed in the room long enough to use the facilities and splash water on her face. Doraliz could be just down the road.

Trees shaded the pavement, winding around the water's edge as she made her way to the restaurant. On the land side of the road sat a variety of shops, hotels, and restaurants. On the water side, patches of beach offset shallow jade fingers of ocean split by verdant hills. Piers with restaurants, bars, and cozy shelters jutted over the calm water.

People sat on steps or leaned on railings, giving off a vibe even more laid back than Ambergris. Where once Belize had epitomized tropical paradise, she now had a new definition. She passed a bar with a sign advertising dollar beer and tequila shots. Maybe she wouldn't go home.

Jessica caught sight of the Papa's Pizza sign and slowed. What if Doraliz was there? If she wasn't and no one had heard of her, she could go home having done her best. She hadn't figured out what she'd do if she found her. She could tell her that her parents missed her and wanted to see her, but Doraliz probably already knew that. If she told her she ought to go home, Doraliz had no reason to listen. Jessica stopped and looked around. Could she tell someone to go back to the desert and the vagaries of family when they had chosen to live here?

Suddenly, her life floated around her in shattered pieces. Who the fuck was she to give advice? Her parents, gone. Her best friends who let her live on their land, probably hanging on by a threat after her latest antic. Her attorney and moral compass, furious with her. Angus? In coming here, in continuing this job when he'd asked her not to, she had told him he hadn't made the top of her priority list.

And yet she was here, about to tell someone else what to do with their life. She needed to listen to Alma and find a new career, instead of this downward slide from real estate to deals to hunting people. She wanted to change, to become more like those she admired, instead of screwing up and screwing them over. Still, she was here.

She slunk up to the restaurant's entrance. A stained wood deck with umbrella'd picnic tables fronted a wood paneled interior. A tall black woman with incredibly shiny long black hair greeted her and asked where she'd like to sit.

Jessica chose a table just inside the restaurant instead of on the patio and sat facing the kitchen and bar. The only other person in the restaurant was a stocky white man behind the counter. Jessica took her menu and ordered a pizza and a beer. No Doraliz, not yet anyway.

While she waited for her pizza, Jessica surveyed the restaurant. It was the opposite of the pizza place in Ambergris with its white tile floors and white painted walls. This was the jungle version of that, all wood and surrounded by trees, with just a slip of sea view when she looked behind her.

Jessica turned from the ocean and watched the man behind the counter. He slid a pizza into the oven. Likely in his thirties, although where along that line she couldn't say, he had platinum hair, dyed the color guys used when their hair thinned. He wasn't bald yet, but his hairline had begun its rearward creep. Could this be Sebastian, man of many countries, who claimed Doraliz as his girl? He had a look, call it aging sexy. He'd gone a little thick around the middle in addition to the retreating hair, but the traces of lines on his face added some needed gravitas. His muscular arms pulled the pizza from the oven and slid it onto a tray in a single swift motion. She'd have done him.

"Alyssa, order up," the man said, prompting Alyssa to walk over from where she'd been wiping off menus.

"Thanks, Sebastian," Alyssa answered.

The pizza arrived bubbling with cheese and dotted with the sausage and jalapeños she'd ordered. Jessica barely registered its appearance. This was the place. She could have scarfed down the delicious pizza, given her hunger, but she ate slowly, chewed each bite. She needed to stay here for as long as it took for Doraliz to arrive.

Fortunately, other people began to fill the tables. Younger than the crowd in Belize, most of the patrons were in their twenties and thirties. No one with kids. Another server showed up, a Latino guy who took over the patio service. Jessica couldn't eat another bite, but she ordered a second beer to help pass the time.

Doraliz arrived and slipped behind the bar. Shockwaves pummeled Jessica. Some part of her thought she'd fail in this task, despite knowing how close she was to finding the woman.

Jessica wouldn't have recognized her if she hadn't spent so much time staring at her photo. The woman had gone from flowing debutante hair to a short cut shaved close on the sides with a lock of thick black hair hanging over one eye.

Her skin prickled with excitement. She'd been incredibly lucky, and the hints from Doraliz's mother had paid off.

She didn't want to show her interest in Doraliz, not yet. Doraliz had escaped her past, started over. The possibility fascinated Jessica, and she clandestinely watched her as if she were an exotic zoo animal.

Doraliz began her set up at the bar, then Sebastian waved her over. He wrapped an arm around her waist and pulled her in for a kiss. When he released her, she said something to him that made him laugh. Then she returned to the bar.

Jessica needed a guidebook on what to do next. Should she approach Doraliz? Just watch her for a while? Indecision held her in its grasp, so she loitered, draining her beer.

"Would you like anything else?" The server unknowingly pushed her into action.

"Could I trouble you for one more beer? I know you're filling up and I'll leave after that."

The server looked at her as if the question had been ridiculous. "It's no problem, stay as long as you'd like. Do you want me to box the rest of your pizza?"

"No thanks. I don't have any place for it, but it was delicious."

The server returned to the bar to give Doraliz her order. Doraliz looked up, finally seeing her. Then she turned her head to smile at the server and pulled a mug from beneath the counter.

Jessica watched, rapt and unable to turn away. Doraliz set the full beer atop the bar and looked toward Alyssa, who'd moved on to assist another table, then she turned to Jessica. Saw Jessica staring. Doraliz grabbed the full mug and approached. Jessica's heart hammered so hard the other woman had to hear it, but no words came.

"You ordered a beer?"

Jessica caught the faint formal Mexican accent in the words. "Thank you," she said as Doraliz set the mug on the table, then returned to the bar.

Crap. What was she supposed to do now? She'd been chasing a fantasy at least as much as a real person. She caught herself blatantly staring at Doraliz again and turned to face Sebastian instead. How had she come here without a plan? Amateur.

Doraliz took Sebastian a beer and talked to him for a few minutes. Sebastian tried to grab her ass when she left, but Doraliz stepped deftly away. And looked up at Jessica as she did. Saw her staring. Again.

Jessica hailed her server and paid the bill. When she left, she stopped by the bar.

"Would you like another drink?" Doraliz kept her voice innocent, but Jessica noticed suspicion in her eyes.

"No, thanks. I'm good. Hey, can I talk to you about something? It's personal."

Doraliz stilled, a pint glass in one hand, drying towel in the other. Her eyes bored into Jessica. "Not here." The carefully placed words accepted no argument. "I will be at the Treasure Trove after my shift."

"Thanks. I'll see you then." The bar with dollar beer and shots. Well, twist her arm. Jessica couldn't think of a better place to hang out than the tropical version of a dive bar.

She went back to the hotel and showered to try and sober up. She should have asked when Doraliz's shift ended. Dragging from the long days, she attempted to grab a nap, but the exhaustion couldn't get past the shaky nerves. Doraliz's parents were jerks. She left a city where women get murdered all the time, something Doraliz actually cared about, had written a thesis about. Now she lived in a beach paradise and apparently had a new boyfriend.

If Jessica's parents had sent someone to find her, well, they knew where she was. She had never left El Paso. They hadn't cared enough about her to hand out envelopes of money hoping to bring her back home. The familiar ache began its work of hollowing her out.

She hadn't wanted to go to Fort Davis when her parents first talked about it. What sixteen-your-old ensconced in high school would? She had friends she loved, something she thought was a future. But high school seemed to go on without her after her parents left. She went to class, studied, but her friends vanished into their own lives, leaving Jessica alone. Except for Angus.

Despite how things had turned out, or maybe because of it, the white-hot anger that burned through her when her parents suggested she move could still singe her skin. She'd yelled at them. Called her dad a criminal. Told her mother she was useless. But if they had sent someone to ask her after those first few months, once she understood about drowning in loneliness, it would have made a difference.

Jessica's mom hadn't cared enough to fight for her. Doraliz's mom wasn't exactly on the hunt either. The Velascos had their money do the work. And, unlike Jessica as a sixteen-year-old, Doraliz didn't look lonely.

Oh! Inspiration hit her like an iron bar. Ruben Velasco had asked her to find his daughter. He didn't ask her to bring her home. She'd bet he wouldn't want her to talk to Doraliz and let her know she'd been discovered. That way, he could bring in his goons and extricate her.

Too bad for him he hadn't given her explicit instructions. Doraliz didn't seem to be in any trouble, so Jessica would extend her investigation and find out more about her life before reporting back to daddy. And, if Doraliz was happy? Who was she to question an adult's decision?

Her attempt at rest only made her brain spin, so she left the room and walked across the street to the small beach. Spikes of green hills stretched toward the sea and framed the curve of a perfect, miniature bay. She snapped a photo and texted Angus. His only response to her photo of Ambergris had been *pretty*. She couldn't blame him. Jessica stared at the screen of her phone, wishing she could take back the image she'd just sent. She hated that she toyed with Angus, wanted to show him her life only to shut him out when he got too close.

She had to stop the back and forth. It only tortured both of them. She'd made her decision, chosen the job, and manipulated Angus to go along. Exactly like her father had done when he chose to do something illegal rather than protect his family. She had spent her life trying not to be like him, and she'd ended up exactly the same. Well, not exactly. It's not like she and Angus were married with children. She wouldn't follow her father there.

She had to end things with Angus.

She turned toward the Treasure Trove. Doraliz probably wouldn't be there for hours, but Jessica had a sudden urge to get her drink on. What the hell, she'd landed in Eden, might as well take a bite of the apple.

Chapter 14

Built on stilts a few feet above the sand, the Treasure Trove's wide wooden deck held colorful, scattered tables that reminded her of fallen piñata candy. Along one side, the bamboo bar had a drink specials sign that mirrored the one on the road. Dollar beers and dollar tequilas, Jessica's preferred libations.

She approached the bar, a thrum of excitement running through her. Instead of being thrilled she'd found Doraliz, recklessness drew her forward. She'd come here chasing some other girl's life. Now that she'd found her, Jessica had no magic way to make Doraliz's life better. Jessica's father had worked with the same people and gotten in too deep. She'd followed his example. She couldn't be trusted with relationships. At least that freed her return to hard drinking and sex with strangers. She'd forgotten the excitement that came with the bleeding edge of drunkenness and danger.

"A beer and a tequila please." She slapped three dollars on the bar. While she didn't know the denomination of the local currency, it seemed everyone here took dollars. She'd become just another American slut on vacation.

"You bet." The bartender had cinnamon skin and ocean blue eyes. Definitely a contender. "Are you here alone?"

"Yes," she answered, trying to sound confident. People needed to learn not to ask that. Why should it matter if she traveled alone?

"Awesome," he said, his smile lingering. "Let me know when you need a refill."

He set the tequila in front of her. She picked up the shot glass and threw the liquid into the back of her throat, loving the burn that spread down her esophagus. Her eyes watered at the harshness. This was not sipping tequila. She set the glass back on the bar. "I need a refill."

He cocked an eyebrow at her, clearly flirting. She enjoyed being back in a game she knew so well. She took her beer and second tequila to one of the bar-height tables on the patio where her view encompassed the beach and the patrons as they arrived. Whatever she wanted tonight, she could have. She deserved the consequences of morning.

As the night wore on, she found herself plied with cheap drinks. The line of men willing to spend a buck to see if they'd get lucky stretched as far as the liquor would last. She'd moved on from the overworked bartender and had several new targets in sight. A rowdy gang of guys in their twenties had taken over one corner of the bar, including a tall guy with ebony skin who eyed her stealthily throughout the night.

A sunburned geezer and his fishing buddy at the table next to her kept trying to start a conversation. She'd heard more than she wanted about their attempts to catch a blue marlin. One of them had bought her two beers already before personally delivering her a tequila and standing at her table like he wanted something.

"You can't buy me enough drinks to go home with you tonight," she finally said. She didn't enjoy being mean, but she needed him to move on.

The wooziness of the alcohol crowded her brain, and she switched to water. She wanted to be sober enough to talk to Doraliz. She could have picked a better night to drink, but this trip to the tropics had shown her the worst part of herself. Instead of confidence and relief at finding Doraliz and finishing the job, the dark part of her knew she would hurt the woman. She had plenty of experience with that. Just ask anyone who cared about her.

After an hour of sipping water and making eyes at the tall guy, Doraliz still hadn't arrived. Jessica ordered a beer and made a deal with herself that if she didn't see Doraliz before she'd finished, she would return to the pizza place.

Five minutes later, Doraliz strode in with Sebastian and the woman who'd been Jessica's server. They walked straight to her table.

"Hello, thanks for coming to the restaurant today. I'm Erica," Doraliz said.

"Hi, Erica. I'm Jessica." She shouldn't have ordered that last beer. She couldn't slip and reveal Doraliz's identity. Jessica's words didn't exactly slur, but they sounded too big for her mouth.

"You've met Alyssa," Doraliz said. "And this is Sebastian. He owns the restaurant."

Jessica smiled at Alyssa. To Sebastian, she said, "It's amazing that you own a place here. Is it easy to buy a business in Honduras?"

"I've got a head for business," he said, an Irish lilt coming through. "The restaurant was a prime opportunity."

Doraliz put an arm around him and gave him a quick squeeze. "Hey, would you get me a drink?"

"Sure. Come on, let's leave these two alone." He took Alyssa's hand and pulled her toward the bar.

Jessica stared at them as they left. She'd thought Doraliz and Sebastian were an item. Now she wasn't sure.

She turned her focus to Doraliz. "How long have you been on the island? Or are you from here?"

"I've only been here a couple of weeks." Doraliz gave her a long look. "What do you want with me?"

"What's it like to leave your life behind and start something new?" Jessica hadn't planned on asking that question, and it had come out with an unexpected longing. If you started over where nobody knew you, could you rewrite your life?

Doraliz's eyes narrowed to focused slits as she considered the question. "I guess it depends on what you've left behind. Why so many questions?"

Jessica must have been drunker than she thought because the response seared through her like a white-hot sword. "I left my family behind." She didn't know whether she meant her mother and father or Angus.

Doraliz's eyes flew open. "Why?"

An excellent, unanswerable question. "I was young." The response sat on the table like an unfinished beer.

"Family can be difficult," Doraliz said. "That is why some people choose to create their own families instead of condemning themselves to the one they were born to."

"Is he your family?" Jessica gestured toward Sebastian. Too late, she noticed his hand on Alyssa's hip.

Doraliz sighed long and heavily. "Love is overrated."

"Doraliz, that is something I can drink to." Jessica tipped her now empty beer bottle in Doraliz's direction and noticed the anger on the woman's face. "I mean Erica."

Just then, the tall guy appeared with a fresh bottle in each hand. He gave one to Jessica and the other to Doraliz. "I'll be right back," he said. "I need to get one for myself."

"Salvavida," Doraliz said, looking at the name on the beer bottle. "Do you know what that means?"

"Lifesaver," Jessica answered. "I've felt that way a time or two about a bottle."

"Well, you're going to need more than a bottle to save you if you ever contact me again. Understand?"

"We need to talk."

"No. We definitely do not. You need to go home. I need to take care of something." Doraliz nodded at Sebastian and Alyssa, now crammed into each other's personal space.

With that Doraliz left, her beer untouched. She marched straight to Sebastian and Alyssa. Jessica couldn't see her face or hear her words, but she caught the echo of an angry voice. Soon the trio passed close to Jessica's table, Doraliz in the lead and Sebastian dragging Alyssa behind him like an afterthought.

Doraliz turned to Sebastian with her hand in the air, stopping him. "Do not come back to the house. You made your choice. Stay with that slut tonight."

Sebastian and Alyssa, and frankly, half the bar, stood rooted to their spot, watching Doraliz stride away. That woman knew how to leave a room.

Now what? She'd blown her chance. Jessica sensed someone at her shoulder and turned to see the tall guy.

"What happened to your friend?" he asked.

"Nothing a couple of tequilas won't cure. Although I need to find her again."

"She works at the dive shop we went to this morning." He pulled a barstool next to hers. "I'm James."

"Jessica. What's the name of the dive shop?"

"West End Divers. It's awesome, you should try it. You have to get up early, though. The tours leave at eight in the morning."

"No thanks. That would be terrifying. I'm not a big fan of the water."

"Then why are you in Honduras?"

"I'm just here to screw up lives and get my drink on. You?"

He gave her a stare, probably trying to figure out if she was worth it. "Bachelor party." Long lashes framed bloodshot eyes, and he smelled faintly of pot. He had beautiful lips, full and dark. Yet, she didn't want to kiss him.

"I'll be right back," she said. She returned with two shots. Set them on the table.

"Not for me," he said. "I'll hurl if I drink that."

Lovely. She poured her own shot down her throat, thinking it would bring her back to herself. She'd been flirting with this guy all night. A guy like this could get Angus out of her system. She closed her eyes, waiting for the tequila to take hold, felt his hand on her knee. She smiled and looked into his face. He'd come closer. She fixed her gaze on his lips, tried to picture him kissing her neck, her shoulder, her breasts. Nothing. A piece of her had gone missing. She'd left it with Angus back in El Paso.

"Hey," she said. "You're really nice, but I've got to go." Then she slid off the barstool and walked into the night.

Chapter 15

Jessica had set her alarm for seven-thirty but must have turned it off without realizing it. She woke just after eight, and her head ached like it had tumbled in a cement mixer all night. Pulling herself out of bed, she downed three Tylenol before brushing her teeth. She made it out the door in ten minutes.

In the hotel lobby, she scalded her mouth on a cup of truly horrible coffee and asked for directions to the dive shop. She jogged down the street, every step pounding nails into her skull. Crossing her fingers, she prayed Doraliz would be there.

She found the blue dive shop with the red and white diver down flag on the beach side of the road. Jessica barely remembered to ask for Erica instead of Doraliz, and the guy behind the counter pointed out the back door of the shop. She glimpsed white sand and blue water.

Stepping out of the shop, she had to shade her eyes from the intense brightness of the sun bouncing off the bay. A group of tourists carrying masks and fins waded out to a small boat. Doraliz stood in the water near the back of the craft, helping an older woman who struggled to gain purchase on the boat's ladder. Dear god. Jessica wanted to talk to Doraliz but didn't need a hoard of tourists talking through her headache and watching her barf from seasickness. This had been a bad idea.

It took fifteen minutes to load the tourists into the boat, and Jessica wished she'd spent them in bed. Fortunately, the overly full vessel left Doraliz on the shore.

"Why are you here? I told you not to follow me." Doraliz said, walking over to her.

"Please, just give me a few minutes."

"Fine. We'll talk in the water where we won't be overheard." Doraliz nodded to a smaller boat a few yards away.

"How about we skip the boat and I buy you breakfast?" Jessica would have done just about anything to stay off the water, especially since her headache still raged.

Doraliz waded ashore. "I already ate. Here, take this." Doraliz handed her a mask and snorkel that she pulled from a crate. "Are your feet a size eight or nine?"

"Nine. This isn't a good idea. I get seasick, and you watching me hang over a boat and barf isn't exactly quality conversation time."

Doraliz pulled a pair of fins from a cubby, then turned to face Jessica, hands on her hips. "You said you wanted to talk to me. No offense, but at the bar last night, you were wasted. This is your only chance. You can go with me on the boat, or you can leave. Your choice."

This woman had a spine of steel. Ruben Velasco had underestimated his daughter.

"Fine." They waded back into the water where Jessica struggled to get into the small boat. It didn't have a ladder and Doraliz told Jessica to heave herself up over the side while Doraliz steadied it from the water. Jessica tried but found herself dangling half in the boat, half in the water, before Doraliz grabbed her ass and shoved her in face first.

"Hey, that wasn't nice."

"You are not an athlete." Doraliz smoothly hoisted herself into the vessel.

Doraliz didn't say anything else, just moved to the back of the boat and started the engine. "Sit down," she yelled to Jessica over the roar. "And face the front, you'll be less likely to get seasick."

The few short minutes it took to reach the ocean edge of the inlet surprised Jessica with their smoothness. But the second they reached open water, the boat jerked forward and sped faster and faster over the now choppy sea. Jessica white-knuckled the side of the boat, using the stiff wind in her face as a ballast to keep from being sick. She glued her eyes to the horizon, trying to keep from blinking. The swaying overwhelmed her when she shut them.

Jessica didn't know how long she'd been on the boat, it seemed like hours, and she wasn't sure whether they had headed north along the shore or east to the middle of the Caribbean. If north, they were probably halfway back to Texas by now. Nothing but clear blue water and a lighter blue sky surrounded her.

A niggling fear that this might not be a snorkeling trip after all invaded her thoughts. She wouldn't snorkel here anyway, out in the middle of the ocean without a sliver of land in sight.

Doraliz cut the engine. It should have been peaceful, but this far from shore, the lapping of the sea on the side of the boat reminded Jessica that only a thin piece of metal stood between her and drowning.

The staccato bumping across waves vanished, replaced by a rolling sway. Oh no. A bout of nausea surged through her. She leaned over the side of the boat and threw up.

"That's disgusting," Doraliz said, uttering her first words since they'd left the bay. "And it will bring sharks."

Jessica scooted to the very middle of the boat. "I am not getting in that water."

"That remains to be seen." Doraliz stood and sprang to one side of the boat, throwing her weight with the movement. The boat lurched, dipping precariously toward the water's surface.

"What the hell are you doing?" Jessica screamed.

"You shouldn't have followed me here."

"What are you talking about? You asked me to come snorkeling."

Doraliz crossed her arms, leaning toward the corner of the boat. Jessica watched the vessel dip again with her weight. A wave of nausea rippled up her gut and into her throat. She swallowed and tasted the metal tang of fear.

"I know who you are, and I know you've been searching for me. I refuse to be found by my family, and if that means leaving you here in the middle of the ocean, then that's what I'll do."

The nausea vanished, replaced by ice cold terror that ran through every cell in her body. "You'd kill me to not have to talk to your parents? What kind of fucked up family do you come from?"

"You must have met my father. I knew this day would come. How much is he paying you?"

"Not enough," Jessica said, motivated to be honest with Doraliz and keep her talking. "Right now, you're acting a lot like him. He tried to scare the hell out of me too."

"I wish it had worked."

"Actually, he threatened me if I refused to find you. You're doing the same because I found you. So, either way, a Velasco screws me over."

"You got yourself into this." An angry sigh escaped Doraliz as she sat back on the bench. The boat rocked with her movement. "I wish you weren't here."

Jessica looked around the endless sea, nothing but indigo and teal under a cyan sky as far as she could see. She fucking hated blue. "Yeah, me too."

"I will not go back to that world. Not ever. I planned this escape for years, and I am not going to let some stupid junior detective from El Paso screw this up. You have no idea how hard it was to evade his clutches once. If he finds me, he'll never let me get away again. My father hates to lose."

"I get that. He seems like a complete dick."

A spark of fire lit Doraliz's eye. Jessica bit her tongue so hard she tasted blood. She had to be more careful about what she said. "Listen, I know what I'm talking about. My dad is a criminal and will wear an ankle bracelet the rest of his life. And I haven't seen him since I was sixteen."

Doraliz cocked one eyebrow. "Not bad. My dad kills people."

"Please don't follow in his footsteps." Jessica's hands ached from her death grip on the seat, but she feared letting go.

"I don't want to kill you. That would make me too much like him. But I'm not sure what to do with you. If you go back, he'll make you tell him where I am."

"I won't tell. I promise." Jessica exhaled for what seemed like the first time in an hour. Just maybe she'd get back to land. "Listen, we have a lot in common. I don't want to be like my dad either. I've made some pretty shitty choices because of that."

"I am making the right choices for me. I get to set my own rules here."

"How's that working out for you?" Jessica wanted to swallow the words back the second she'd uttered them. Doraliz probably pictured the same image of Sebastian hitting on Alyssa that Jessica remembered.

"It's fine." Another sigh. "Here I deal with normal stuff—cheating boyfriends, slutty coworkers, making a living. In Juarez, my world re-volved around politics, power, and death. It was not a life worth living. I can make something out of this."

"Sounds lonely," said Jessica, seemingly determined to insert her foot into her mouth until Doraliz threw her from the boat. "And your mom seems nice."

"Ay, pendeja." Doraliz shook her head, disbelief plastered across her face.

"I speak Spanish." Jessica hadn't expected Doraliz to curse, or to call her a stupid bitch.

"First, if you actually met my mother, you would not call her nice. She is either a judgmental ice queen, or she cowers in front of my father like a little mouse. She knows he is filled with evil, yet she chooses to stay with him and would have me do the same. Second, how can you possibly talk to me about being lonely? I saw you last night. At the bar, you were all alone, drunk as shit, and scanning the scene like a broken-hearted puta."

For the first time, Jessica thought about jumping out of the boat instead of waiting to be pushed. Everything Doraliz had said was true. She'd worn the slut label proudly until now. Pairing the word with bro-ken-hearted brought a truth she didn't want to investigate. The things she wanted, she couldn't allow herself to have. Her life totally sucked, maybe even more than Doraliz's.

"You need to figure out your own thing and stay away from my life," Doraliz said.

"I do need to figure out my life. How did you decide running was the right thing for you?" Jessica gestured toward the surroundings, then realized there was nothing out here but an ocean, vast and lonely. They were both screwed.

"I will never tell you anything about why I am here. I cannot tell you anything my father will get out of you."

"I guess that means you're going to keep me alive." Jessica no longer believed Doraliz would leave her to drown. The fear retreated, but the nausea remained, paired with regret and longing and no clear path forward.

"I don't know what I'm going to do with you." Doraliz gazed out at the ocean. She deflated, like she'd lost some battle she didn't want to share. She looked the way Jessica felt.

"I went to Boston and looked at your thesis. It must have been hard to live in Juarez with that going on. Did you ever try to do something about it?"

Doraliz's eyes clouded. "There are more questions around the femicides than can be answered. And the questions asked are often wrong. People used to talk about finding a killer, but it's been thirty years and hundreds of women. It's not one person, it's the entire system. Everyone's hands are bloody."

"Do you mean your father?" That would be enough to cause a daughter to run away.

"I mean everyone. Juarez lures poor, mestizo women from the interior of the country to work in the factories or try to cross to the US. They are desperate to improve their lives. The desperate become easy victims."

"What can we do about it?" Jessica asked, thinking about the work Alma did.

"You mean like change the systems across the world that devalue women? This isn't a Mexican problem, it's a humanity problem. No country exists where women have equal power to men. In some places, religions or family systems or history make it worse, but it is bad everywhere. That's why I'm here, you stupid girl. I had to break my own system first."

The thought stopped Jessica cold. Doraliz hadn't just escaped her family, she'd escaped the social system that had formed her. Jessica had always known she could flee El Paso to someplace her father's stain wouldn't reach, but she could never flee what they'd done to her. And she'd lose what little support she had.

"Will you ever go back?" Jessica asked.

"I don't think so."

They rocked in the boat, Jessica thankful for the thin blue tarp that kept the worst of the sun off them. Doraliz's view of the world seemed devoid of hope. The system she'd run from remained. The only one she'd saved was herself. Jessica blamed her problems on the easy target, her parents, and she'd never escape their decision. Everything seemed hopeless. "Can we go back now?"

"No, it is my turn for questions. How did you find me? Who told you where I was?"

"No one. At first, I thought you'd been kidnapped or killed. I tried to learn something from your friends in Juarez, but I got drugged and beaten up."

"Is that true?" Doraliz's face lit up with a broad smile.

Jessica hadn't seen her smile before. The knowledge depressed her. Escape hadn't brought Doraliz happiness. Only a story from home had done that. "Yeah, I woke up on a bathroom floor with a bloody nose and black eye."

"Wow. Most people would have stopped after that."

"Well, it just pissed me off. Made me more determined. That's when I decided to go to Boston."

"No one there could have told you where I was. Who did you meet with?"

"Professor Gold. I tried to talk to Lauren Feldman, but she slammed the door in my face."

"Good for her, although she didn't know I'd left."

"Yeah, but she didn't seem surprised."

"Hmm." Doraliz stared at the blue water as if it could give her the answers she needed. "I first thought about leaving when I was at Harvard.

Before then, I thought all families were like mine. Lauren's family, they argue around the dinner table like equals. I'd never seen that before. Every word my dad utters is a decree. My mother is made of nothing but lies and judgment and instructions on how to be the perfect wife and daughter. Heaven forbid a woman have an opinion or an original thought."

Jessica's family had probably been more like Lauren's once. Her dad's book smarts didn't stand a chance against her mother's ability to read people. Her mom used sheer will to get anything out of anyone, and they all left thinking helping her was the best part of their day. Of course, her mom helped right back. When Jessica was little, she believed her mom knew everyone in town. They never made it through a shopping trip without speaking to half a dozen old friends along the way. Jessica understood why her dad had loved her mom so much. People like her and her dad needed that kind of light in their lives.

"Are you more like your mom or your dad?" Jessica asked.

"I'm not like either of them. That's why I need to live my own life. They thrive in the Mexican upper class. It built them and they define it. I can't stand the boundaries. I will make my own way in the world."

"That sounds hard."

"It doesn't sound any harder than working for guys like my dad, and you do that willingly. I didn't get to choose who birthed me."

"Touché. Although not everyone can just walk away from their life."

"Why the hell not? You told me you haven't seen your parents since you were sixteen. What's holding you back? Are you married or something? You weren't acting married last night."

"I'm not married. Not now, not ever. Unlike you, I'm like my parents, or at least my dad. We tend to blow up family and not look back." With that, Jessica leaned over the side of the boat and retched again.

"We're not even moving. How do you get so sick?"

Jessica's stinging eyes filled with hot tears. She'd have given anything for an end to the swaying.

"How did you find Lauren?" Doraliz asked.

Jessica glared at the woman who looked completely at ease on the boat while Jessica suffered. "She was on your social media account. That's also how I found out you liked to dive."

Doraliz hung her head. "I was afraid of that. I've documented half my life there. If I delete those accounts, it will be like I never existed." The fire that had burned through Doraliz went out. She suddenly looked smaller and ten years older.

"Don't you still have the photos?"

"I don't have much of anything anymore. I needed to leave the past behind so I wouldn't get caught." The loneliness in her voice was as immense as the ocean.

"That sucks. I'm really sorry. Is there anything I can do to help?"

"You are the last person in the world I want help from. My dad owns you."

"He does not." Although, when she'd tried to quit, he hadn't let her.

"I see it in your eyes. You are afraid of him." Doraliz's gaze filled with contempt. "Don't worry, tough girl. The strongest men I know are afraid of him. But you've put both of us in a bad position, because you know where I am, and he wants that information."

"I don't have to tell him. My lawyer knows how I can get out of the contract."

Doraliz laughed, loud and cutting. "Contract. What does a contract mean? Did he actually sign a paper with his name on it? That doesn't sound like him."

"It's a verbal agreement."

"He owns you. And you will tell him where I am."

"I won't." Exhaustion overwhelmed her. The late night and too much drink, followed by this horrible nightmare of hours on the ocean almost reduced her to tears. "I don't want to tell him. I want to protect you."

A mean laugh escaped Doraliz. "You won't have a choice. He'll get the information out of you. He has tactics. You won't like them."

A snake of fear curled in the pit of Jessica's stomach. There was plenty of room for it now that she'd barfed her guts out. "I'll find a way."

"He preys on people like you. You don't stand a chance."

The woman's derision finally broke through Jessica's fear. Screw the ocean. Screw this bitch and her father. "You don't know what tough is. I've been on my own for years. You've been out here for three weeks, and probably have a good amount of daddy's money stashed somewhere. You act tough and whine that your life is unfair. But what have you gone through that's so hard? I'm pretty sure daddy's money and influence paid for Harvard. All your travel and dive trips weren't free. You don't know what it's like to work your way through school and support yourself as an adult. I bet your job at the pizza shop on Ambergris was your first real job, and you probably only got that because you were sleeping with the boss." She took a ragged breath. "Do not lecture me on tough."

Jessica's body trembled with rage. How dare this spoiled bitch threaten her? She might be able to swim to shore on anger alone if she only knew which direction to go.

"I've worked before." Doraliz tried to stare through her, but Jessica saw the doubt behind her eyes.

"You worked for daddy. That doesn't count."

The fight left Doraliz. "How did you know about Ambergris?"

"Your mom dropped some hints. And Instagram."

"I've got to delete my account."

The word forlorn had always made Jessica think of coyotes howling in the desert. Doraliz wore that look of hunger and loneliness as she turned toward the engine. It roared to life, ending further conversation. Jessica turned back to the front of the boat as it lurched forward. It must have been the wind making her eyes water.

She wanted the boat ride to end, to get her feet back on solid land. But part of her wanted it to go on forever. When they returned, she would have to make decisions. She had already decided not to tell Doraliz's dad his daughter's location, or even that she lived. If he knew she was alive, he wouldn't stop searching until he'd dragged her back to Juarez. Jessica vowed to die before she told him. At least one of the women in the boat should have a future worth living.

A line of green formed on the horizon, and wave by choppy wave, the green grew into trees, into an island. It surprised Jessica when they pulled up to an unfamiliar beach.

Doraliz cut the engine twenty yards from the sand. The boat slunk forward a few yards before running out of momentum.

"You're getting out here." Doraliz's voice was firm.

Jessica turned and straddled the seat so she could look at Doraliz. "Where are we? Is this Roatán?"

Doraliz rolled her eyes. "Yes. This is West Bay Beach. The main road is just past the sand. Turn left. It will take you about an hour to walk back to West End."

"Seriously? You can't just take me back to the dive shop? You have to go back there anyway." It had been a long day, and Jessica didn't want to find her way back to the hotel, but Doraliz likely wanted a head start on her next move.

"What I do from the moment you leave this boat is none of your business."

"You know, you've only been gone three weeks. What happens when you're tired of your vacation?" Jessica almost spat the words. Doraliz seemed to think she could head down to paradise and leave all her problems behind. Life wasn't that easy.

"This is not a vacation, but in many ways, it's been the best three weeks of my life. Because it is *my* life. I have the freedom to make my future anything I want it to be, and I've never had that before. You've had that freedom for years and didn't even know it."

"So, you're just going to wander from place to place never letting anything tie you down and call it freedom?"

"No. I am searching. I love the idea of family, but I want to build it my way. I will never be allowed to do that in my parents' orbit. Somewhere out there is a man I will fall in love with and a place I will want to be forever. I just have to find it."

"How long will you search?"

"It doesn't matter. It may take three years, or thirty. I don't care. I'm already becoming the person I want to be, someone free from the constraints that have ruled my life. I'm just discovering this person, but I love her already because her life has meaning." Tears formed in Doraliz's eyes. "You jeopardize all of that."

"I'm sorry." This stone should have remained unturned. For a moment, Jessica wished she could trade places with this woman, start her life over and do it right this time. The lure of a life with meaning pulled at her heart. But Jessica carried such heavy baggage, dragging the burden of her family behind her, despite cutting her ties to them years ago. Hopefully, Doraliz's journey would be easier. "I hope you find what you're looking for."

The other woman didn't answer, just nodded toward the water. Jessica sidled over to the edge of the boat and turned to drop one foot into the sea.

"For god's sake, just stand up and jump in. A Chihuahua could paddle to the shore from here."

Jessica cut an angry look at Doraliz. She saw the smile on the woman's face, not mocking, but friendly.

"Sometimes you have to take risks," Doraliz said.

Jessica half stood, her hands gripping the side of the rocking boat. She put one foot up on the wooden plank she'd used as a seat for leverage, then lunged forward into the water. She clipped a foot on the edge of the boat going in, and it hurt like a mother. The taste of ocean brine almost brought up whatever remained in her stomach. She couldn't touch the bottom, which brought a moment of fear.

Then Jessica relaxed. The warm water buoyed her, and she treaded easily. As she cycled her legs, she stirred up a cooler layer of water below. The gentle roll of the sea caressed her without trying to drag her under. She'd been so afraid of the ocean, she hadn't bothered to get in. The water was amazing, and she'd missed out. A grin plastered on her face, she turned to Doraliz.

"See, it's not so bad." Doraliz matched her smile. "You can discover a lot about yourself when you open yourself to new opportunities."

"Goodbye, Doraliz." Jessica turned and paddled toward shore.

When she got close enough to stand up and turn around, she looked to see if Doraliz had gone. The little boat swayed halfway out in the bay. Jessica waved. Doraliz didn't wave back. Instead, she started the engine and drove out of sight. Jessica wished her luck, then waded to shore.

Chapter16

D oraliz had been right. It took Jessica an hour and ten minutes to walk back to her hotel. She bought two coffees and a muffin at a nearby stand, then took them to her room and locked the door. Too many thoughts rushed through her head. She took a long sip of the first coffee, needing the caffeine but hating the searing temperature. Her day in the sun and walk to the hotel had overheated her, and the warm liquid added another layer of sweat. Still, the caffeine would quell her headache.

She turned the air conditioning a degree colder, stripped and showered, and tried to rid herself of the long day, the drunken night, the weeks spent chasing someone who didn't want to be found.

After the shower, she tested the coffee again. It had become tepid under the blow of the A/C, and Jessica chugged both cups. She ate the muffin, then climbed into bed, determined to rest and give her brain the chance to sort out what the hell had happened, and what she should do next.

When she woke, the brightness of the sun coming through the windows had dimmed. She grabbed her phone. Six o'clock. She'd slept through the rest of the day. Tomorrow, she'd board a flight back to Belize City and then another back to the States. Back to Angus.

He hadn't replied to her most recent text. She called him. He answered on the first ring.

"I found her."

A few seconds lapsed before he responded. "Well, that's what you set out to do."

"She took me out on a boat to the middle of the ocean. I was terrified, but we had a long talk. She doesn't want to be found, and I'm not going to tell her dad where she is."

"Okay."

"Angus, what's wrong? You didn't answer my text, and now you're being weird." Not that he didn't have a right to be. She remembered the guy from the night before, how she hadn't been attracted to him. How she'd thought about Angus almost every moment since she'd left home. How much her need for him scared her.

"I'm glad you're safe. I guess I hoped maybe Doraliz wouldn't be the only woman you found down there."

"What do you mean?"

"Jessica, what are you doing with your life?"

Why the fuck did everyone she knew ask her that? "I'm trying to make it through. How can you ask me that? What great thing are you doing with your life?"

"I'm doing exactly what I want to do. I own a record shop. I love helping Sarah with the kids and the horses. When I see them opening up, well, it's something wonderful. I feel really good about my life."

She voiced his unsaid words. "Except for me."

"You aren't my responsibility."

The words settled heavily onto Jessica's chest and made it hurt to breathe. She wanted to say something, to contradict his lie, but she could only draw one ragged breath after another. If he wasn't there to pick up her pieces, would she remain shattered?

"You enchanted me the very first time we met," he said. "You pulled me off the monkey bars in kindergarten because you wanted a turn. When I hit the ground, I was ready to cry or attack the kid who'd done that. Then I saw you."

Jessica held her breath to keep from crying. Memories of playground dust and green monkey bars rebuilt the forgotten scene.

When that whole thing when down with your dad, I thought I needed to save you, to keep you from hurting. I've been doing that ever since, even though you always insist on saving yourself." He sighed as if he had to gather his strength to keep talking.

"Angus, I'm sorry."

"Let me finish. I had a long talk with Sarah. I've been so worried about you. You seem to keep getting deeper and deeper into trouble, and I don't know how to save you anymore. She told me you couldn't be my responsibility. You're an adult, and you get to make your own decisions. I'm always going to be here for you, but I'm not going to hold you back anymore or try to turn you into the incredible woman hiding beneath all that pain and anger."

Her breath released in a wrenching sob that threatened to rip her in two. Why was happiness an impossible goal? "I don't know how to get from here to there."

"I don't think you do it the way Doraliz did, by running away from your problems."

"Yes." She could see the pattern now, the trap. The drinking, the sex, even the job kept her from facing the things that really bothered her. Her parents. The meaninglessness of her life.

"I've got to go," Angus said.

And she let him.

———————

By the time hunger drove her from her room, the night had gone black. Low-slung clouds covered the stars and the moon. Without their reflective glow off the ocean, the island seemed ominous. She walked by the pizza restaurant, scanning for Doraliz. Jessica wanted to let her know she'd made it back okay and wouldn't tell her father anything.

From her place on the dark street, the interior of the restaurant glowed with warmth. Happy people ate. Alyssa and the other server rushed between tables. Sebastian sweated back by the pizza oven. She didn't see Doraliz.

Jessica slipped into the restaurant. She had to ask.

"Table?" Alyssa asked.

"No, is Erica here?"

Alyssa gave her a smirk, then called out across the restaurant. "Hey, Sebastian, esa loca wants to know where Erica is."

Sebastian's face grew dark. He wiped his hands on his apron, then stalked across the room. "What did you do? What did you say to her? She left. All her stuff is gone. She didn't even leave a note."

"Aren't you the one who was half in Alyssa's pants last night? If I remember correctly, and honestly, I don't remember that much, she yelled at you not to come back."

"Get out of my restaurant." His icy whisper didn't match the rage on his face.

Jessica retreated. Doraliz could do better than this guy. Jessica wished her luck, then found a restaurant at the end of a pier for dinner. While she ate, a breeze became wind became rain, a fitting end to her time in paradise.

She stopped by the dive shop the next morning. There, she heard the story of Erica quitting and leaving them short staffed. Jessica wondered if she'd see Doraliz at the airport, heading to the next stop in her search for something worth sticking around for.

———

Jessica searched for Doraliz until the gate agent took her ticket and she boarded the plane. A brief flutter of desire prompted her to make a different decision, to follow Doraliz into the unknown and start over, but Jessica's future lay north in the high desert mountains. She had to go back to move forward.

As the plane backed out of its slot, she noticed a commotion outside the window. On the tarmac, near a small, sleek jet, Doraliz and Tomás faced off, arguing. What the hell!

Jessica's sat forward and pressed her face to the window as her plane rolled by. Tomás grabbed Doraliz by the arm and pulled her toward the jet's stairs. She jerked away, then Tomás seemed to yell at her in anger and turn toward the plane. Doraliz followed.

Jessica craned her neck to look back, but the jet blocked her view. Soon, her own plane sped down the runway and away from the treachery beneath her.

Doraliz hadn't looked afraid of Tomás, only angry. Had he been in on this all along and would take her to her next hiding place, or would he deliver her to her father?

None of it made any sense. Why had Tomás suggested her for the job when he knew Doraliz's location all along? Had he wanted updates from Jessica so he'd know when she got too close to Doraliz? But, if that were the case, why had Doraliz resisted going with him?

No matter how many times she turned the problem over in her mind, she couldn't find a plausible explanation. She couldn't do anything about it anyway, stuck for hours on a plane. She'd call Tomás when she landed. Doraliz didn't seem to be in danger, and Jessica needed to address her own problems.

Chapter 17

When Jessica arrived in El Paso, she called Tomás, but his phone went straight to voicemail. She left a message saying she'd seen him with Doraliz and told him to call and tell her what the hell was going on.

She didn't want to go home and deal with black SUVs and whatever else waited for her there. Instead, she texted Alma from the airport and asked if she could stop by. Alma responded immediately, telling her to come to the house.

Night had arrived in El Paso, but unlike her final night in Roatán, here stars filled the sky while the twinkling lights of civilization lit up two countries. Even the black mountain, a dark slash through the lights of the city, wore a manmade star of huge lightbulbs that decorated the southern slope. The comfort of home sank into Jessica's bones.

The taxi dropped her at a home high up the side of the mountain, with a view that, during the day, could stretch to mountains dozens of miles away. Tonight, she could only sense the distance stretching before her like a velvet carpet with appliqué rhinestones. She could breathe more deeply in the desert's thin air while the aroma of creosote and sage opened her lungs.

She noticed extra cars in the driveway. Sure enough, Alma led her to a dining room where her sisters Luz and Paz sat at a table with Alma's two kids, Beto and Elena. Maria Grande, the women's mother and one of Jessica's favorite people on earth, stood at the doorway to the kitchen. Maria Grande earned her name "Big Maria" after naming each of her three daughters Maria as well: Maria de la Luz, Maria de la Paz, and Maria de la Alma.

"Hola, Jessi." The older woman smiled and opened her arms for a hug. Jessica obliged and wrapped herself around the tiny woman. As always, she smelled like cinnamon and pasilla chiles, a rich aroma that reminded Jessica of baked goods and enchiladas. Little arms wrapped around her waist, and Jessica caught Elena's gap-toothed grin smiling up at her.

"It looks like someone got a visit from the tooth fairy!" She reached down and swung the girl onto her hip. Elena had grown since her last visit. It had been too long.

"Guess what, Jessica? I get to start riding lessons with Aunt Sarah!"

"That's fantastic! Are you going to ride Bosco?"

"Yes, on Saturday!"

Jessica slid the girl down her leg. Maria Grande had disappeared into the kitchen and returned with a plate of homemade gorditas, rice, and beans for Jessica. She'd eaten this woman's food for years, and it tasted closer to home than anything she could remember. She tried to think of her favorite foods her mom used to cook but came up empty.

Tonight, the warmth and love of this family seasoned the always amazing food. Jessica looked around the table: sisters, mothers, children. Her heart pounded beat by slow beat, filling her with the need to be a part of something. She broke free of the thought. She had a different life. She rocked at sea somewhere between Doraliz's stark solitude and the multigenerational ties that bound this room with love.

"Hey, where's Tucker?" Jessica asked, noticing Alma's husband missing from the room.

"He had to fly to Phoenix for the week. He's got some big real estate deal there."

Alma's husband had been nice enough to help Jessica get her first job in real estate. He'd since moved on to a large international firm. He'd asked Jessica to come with him, but she'd insisted she needed to make it on her own. Looking back, making it on her own seemed to mean making everything five times more difficult than necessary. After he'd left, the company struggled to get by, causing Jessica to branch out into other ways of helping people. Look where that had gotten her.

She'd have more money, more security, and wouldn't be doing dangerous jobs for people like Ruben Velasco if she'd followed Tucker. She really needed to rethink her loner, tough-girl act. It wasn't getting her what she wanted.

"Hey, I've got to go," Paz said. "Lucía studying at a friend's house, and I need to pick her up and get home."

The oldest of the three sisters, Paz, had been through a nasty divorce and now lived alone with her high school-aged daughter. Paz had struggled to make a living, eventually ending up working for Alma as a paralegal, but mother and daughter remained close. Jessica had always looked at them with envy. That's how things should have been with her mother.

Alma rose from the table after Jessica finished her meal. "Mamá, we're going to talk in the living room."

"Bien, bien," María Grande said. "I will get the children ready for bed."

The kids grumbled, then circled the table passing out hugs like candy. Maria Grande planted a kiss on the top of Jessica's head and squeezed her shoulder before herding Beto and Elena to the back of the house.

"I need to get out of this job with Ruben Velasco," Jessica said once they had settled into the living room.

"I can help you with that. Are you willing to return the money?"

Before Jessica could say yes, Luz broke in. "Did you find his daughter?"

"Yes to both. But I can't let him know I found her, or where she was. She's gone now anyway."

"Where was she?" Luz asked.

Jessica debated telling them about Tomás, but she needed to understand it first. She might not be able to help Doraliz, and perhaps Doraliz did not need her help. But the time had come for Jessica to face her own ghosts.

"She's safe and searching for a better life. We had a long talk in the middle of the ocean where she threatened to throw me out of the boat, so she is her father's daughter."

Jessica didn't think she could say the rest of it. Something about seeing Doraliz's lonely future had scraped away the woman Jessica thought she'd been. At least Doraliz had chosen her path. Jessica had bumped along hers, one eye always on the rearview mirror.

It had been hard to admit to herself that she needed to change. Admitting it to others made it real, but that's why she'd come here tonight. "Doraliz is determined to find a better life for herself. I also want a better life. I thought, briefly, about following her. But for me, things won't get better until I deal with my past. I need to go see my parents."

Luz took a deep breath. "It's about time."

"That's great," Alma said. "When do you want to go?"

"Now. There's no reason to wait."

"Don't you want to warn them?" Alma asked.

"They won't care," Luz said. "They'll do anything to see you again."

Confused, Jessica looked at Luz. "Why do you think that?"

Luz fidgeted, running a hand through her hair, then sighed. "Sarah and I talk to your mother every Saturday at four o'clock."

Betrayal slid through Jessica's bones. Luz and Sarah had been her friends, were on her side. That truth had sustained Jessica through so many hard days. Hard years. She thought she could always count on them, had dreamed of them being her real parents. Had all of that been a lie? "How long have you been talking to them?"

"Forever. Since your parents moved to Fort Davis."

A lump as big as the desert lodged itself in Jessica's throat. She had trusted these women. Had they been proxies for her parents all along? Had they been paid to look after her like a child? She'd prided herself on building an independent life. She'd based her self-worth on a lie.

"Nice timing, Luz." Alma shot her sister an irritated glance. "Your parents wanted a few people to look after you, that's all. You were so young when they left."

"So, I was just a job for you guys? I mean, I know you get paid for being my lawyer, but what about you and Sarah?" Jessica turned her attention toward Luz.

"It's not like that. They don't pay us. They just want to know how you are doing." Luz perched on the front of her chair, clearly frustrated.

"I'm moving out the second I get back." Jessica's anger burned through the lump in her throat. "In fact, can you give me a ride back so I can get my truck? I'll be out of your hair soon."

"Don't be like that," Luz said.

"I've just learned that what I thought was a friendship is actually only a transaction set up by my parents. Is that why you started happy hour, so you could see me once a week and report back to my parents the next day?"

Alma rubbed her temples, eyes downcast. "You've got this all wrong," she said, looking up at Jessica. "We love you. All we want is for you to be happy. You know Sarah and your mom have been friends for a long time. When you refused to go to Fort Davis with them, we told your mom we'd do our best to look after you. We've tried to do right by you."

Nausea surged through Jessica just as tears arrived, but she refused to let them fall. The urge to find a dive bar and drink until she couldn't see straight then find a stranger to fuck pulled at her hardest of all. It made the pain go away every time, if only for a few hours.

Instead, she faced Luz's words. She needed to face all the ugliness she'd buried over the years. If she brought it out and examined it, maybe she could control how much pain it caused. She hurt now, but the pain wouldn't kill her. And it would let her know what in her life was true and what she had imagined.

"How many other people check up on me? Angus?"

Luz laughed. "Angus is just a kid. He doesn't know about any of this."

Jessica leaned back into the plush chair, and something unhitched in her chest. Angus had no part in the deception. Luz and Sarah had deceived her, maybe not maliciously, but they had hidden their communications with her parents. That hurt.

Jessica closed her eyes and examined her feelings. This sliver of hurt didn't compare to the gaping wound she'd let fester for years.

"Okay," Jessica said, opening her eyes. "I'm still going to see them. I'm not like Doraliz, but I am as determined as she is to make something of the shambles of my life. For her it means running, for me, it means facing my past. Can you give me a ride back to the house?" She directed her gaze at Luz.

"Why don't you spend the night here and leave in the morning?" Alma asked. "We can go by my office first and prepare the documents for Ruben Velasco, then you can leave. It's a three-and-a-half-hour drive. If you tried to go tonight, you might not get there until midnight."

"I should go home and get some fresh clothes."

"I agree with Alma," Luz said. "That Suburban is still hanging around the ranch. Don't let them know you're home."

"But I have to get my truck."

"You can take mine," Alma said. "Tucker will be gone all week, so I can use his car.

Maria Grande appeared at the living room entry. "Jessi, I will put your clothes in the wash."

"Maria, I can wash my own clothes." Jessica smiled at the woman who'd clearly been eavesdropping.

The older woman waved a hand in her direction, then disappeared, probably on the hunt for Jessica's duffel. A fresh pile of neatly folded clothes would likely await her soon.

"I feel like you guys are conspiring, but I can't figure out if it's for me or against me."

Luz leaned over and pressed a hand against Jessica's knee. "We've been waiting for you to decide to see your parents for a long time. They really miss you."

"I'm still angry that you know things like how much they miss me. How could you pretend to be my friend, and then talk to them behind my back?"

Luz looked down at her hands, then glanced at Alma, seeming to search for a way to answer the question. Finally, she returned her attention to Jessica.

"We used to talk to them every day after they moved. You were just a kid, and it seemed like the right thing to do. After that, it just became a habit. Honestly, I'm ashamed to admit I never looked at it from your perspective. I'm sorry about that."

Luz's statement rang true but didn't take the pain away. "I haven't been a kid for a long time. I thought you were my friend, but you chose my parents' side."

"It wasn't like that, I swear. It didn't feel like we'd taken sides. There was this huge chasm between you and your parents, and sometimes I felt like Sarah and I held on to the tiniest line of dental floss connecting the two of you. You see, from where I sit, neither side is complete. You hurt. Your parents hurt. If we'd let go, let communications go completely dark, I didn't know whether any of you could have recovered that part of yourselves."

Jessica sat, arms crossed, willing the words to bounce off her. They would have, once. But her barricade seemed softer, allowing the barbs into her heart.

Luz tried again. "If we'd told you about the phone calls, you might have left us, and I wasn't willing to let that happen. We love you. Please believe we only want what's best for you. If you go to Fort Davis and it doesn't work out, I'll stop talking to them. I can't speak for Sarah, but she'll probably agree. But I think you'll find that missing part of yourself instead."

"It may not go well," Jessica said.

"That's probably guaranteed." Luz sighed. "But anything is better than hanging around here with Ruben Velasco's guys following you."

"Yeah, that will be a good one to be done with," Jessica said.

Later that night, Jessica snuggled into an unfamiliar bed and worried about how to approach her parents in a way that would result in something better than a five-minute meeting that ended with a door slammed in her face. They could spend a little time talking about what they'd been up to in the past decade and a half. Jessica guessed her parents wouldn't have much to say since her dad had been unable to leave the house most of that time. And her mother had been unable to leave him.

She could talk about herself, but there wasn't a lot she wanted to share. Besides, with weekly reports, her parents knew far more about her than she did about them.

The only thing she really wanted to know was why they had left her behind. Why had they cared so little? Maybe they didn't need anything beyond progress reports. They didn't need to see her or touch her or listen to her. They hadn't cared, so she'd searched for fulfillment from strangers in bars. It's no wonder she turned out the way she did.

Maybe none of it would matter. She'd visit them, learn they didn't really care about her, and nothing in her life would change. At least anger had been something to hold on to. She risked being left with nothing at all.

Chapter 18

The next morning, the smooth ride of the Lexus lulled Jessica down the freeway. Interstate 10 heading east from El Paso was a long straight shot of nothing, or everything, depending on how you looked at it.

Jessica had spent the first part of the morning at Alma's office. Getting a cashier's check for ten thousand dollars had hurt. Jessica had spent a couple of thousand dollars on her trips to find Doraliz, but Alma insisted she repay the full amount. There couldn't be a hint of Jessica owing him anything. While she procured the money, Alma prepared a three-page letter for Jessica to sign, terminating any verbal agreement between the parties. A woman in the office notarized the document. Jessica hoped hiding behind Alma's legal skirts would be enough to get Velasco out of her life.

She told herself she was ready to be done with the whole thing but couldn't keep from leaving Tomás another message before she started the car. It went straight to voicemail. She closed her eyes and wished for Doraliz's safety. She wouldn't give up on Doraliz, but if she couldn't face her own problems, she had no hope of helping anyone else.

She drove east, glad the sun had risen high enough to offer an unobstructed view of desert. Purple mountains rose in the distance, and sage and cacti dotted beige sand darker than the pale grains that ringed the beaches of the tropics. The desert held its own beauty, with subtle shades flowing into each other instead of the saturated blues and greens of the sea and jungle. She fit here, where the land stretched forever and the open sky made any dream seem possible.

Her dreams before had been small and petty. She realized that now. She'd refused to communicate with her parents, yet wanted to show them she could make it on her own. Ridiculous. Maybe if she'd thought they could see her success, she would have reached farther. And then it turned out they'd known after all. They'd used her friends to follow her life.

Doraliz had shown her how big dreams could be. Reach for everything, regardless of the cost. Jessica needed to find a path in the middle. She had to learn to reach for what she really wanted and base those desires on things that would give her life meaning. Showing how tough she was, how she made it despite her circumstance, was a fool's game. Someone who was truly tough wouldn't stay shackled to distant mistakes.

The chip on her shoulder had grown into a mountain, and she needed to lay it down. Every step she'd taken since her parents left had been to get back at them. Every drink, every bad decision, every lonely night.

Thank god for the dog who never judged her. She missed Tela, but Luz had promised to keep her at the house with the ranch dogs.

It wasn't just the dog. Gratitude swelled around her as the miles rolled on, taking away the sting of anger. Luz and Sarah contacted her parents because they loved her. She relaxed into the comfortable leather seats. Alma would do anything to help her. Angus loved her, despite how she pushed him away. Not everything in her life had been bad.

She wished she didn't have to make this drive to set her burden down, but it would never be gone unless she faced her parents. So, she kept driving, forcing herself to keep going every time she wanted to turn around.

After a hundred and fifty miles, she reached Van Horn, a tiny town lost in the vast desert. She turned south off the freeway and onto a two-lane road, at first intersected by streets named after cattle, Hereford, Brahman, and then nothing but straight road for another fifty miles.

By the next turn, she had reached truly desolate country. The green relief of sagebrush and cacti had disappeared, replaced by a shallow basin of gold, brittle grasses that looked like they hadn't seen rain in a century. A solitary metal sign marked an intersection. Why had her parents fled so far?

She traveled under a blue sky unblemished by clouds. Slowly, the mountains on the horizon grew larger. She imagined herself on some ancient journey, trekking through the desert while traveling back in time. Perhaps she'd cross the river Styx, although her luck with water wasn't so good.

Finally, the road began to curve around lumps of gold grass-covered mounds that no one would call hills. She noticed a herd of Pronghorn antelope grazing not far off the road, their golden backs matching the grass but softened by white underbellies. She stopped and took a photo of them and texted it to Angus, documenting the fantastical beasts in her otherworld journey. And at the end of the road there'd be a dragon to slay, the very one who traveled with her. Perhaps the desert had stolen her sanity.

Eventually, she turned onto a road occasionally graced by a proper tree. Then buildings sprang up, and she began passing other vehicles. Soon fences carved fields of varying colors, and electrical lines carried the promise of civilization.

It took about thirty seconds to drive through town. She followed a sign to a historic site and drove by what had to be an old army base, the fort in Fort Davis. She turned around and noticed a sign proudly displaying mileage, two hundred miles to El Paso, four hundred to San Antonio, thirty seconds of town, and a lifetime of hurt to address.

The hours on the road left her numb and unprepared. Food first, a repast during which she'd figure out what to say. She chose one of two Mexican diners out of the four restaurants in town. She devoured a plate of tacos, finishing much too quickly. Then, she had nothing left to do but go see her parents.

Alma had written down the address, and Jessica keyed it into her phone. Half a mile. She could walk but preferred the bulky armor of the Lexus.

The main road through town seemed to be the only one with asphalt. Jessica turned the Lexus onto one dirt road, then another, then pulled to a stop in front of a cute slate blue house with white trim.

She sat in the car, hands gripped on the steering wheel, trying to control her breathing. So many years. So many awful feelings. So much regret. The door to the house opened, and Jessica saw an older version of the memory of her mother.

She wanted to cry, wanted to return to sixteen and crawl into her mother's arms and beg her to stay, to love Jessica forever. But the story hadn't happened that way.

Jessica got out of the car. Her mother started down the steps, then stopped midway. Jessica would have to be the adult. She walked to the gate, opened it, and walked through, each step harder than the last as she fought her way through the past and into this new present.

"Hi, Mom."

A flow of tears reflected off her mother's cheeks. "Baby."

God damn it. Water trailed unbidden down Jessica's face. Her mom's face showed new lines and appeared softer without makeup, just a little lipstick. Her mother never left the house without lipstick.

"You're so beautiful, so grown up."

Neither woman crossed the thirty-foot threshold between them. Jessica had no idea what to do. She wanted to hug her mother and cry just slightly more than she wanted to slap her and accuse her of abandonment. So, she stood, awkward in her indecisiveness.

"Please, come inside and see your father."

A gut punch, the words made Jessica's heart ache and her stomach roil. He'd caused this. She chose him over her daughter. Her stomach burned. She shouldn't have eaten the tacos.

"Okay." It was the only word she could muster. She trudged after her mother, getting close when her mom held the door open but making sure not to brush against her. She entered a room, also slate blue with wood floors and a low white ceiling. And her dad, seated in a wheelchair and so very much older than her memories.

"Hi, Dad."

Her father raised one arm, smiled with half his face. Jessica turned to look at her mom, wanting an explanation.

"He had a stroke a few years ago."

The explanation gutted her. The parents in her mind had not been mortal. They had maybe aged in theory, but not like this. The ache of wasted time pierced the left side of her chest. Perhaps she'd have her own heart attack. Maybe that's what it took to slay a dragon.

Jessica couldn't bite her lower lip hard enough to stop the crying, so she let the tears come. First, she stepped into her mom's embrace, then she knelt in front of her father, took his good hand in hers, and hugged him. He shook with sobs.

How could they just be people? She'd built them up in her mind into giants, evil and strong, with the power to hurt her deeply and forever. She'd expected a version of Ruben Velasco and his ice queen wife. Instead, she'd found her mother's kind face and her father's broken body.

"I'm so sorry, baby," her mother said, managing to wrap Jessica and her father in a hug. They cried it out, years of tears washing through each of them. Jessica ended up sitting on the floor, her hand still locked in her dad's. Her mom crouched beside her. Jessica let time pass until it slowed her tears and relieved the ache in her chest. They had rocky ground to cover, and she needed to go slow, broken as they all were.

Her dad spoke, his voice slushy, whether from crying or the inability to move his face she did not know. "I'm sorry."

Jessica wiped her eyes, stood, then helped her mother up from the floor. "Let me go freshen up." There was so much to say, but she needed a minute to compose herself and accept this new reality so different from her imagination.

Her mother led her to a small bathroom and Jessica splashed her face, looking for her parents in her features. The curve of jaw and shape of her eyes matched her mother's, her raven hair and height both things her father had lost. Anger still burned for the injustices she'd suffered at their hands, but regret now matched it, mixing a powerful cocktail. She heaved a sigh and returned to the black river of tears and regret.

"Can I get you a drink?" her mother asked. "I've got some iced tea."

Jessica wanted bourbon. Tea would have to do, at least it looked kind of like bourbon. She could pretend it's a tall, sweaty glass of bourbon.

"Let's sit in the living room with Dad." Her mom paused at the word as if she wasn't sure what to call her husband.

It was all one big room, with the front door serving as the dividing line between the kitchen and dining area and the living room. Jessica obliged. She couldn't remember why she'd driven all this way. Something about facing her past to forge her future.

But her parents were just people, and they couldn't erase the past fourteen years. What had she thought she needed from them? Forgiveness? Understanding? She couldn't expect others to bring meaning to her life. Jessica perched on an unfamiliar armchair, wrestling with emotions, bereft of words, and sorely wishing she was back on the road.

"We're really glad you came." Her mother sat on the couch, near enough to her father to keep a hand on his bad arm. "We've been hoping you would come for years. We know how angry you must be, and we're sorry for everything that happened. Your dad, well, he's been miserable about, well, everything. For such a long time. He just—"

"Why did you leave me?" Fourteen years of frustration rang through the sentence. She hadn't meant to speak, but her mother kept prattling on, and she couldn't take another word.

Her mom drew back in snakebit horror. "Jessica, I begged you to come with us! All I did was fight and beg and scream to get you to move here. You refused. I could have forced you, but you told me you'd run away. Leaving you was the hardest thing I've ever done, and I've regretted it every day of my life. The only thing worse would have been bringing you here against your will."

Jessica's chest rose in defiance, and she lined up each of her words to deliver their blow. "It's been fourteen years. You haven't seen your daughter in fourteen years."

Her dad let out the moan of a wounded animal, her mother began crying again. Jessica held on to her bitchy power with all her might. They deserved this. Perhaps she'd come here to break them, to show them she'd turned into someone who could break people. Just the way they'd taught her.

"You didn't even come see me." One last blow in case they had any righteousness left.

"I begged you to come here. I wrote you all the time. I still do. Every week." Her mother returned to the fight, but her father sat still as stone, both sides of his face drawn down.

"I've never read your letters." She had stoked her hate with them instead, ripping them in two and throwing them in the trash the moment they arrived.

She watched her father dip his head into his good hand as if it were too heavy for his meager shoulders to hold. Her mother jerked back, one hand flying to her chest. Great, she'd probably just caused her mother to stroke out. The silence dragged uncomfortably long. This had been a mistake.

"Don't go," her mother said as if she could read her mind. "I couldn't come see you. I couldn't leave your father. He wears an ankle bracelet. He can't leave the house. He, he tried to kill himself not long after we left. I had to take care of him. I was afraid to leave. Four years ago, he had a stroke. After that, well, I'm the person who cares for him."

Jessica shielded herself from the words. Focused on the origin of what had gone wrong. They shouldn't call it a bracelet like a piece of jewelry. Call it a tracking device or something akin to handcuffs. Something that blared about how this person committed a crime. She looked down at his ankle, imagining the device beneath his pants leg, anything to avoid her mother's words and stare. A balloon of hurt welled in her chest.

Finally, Jessica built up the courage to deliver her final blow. "Well, you made your choice."

"No!" Her father's desperate rage flew across the room. He struggled like he wanted to rise from the chair.

"Honey, calm down, it's okay. It's going to be okay." Her mother's soothing voice focused only on her father. Eventually, he stopped scrambling and became a quiet, trembling mass in the chair.

Her mother turned to address her. "This is why I've been afraid of you."

Afraid of her? She'd been a child.

"I knew you wouldn't understand." Her mother's voice hovered just above a whisper. "I had to split myself in two to come here. And I left the most precious part of myself back in El Paso. What was I supposed to do? I wanted you here with me. I needed you. But you hated us. Everyone hated us, but you most of all."

"Don't you dare blame me for this. I was a kid."

"Yes. And we were the adults who screwed everything up. Threw both our lives away. I would not throw yours away as well. The only thing I could possibly give you was the freedom to live a life untainted by our mistakes."

"My mistake." Her father's voice lacked clarity but bore meaning. "My mistake."

"Freedom? It wasn't freedom. Your mistakes imprisoned me. They influence everything in my life." Jessica turned to her father. "I'm sorry, Dad, you shouldn't have broken the law and ruined our lives. But you," she turned on her mother, "you chose your husband over your child."

Jessica stood, buoyed by self-righteousness. She looked down at the parents who had haunted her all these years, now shrunken and gray. She strode out of the house, not even bothering to slam the door on her way out.

She made it all the way to town before she pulled the Lexus to the curb. Four blocks. She slammed the steering wheel with her hands, slammed it again and again until her palms ached. The hurt brought her back to herself.

"God damn it!" she shouted. Then she steered the car back to the small blue house.

Her mom opened the door as she walked up the steps.

"I'm sorry," Jessica said. "There are a lot of emotions buried in fourteen years."

"Yes. Can we take a break? I'd like to put your father down for a nap."

"Sure, that sounds like a good idea. Do you need help?"

Jessica's mother gave her a long look that clearly told her she hadn't been around to help before, so why start now. "No, honey, I can get it." The look changed to one of uncertainty. "Will you stay the night? We have an extra bedroom."

Jessica balanced on the cliff edge. Forward or back? Her bag waited in the back seat of the car. She knew the exhausting, dangerous life that lay behind her. Surely, forward was the better choice. "I'd be happy to stay. Let me get my stuff."

Her mother showed her to a room with familiar muted lavender walls, the exact shade of her girlhood bedroom. A quilt of pinks and yellows and baby blue topped a blond, wood-framed bed. They'd furnished the bedroom for the girl she used to be. It broke Jessica's heart.

Her mother had given her an hour before her dad would wake, so she climbed into the double bed. Smells from her childhood, a mix of laundry detergent and her mother's perfume, stilled an ache in her chest. The drive, the tears, and the trip to find Doraliz caught up with her, making her eyelids heavy and her breath shallow.

Jessica woke to the faint sound of her mother's voice. If she kept her eyes closed, she could pretend her way back to childhood before anything had gone wrong. Pots clanked, and she heard her father's voice, so changed from the quick staccato of earlier years. She promised herself not to hurt them again, but she needed to learn what had happened.

Chapter 19

"I can't tell you how wonderful it is to see you in this house. I know we have a lot to get through, but from the bottom of my heart, thank you for coming to see us," her mother said.

"Momma making stew and carrot cake." Her dad struggled with the words.

Beef stew and carrot cake, Jessica's unlikely birthday meal. She'd wanted it every year, despite the August heat in El Paso. It represented a peace offering from celebrations past.

"Did you sleep okay?" her mom asked.

"Very well, even though I didn't expect to fall asleep. That's a comfortable bed."

"Well, it's yours any time you want to come visit."

"Thanks, Mom. And thanks, Dad, for letting me intrude on you guys."

"No trusion. We love you." Her dad took a deep breath, and when he spoke again, his voice broke. "I am so sorry."

Jessica made her way to the table and fell heavily into a chair. "I need to understand what happened back then. And I want to know what you guys have been doing since. I'm not sure where we go from here, but there are things in my life I'd like to change, and this is one of them."

Her mother served up stew, and her dad rolled to his place at the head of the table. Jessica needed answers, but so, apparently, did her parents. They sat at the table for hours, Jessica's mom plying her with questions about her life. Things long past held her mother's interest the most, how she'd liked college, who she'd dated, what teachers she'd had.

Jessica could tell her mother had a very different college experience than she, even though they both attended UTEP. Jessica had worked and studied, grinding out each day. Her mom had joined a sorority, ridden horses, and had a social life packed with events and people. Jessica had kept her head down in the hopes no one would recognize her. Like that one poly-sci professor who had discovered her name on the roster and proceeded to detail her father's crimes to the class. Horrified, she'd sat stone still, even when he asked her whether she thought her father's punishment had been fair. She'd been the first one out the door the second class ended, only stopping to puke her guts out in the bathroom before heading to student services to drop the class.

"Mom, I'm not here to talk about college." She'd meant to keep the derision from her voice.

"Jessica," her father said, maybe to placate, maybe to admonish. The stretchy roughness of the syllables failed to deliver their meaning. "You're in real estate?"

"Yes. Commercial real estate, not houses," she said, before remembering he probably knew the details. And most of the people she worked with.

"Is it hard?" he asked. Not at all the question she'd expected.

She pushed her empty bowl away and leaned back against the wooden spindles of the chair. Was it hard? Not technically. It required familiarity with the area, but contracts weren't difficult once you'd seen a few. Being the lynchpin between American company owners and Mexican landowners could be fun, or at least had been in the beginning.

"The work's not hard," she finally said. "But it can be hard to find enough work now that all the companies are moving to Asia. And it's not exactly soul-filling work." She hadn't meant to say the last sentence, the one she'd been saying to herself for a while now.

She quickly covered the words with pretty paper. "I serve on several chamber of commerce committees and helped set up the local branch of the World Trade Center a couple of years ago." The achievements sounded hollow.

"People trust me with information. I'm asked to deliver checks and documents when clients don't have confidence in others." Why couldn't she quit talking? Each thing she said sounded less important than the last. A desperation to prove her work had meaning left her aware of everything it lacked.

Jessica's mother smiled and nodded at her words, but her father's face darkened. As if in judgment. When he had no right. She reached for a knife and busied herself with buttering a roll. She delivered the words that would cut him far worse than a knife. "It was going well for a while, but I've had a little trouble lately. I work quite a bit for Tomás Garcia, and he put me in touch with a new client, Ruben Velasco."

Jessica jumped when her father slammed the table. "No! Bad man."

"Yes, I have learned he is a bad man." She stared into her father's eyes, spreading her trauma to him. "His daughter disappeared, and he hired me to find her. He thought I'd have more success than his henchmen since she's just a few years younger than me."

Her father's face darkened to a bloody red. Her mother eyed him nervously.

"It became a bit of a problem, but Alma helped me fix it."

Jessica's dad fidgeted in his chair. She'd upset him. A sliver of triumph slid through her veins. Her mother reached a hand to his arm. Jessica watched him struggle with emotion, trapped in a body that wouldn't let him express himself. He had always been the smartest man she knew, at least until he blew that perception apart with an act of sheer stupidity.

She wanted to ask why. But he'd never really be able to answer her now. She'd come too late, unless he had shared the details of his crime with her mother. It didn't seem fair to ask her with him sitting here, unable to fully participate.

Hurting them came so easily. Jessica guiltily steered the conversation to safer ground. "So, what's it like living in Fort Davis?"

Her mom seemed relieved by the question. "It's quiet, but we've made some good friends."

"What do you do for fun?"

"At night, we usually play a board game or watch TV. During the day Dad can sit in the garden or come to the art studio with me."

"Art studio?"

"Oh, it's nothing. I took up painting a few years ago. It's just a hobby."

"Show her." Jessica's dad now patted her mom's arm, reversing the calming gesture. He'd relaxed and warmth lit his face as one cheek curved into a smile. He looked happy for the first time since she'd arrived.

They ate the carrot cake, almost without conversation. Jessica closed her eyes after the first bite, the flavors of cinnamon, pecans, and coconut jolting her back to a time when she'd been wrapped in love. She thanked her mom, managing to climb back up to that place where she balanced between love and hate.

After they ate, Jessica helped with the dishes, and then her mom led her past the bedrooms to an enclosed back porch. When her mother turned on the light, an explosion of color cascaded over Jessica. Paintings stacked along the floor formed a baseboard of color. Several easels carried half-finished works, and hardly a bare inch of building remained visible behind a wall of varied hues.

Amped up desert colors covered each canvas. A royal blue afternoon sky, sable and terra cotta mountains breaking like glass shards against the landscape, slashes of occasional green setting of amethyst shadows. The bold works conveyed the harshness of the wild land, with beauty an afterthought. They stopped Jessica cold. Her mother had painted the inside of her soul.

Goosebumps marched across her forearms and shins. Each canvas mirrored a thought, anger, hopelessness, resolve. Her mother's journey had been laced through with Jessica's own emotions.

Her dad harrumphed behind her. She turned, remembering they were in the room, unsure how long she'd stared at the paintings. "They're amazing, Mom."

Her mother stared at her, a half-smile on her lips and her eyes brimming with tears. "I think of you when I paint. I think of all the things that should have been."

Jessica reached out to hug her. Regardless of who'd caused the pain, they'd both suffered. Their paths through the desolate space and time had left them fractured, but still breathing.

"There's an art show at one of the galleries tomorrow. I've got a few works in it if you'd like to go."

"Sure, Mom. I'd love to go." She'd planned to leave in the morning. She'd come for answers, but the only thing left to mine seemed to be heartache and bad feelings. But now, because of the paintings, she had accessed some deeper connection to her mom.

Later, after both her parents beat her at Scrabble, after they'd turned off the lights and the noises in the house quieted, Jessica returned to her mother's studio. Enough starlight filtered through the porch windows that she didn't need the overhead light. She sank to the floor, surrounded by paintings now muted in the dark, transfixed by the colors that painted her soul.

Her phone dinged.

"How are you?" Angus texted.

An ache lanced through her, the question impossible to answer. "Busted into 1000 beautiful pieces," she answered. Then, "I miss you."

"I'm here."

"Can I call you?"

"I'm here - ur parents house."

Chapter 20

Jessica scrambled off the floor, then tiptoed through the house and swung the front door open. Angus's shaggy mane glowed with starlight. She closed the door silently, then ran down the stairs and leaped into his arms. The chaos of the last few hours melted away as she gazed into his kind face and found herself in his strong embrace.

"Why are you here? How did you know where I was?" she whispered into his ear.

"You sent me a photo."

Jessica pulled back and looked into his face. "You saw one photo of this entire desert and knew to come here?"

"No, but I had an idea, so I called Sarah, and she told me you'd gone to your parents." He took her hand and led her from the small yard to his car. They leaned against the hood, still warm from the drive and comforting in the cool desert night.

"Thank you for coming." Jessica wrapped an arm around him and held on. She wished she never had to let go. He could protect her from all her bad decisions.

"Hey, you know everything's going to be all right. I'm so glad you finally came here. Did it go okay?" Angus stroked her hair, her back, each warm pass of his hand spreading his calm into her body.

"They're so old. My dad had a stroke and is in a wheelchair. He can't talk very well. I came here to find out what went wrong back then, and he can't talk."

"Hey," Angus pulled back just enough to look into her eyes. "It's going to be okay. All the answers you need are already inside you. I'm so proud of you. You faced your biggest fear."

His words didn't make sense, except that they did. Still, she'd held onto her belief that someone owed her an explanation for so long she couldn't quite see past it. "I came here for answers."

"And if you don't find them?"

His quiet words sank into her heart. Even if her father could talk, he wouldn't give her the answers she wanted. They couldn't rewrite history. Something crumbled inside her like a dam breaking. She hoped it wouldn't bring water—she'd cried enough.

"You're right. I can't rely on others for answers. But then what comes next?"

"Let's talk about it. I've got a hotel room in town. Let's see if we can get some coffee and talk it out."

They made the quick drive to the hotel, a two-story limestone building, a remnant from an earlier century. They looked for coffee, but even though it was only nine-thirty, everything seemed closed for the night.

Giving up the search, they went to his room, another place out of time with its patchwork quilt, flowered armchairs, and china plates hung on walls. Angus avoided the bed and pulled the two armchairs to face each other.

"Sit," he said. "Tell me the story of your parents."

"I don't even know where to start."

His familiar brown eyes and the smile hovering on his lips welcomed her to share her burden. She wanted to put into words all the feelings of the last weeks. She'd been floating in a constant push-pull of escaping and finding. But the things she escaped transformed into ghosts, and those she'd found had changed from the hopes and nightmares she'd originally sought.

"I found Doraliz. She wanted to escape her family. She could have been me sixteen years ago. I'm not sure whether it's frightening or brave, but she took off on a lonely journey with no support at all. At least I think so, I'm not really sure anymore." She pictured Tomás at the airport, then shook the thoughts away. "But she believes she'll find love and create her own family. I don't know where she's headed now. Maybe back to Juarez."

Jessica bit her lower lip, deciding when to continue with the one thing she didn't understand. "A strange thing happened when I left. Tomás, the guy who first contacted me about finding her showed up. I think she left on a plane with him."

"She's not your problem anymore."

"I'm still worried about her, but somewhere along the line, maybe just right now, I realized how different Doraliz and I are. All those years ago, when my parents' lives fell apart, I pushed them away. It was a test. I wanted them to come back to me. I wanted to see how much they loved me. And when they didn't return, well, it broke something in me."

Jessica slumped back against the chair. "I was so mad at them for that." She chuckled under her breath. "I drove up here thinking I was going to slay these dragons that have haunted me for so long. I would tell my parents how badly they'd hurt me and confront them with their wrongs. Yet when I got here, I found two old people even more broken than me."

"No dragons?"

"So far from dragons. So far from the people I remembered. When I arrived, we just cried. For a long time."

"And now?" He leaned forward and held her hands.

"I haven't figured out now yet. Or what's next." She sat up and leaned toward him, wanting to say the hardest words. "I want to change."

"What does that mean?"

"I want my life to mean something. I definitely want my work to mean something." She surveyed Angus. "I always thought you owned a record store because you didn't want to grow up after high school. You were always in a band and loved playing guitar. I just . . ."

"I know. You thought I was too lazy to get a real job."

"Kind of."

He smiled so wide dimples formed in both cheeks. "I love having a record store. It's definitely more nostalgic than practical, but I get by, and it's a hell of a lot of fun. I get to help kids pick out their first electric guitar and place awesome special orders for some of the musicians in town. Maybe I should worry more about saving for retirement, and I'm working on a plan. I'll get there someday, but I'm just not there yet."

"My job's not exactly setting me up for retirement either. If I could go back in time, I'd have gone into corporate real estate with Tucker. Alma and her husband really seem to have their lives on track."

"Let me ask you something. Do you get any pleasure out of selling someone an industrial building or delivering documents across the border?"

Jessica considered his question, forcing herself not to retreat to throwing barbs about how at least she supported herself or dipping into self-pity. "No, I don't. I've been thinking about that too. If I could do anything, I'd follow in Alma's footsteps."

"Then do it."

"I can't go back to school. I can't afford to."

"Maybe your parents could help."

"I doubt it. They're not exactly living large here. Besides, I talked about it with Alma once. They don't have any way of making money. My mom never worked, and my dad, well, he can't even leave the house, and now he can barely speak."

"If you want to go to law school, I'm sure there's a way."

"Maybe. But right now, I've got other things to think about."

"Like what?"

"I don't know. It's just been a lot." She crawled forward, placing her knees on either side of his slim hips and lowering herself onto his lap. Taking his head in her hands, she met his lips with hers. She ached with want, with the need to replace loneliness and confusion with sweat and lust.

He snuck a hand between them and gently pressed her away. "Hey, I'm here to support you, but I don't think we should do this."

"What are you talking about?" Surely, he wouldn't reject her. "We've had sex a hundred times."

"Sixty-three, actually."

She laughed. "You've been counting?"

"Of course." He sounded proud.

"Do you count each time we're together or each time we do it? I mean, sometimes you're a machine."

He leaned back, his grin so wide it crinkled the corners of his eyes. "Each time we're together. There are too many permutations to count any other way."

His attempt to soothe her with words and memories partially worked. "Well, if you're not here to make me feel better, what are we supposed to do?"

"I am here to make you feel better. I want you to feel better here," he touched her temple, then smoothed her hair back from her face. "And here," he ran his hand down, stopping above her heart.

She slunk back to her own chair. "You know, sex makes me feel better everywhere."

"No, it just lets you avoid the pain for a while. Can you imagine how great sex would be if you didn't use it to cover where you hurt?"

"That's just mean." Her words came out in a whisper, the truth too close to the pain.

"I'm not trying to be mean, and I don't want to hurt you. I've spent so many years trying to help you cover your hurt. I don't want to do that anymore. You did a brave thing today, and I am so proud of you. If you can face your problems instead of covering them up with booze and sex, you can get beyond them. I'm here for that."

Jessica sat in her indecision. Part of her wanted to jump on top of him again to see if she could get her way. She probably could. He'd never really denied her anything. Part of her wanted to hide from the rejection. But some small piece of her considered his words. At the very least, it would be a new way to deal with things, just like driving out here and facing her parents.

"So, you drove for three hours straight, and you don't even want to get laid?" The question kept her options open.

"Today, I just want to be here for you. I wasn't sure how it would go, but you seem all right."

"I'm not sure there's an all right with this one. It kind of is what it is. So much time has passed that they're not the people I remember. If they ever were. My mom's an artist now."

"Really? That's awesome."

"Yeah, she's actually really good. She's taking me to a gallery showing her work tomorrow. You should go with us."

"I'd love to." Angus kicked back his chair a little, pulled off one of Jessica's boots, and began to massage her foot.

"You know, if you don't want to sleep with me, you probably shouldn't be doing that. It feels really good."

"Just relax. Haven't you ever gotten a massage? It's not like you want to sleep with your masseuse."

"I do want to sleep with them. Every time."

"You may need more help than I can give." He reached down for her other foot.

"I didn't know I had so many knots in my feet." Jessica relaxed into his touch, and he rubbed through each kink until it melted away.

"Your whole body is probably like this, but there's no way I can massage all of you and maintain my pure thoughts."

She laughed at that, relaxing even more into the warmth of his hands. Thoughts came unbidden, as if he worked through the rough patches in her mind as well. "It really made me mad when I found out Luz and Sarah talk to my parents every week. They give them updates on me. Did you know about that?"

"Nope, but it makes sense." He went back to the first foot. "Just because you didn't want contact with your parents doesn't mean they didn't want to know about you."

"I guess, but I trusted Luz and Sarah."

"If you had asked them, I'm sure they'd have told you the truth. I think everyone's been afraid to talk to you about your parents."

"Hmm. I guess that makes sense." Jessica's eyes closed, and she concentrated on his warm hands rubbing and pulling. She could sleep right here.

"Hey, wake up. Let me take you back to your parents' house."

"I'd rather stay here with you." She'd rather not move at all.

"It would hurt your parents if they woke up and you weren't there. Come on, sleepy."

They drove back through the silent town and stopped in front of the blue house. She didn't move. The car was a safe haven, a boat in a sea of regret.

"There are so many stars here," Angus said. "No light pollution."

"I don't want to go in. It's just so sad." But she had to. She kissed him first, thanked him. She'd always thought of herself as the one with the power in their relationship. Tonight, that dynamic had spun the other way. He'd used his quiet strength on her for years, and she'd relied on it without awareness. She'd always known he was the better of the two of them, but for the first time, she realized he made her better than she could have been without him.

She'd been so proud of herself, always thinking she'd done everything on her own. She'd never have accomplished half of what she had without Luz and Sarah and Alma. And she certainly wouldn't have without Angus. Without him, she'd have gone completely feral.

"It's hard to leave you," she said as he walked her to the gate.

"I'm right here by your side."

Chapter 21

The next morning, Jessica woke to the sounds of clattering in the kitchen. Before her eyes could open, she caught a whiff of lemon Pledge, a scent from her childhood. The nostalgia disappeared the moment her eyes cracked open. She needed to tell her mother to get rid of the periwinkle walls. As a child, they'd made all of Jessica's friends jealous, but now she'd grown up, and the infantile color gave her a headache.

She sat up, rubbing the pain from her temples. It had been too long since she'd slept in her own bed or played with her dog. She'd spend some time with her parents this morning, go to the gallery, and then head home. She wished she could ride home with Angus, but she had to return Alma's car.

When Jessica entered the kitchen, her dad sat in his wheelchair watching her mom pull a batch of biscuits from the oven. Butter and honey rested on the tablecloth. Another favorite meal from childhood. She wondered again how her mother happened to have all her favorite things on hand. Probably Luz or Alma had called. If so, she'd have to thank them. Yesterday had been hard enough. If they hadn't expected her, it would have been worse.

"Hey, Mom. I've got a friend in town. He drove up yesterday to make sure I was okay."

Her mom put a hand to her heart as she turned around as if scared by the new voice in the house. A frightening thought flitted through her. If her mom had a heart attack, would Jessica have to take care of her father? She would not move to this house in the middle of nowhere that would never be home. She pushed the morbid thought away. Stop. Just stop.

"Is it Angus? Where is he?" her mother asked.

Jessica's hand rose to her chest, mimicking her mother's action. Her parents knew far more about her life than she'd imagined. "Yes, it is Angus. He's staying at Hotel Limpia."

"Would he like to come over for breakfast?"

"I'm sure he would." Jessica forced a laugh. It came out stilted, exactly how she felt. But Angus could always eat, and her mom had gone from heart attack territory to overly curious. At this late age, Jessica was bringing a boy home for the first time.

She texted Angus about the invitation, and he responded immediately with a thumbs up. He arrived a few minutes later, as if he'd been waiting for the call. Jessica trotted down the steps to meet him.

"Be careful. I think my mom's going to interrogate you." Her heart raced. Surely, she wasn't nervous about Angus meeting her parents.

"It'll be fine." He brought her hand to his lips and kissed her knuckles.

"Don't start acting like my boyfriend." She cut him a look, but he just grinned back at her. For a moment she could picture herself bringing him home as a teenager, his shaggy hair the same as it was today. She could have lived a normal teenage life with them sneaking around and kissing in hallways. She shook her head. Life was infinitely more complex than that.

Angus followed her through the door. "Good morning Mr. and Mrs. Watts. Thanks for inviting me over."

"Angus Delgado, is that you?"

"Yes ma'am."

"Don't call me ma'am or Mrs. Watts. Clarice is fine. I can't believe how much you've grown. How are your parents?"

"They're doing well. They'll be happy to know I got to see you."

"Yes, please tell them hello for us. And come sit down." She gestured to a chair at the foot of the table opposite Jessica's dad.

Angus walked to her father first. "Good morning, Mr. Watts. It's nice to see you."

Jessica watched as her father reached out with his left hand, his one good one. Angus covered the man's hand with both of his own. He smiled and nodded when her father grunted out a good morning.

Her father took a deep breath and tried again. "Welcome," he said much more clearly.

Jessica noticed how much more relaxed her mother appeared with Angus in the kitchen. She peppered him with questions about El Paso, and he answered each one in his usual laid back way. With Angus at the table, the accusations, hope, and emotion from earlier conversations dissipated.

She still had questions for her parents, but they mattered less in the morning's light. She had to come to terms with the fact that she'd probably never get the answers she needed, and she'd have to figure out how to move forward without them. At least the biscuits were delicious.

"Hey, Mom." The conversation stopped dead, and everyone looked at Jessica. "I think after the gallery show, I'm going to head back to El Paso. I've been traveling, and it's been a long time since I've slept in my own bed."

Her mother reacted immediately, every emotion visible on her face as her cheeks turned red and her eyes filled with tears. She couldn't gauge her father's reaction, but he stared back at her with her own blue eyes.

Jessica's heart turned to dust, and a wave of nausea rolled through her. How could three people have hurt each other so badly that mere words sowed tragedy?

"Excuse me," she said and ran from the table. In the bathroom, she took great gulps of air, trying to get her balance back. Maybe this was a seasickness hangover from that day on the boat.

She shuddered, the thought of Velasco and his daughter only adding to the pressure both weighing her down and threatening to burst her open. Hopefully, he had received the documents terminating their relationship. She did not want to see him again.

Jessica splashed her face with water, willing the thoughts away. She wasn't sick, she just needed time and perspective to sort through the chaos her life had become.

"Sorry," she said when she returned to the kitchen. "I got a horrible bout of seasickness in Central America and possibly picked up a stomach bug there."

"Central America?" her dad muttered, Jessica barely understanding the words.

"Yeah, I went there looking for Ruben Velasco's daughter."

Her dad's anger from the previous day returned, and he slammed the table again. "No."

"Dad, I know you don't want me working for him. Alma's helping me get out of the contract."

"Stay away from him." It came out like a groan, or maybe that's just how someone with a stroke sounded. Jessica wondered if her mother could explain why her father hated Velasco so much.

"I'll do what I can, but Dad, I'm an adult now."

Her father glared at her but said nothing more. An awkward silence stretched across the table.

"Honey, I'm sorry you have to leave today," her mom said. "Please know you can come back anytime. You too, Angus. The gallery opens in about an hour, so we might want to clean up. Jessica, will you help me with the dishes? And Angus, I usually take Joe out back to the garden before it gets too hot. Would you mind doing that? Just go straight back through my studio and you'll find the ramp."

"Happy to," Angus said.

Jessica helped her mom clean the kitchen. "Why is Dad so angry about Ruben Velasco? He gets furious every time I mention his name."

"Ruben Velasco was involved when your dad got in trouble."

"Dad didn't get in trouble. He broke the law."

"He broke the law, and he paid for that. I honestly don't know everything that went on, although I know it had to do with getting rid of official files. I didn't want to know at the time. I was so damn mad at your dad when this happened." Tears filled her mom's eyes.

Jessica removed her hands from the soapy dishwater and took a plate and the dishtowel from her mother's shaking hands.

"I had a life in El Paso. Friends. A daughter." Tears streaked down her face. "Ruben Velasco was afraid your dad would tell the truth or had hidden copies of the files he erased. He kept sending threatening messages. Once, a man showed up at our house in the middle of the night. It scared me to death, scared your father too. It was one of Velasco's guys."

Jessica closed her eyes, but the image of Ugly stayed with her. Maybe he'd scared her parents and now worked on the second generation. Maybe it had been someone just like him.

Her mom kept talking. "He didn't just threaten us, that night he also threatened to kill your dad's secretary. The next day, your dad confessed. We put in a brand new security system and got Jaime Castro to move in next door. Later, Paco Rey moved in across the street."

"Luz and Alma's dad?"

"Yes. Jaime is on the police force and Paco had retired from the sheriff's office. Maria Grande had kicked him out of the house for having an affair. Unfortunately, he died right after you started college."

"Huh, I never made that connection. I remember the guy who moved in across the street, but I didn't know he was Luz and Alma's dad. I thought he had died a long time ago."

"They don't talk about him much. He didn't just have an affair, he had a whole second family. Maria Grande was furious. She didn't want her daughters growing up with that kind of man around. I think his girlfriend kicked him out too. It worked out for us. He had plenty of time to keep an eye on the house. And on you after we left."

"Luz said Jaime was a friend of Dad's also."

"Yes. We did what we could to protect you." Her mother's head dropped toward the floor. She looked look exhausted. "I know it wasn't enough."

Evidently, they'd kept a lot of eyes on her after they left. It still didn't mean as much as being there. The hurt swelled again. She might never get beyond her endless supply of misery.

"Mom, I'm not trying to make things worse between us, but why didn't you stay with me? It seems like, for all the people you paid to watch over me, you could have gotten someone to bring Dad groceries. Or why didn't you both stay in El Paso? I mean, you said he confessed to get Velasco off his back. Dad may have been embarrassed, but he kind of earned that."

Her mom put her hand to her heart again and stumbled to a chair at the table. For the second time, Jessica thought she'd broken her.

"Sit," her mother said. "Why didn't you ever read my letters? I explained all of this over and over. You've spent all these years thinking I chose your dad over you. I would never do that. You were, you are, my princess."

"Stop." Jessica couldn't help holding her hand up against the words. "I stopped being a princess even before you left. I'm certainly not one now. You don't know—"

"Jessica, shut up and let me finish." Anger flashed in her mother. "Even after your dad confessed, Ruben Velasco kept threatening us. That's why we left. We thought we could keep you safe in El Paso. I was supposed to go back and forth between El Paso and Fort Davis. That's where I screwed up."

Nausea rose in Jessica like hate. It wasn't a screwup, it had been torture. Jessica excused herself. She thought she had wanted answers, but she couldn't face her mom's excuses.

She wandered to the back of the house and peeked into the backyard. Angus sat in a green plastic garden chair, speaking with her dad. Angus had such patience. It made Jessica want to try harder. She returned to the kitchen to pull the Band-Aid off a little further.

Her mom still sat at the table. Jessica took the chair across from her. The anger that lived just under her skin welled up. "So, you got Dad out of town and thought you'd come back and spend time with me. But then what? The majesty of Fort Davis entranced you, so you never made it back?"

"It wasn't like that. In every single letter, I asked when I could visit. With every phone message, I pleaded with you to set a date."

"I erased your calls. I was sixteen. You left me. I was hurt."

"You were furious. Do you remember how many times you told me you hated me in the weeks before the move? I believed you. I still do. I thought your hate would fade, or at least you'd get to a point where you wanted to see me as much as you hated me, even if it was just to yell at me. Instead, your hate grew and grew, until it became insurmountable. But I should have tried anyway. I completely failed you. In doing that, I failed our family, failed myself. You were the one thing in my life I wanted to do right." Her mom's whole body sagged at the admission.

Jessica wished she could lay her head on the cool wooden table and sleep, somehow make all of this unhappen. The right thing would be to forgive her mom and put the past behind her. But anger and pain were such familiar friends. "You act like you know what I was thinking and feeling. You had people spy on me instead of caring enough to find out yourself. Yeah, I was angry. What kind of mother does that to her child?"

"You can't possibly hate me as much as I hate myself. I deserve this exile."

Jessica closed her eyes, waited a few beats to let her heart settle. This didn't need to become a screaming match. Honesty would hurt her mother the worst, but it would also scrape away at the dirty pieces of herself she most wanted to hide. "I've spent a lot of time with that hate myself. Funny how you can't drink it away, fuck it away, chase it away with danger. It's always there, kicking you when you're down."

Forgiveness might be outside the realm of the possible, but Jessica could meet her mother where she wallowed. It wouldn't help. In fact, she could tell it made her mother feel worse, but at least it wasn't lying.

"You weren't supposed to have that kind of life." Her mother sounded exhausted.

"Things don't always work out the way we want them to." Jessica stood. "I'm going to pack, then we should probably get going. I'll drive straight back to El Paso from your show."

Jessica had almost escaped the kitchen when she heard her mother's voice. "What about Angus? Does he make you happy? He seems like a nice young man."

A smile touched Jessica's lips. She and her mother had just emotionally annihilated each other, yet mom programming insisted on asking about the boy. "Angus has been a good friend to me."

They heard voices coming through the back door. Angus pushed her father through the house. Her father spoke to him in his faltering way. She thought she heard "sounds like a good investment," but she couldn't be sure.

Jessica's mom shuffled over to the wheelchair like an old woman and took the handles from Angus. "I'm going to put your dad down for a nap. Why don't you kids head over to the gallery, and I'll meet you there in a few minutes." She disappeared into the back of the house.

If Jessica had known him a little better, she'd have thought her dad was protesting as he rolled from the room. But she didn't really know these people at all.

"Feel like going to the gallery?" she asked Angus. "I'm going to get my stuff and head home after that."

"Sounds good."

———

They'd been at the gallery for almost an hour before Jessica realized her mother wasn't going to show. A steady stream of people stopped by to look at the art, most of them in their sixties and older. The walls displayed the work of five artists, all desert landscapes. The other four artists stood by their work, eager to speak to anyone who glanced at a painting. All the paintings, except her mother's, could have hung in the rooms of a low-budget motel.

Her mother's works tore into her with shards of color. It hurt to look at something that so closely mirrored her psyche. Beauty ripped apart. She'd have liked to ask her mother about the paintings, but once again, her mother had disappeared.

"I don't think she's coming." Jessica finally said. "We should get on the road."

"Are you mad she didn't come?" Angus asked.

"So fucking pissed."

"Then go tell her."

"No. I'd rather just be done with it."

Angus took her by the shoulders, grabbing hard. "You will never be done with this unless you tell her what you think. You aren't sixteen anymore. Take control."

An unexpected spark of revenge-tinged joy lit and spread through her. "I can't believe you're telling me to go chew out my mother."

"Those weren't exactly my words."

"Want to see the fireworks?"

Angus released her shoulders and nodded. Jessica took his hand and pulled him toward the door.

They jumped into the Lexus and sped through the sleepy town. Jessica skidded to a stop on the gravel road in front of her parents' house. Wincing, she realized she should be more careful with Alma's car. She honked the horn to let them know she'd arrived.

Approaching the gate was harder. She stood, hands on hips, looking at the cute blue house and unsure whether she wanted to enter the viper's pit. She glanced at Angus, halfway out of the passenger seat. Then she started yelling.

"What's wrong with you? It's not enough to abandon your daughter once, you have to do it again when she finally comes to see you?"

A curtain moved in the home next door, and the pale face of an ancient woman peered out. She and Jessica stared each other down for a few seconds, then Jessica heard her parent's door open. Her dad, sitting in his wheelchair, wedged himself in the doorway.

"Come in."

"No. I am done coming in. You can tell my mother that all that bullshit she fed me about how much she loved me and wanted to be with me was lies. She couldn't wait to get rid of me again."

Her father craned his neck over his shoulder and looked into the house. "Come here," he bellowed.

The door opened wider. Her mother perched behind her dad, refusing to step out. Tears flooded down her face.

"What do you have to say for yourself?" The sneer in Jessica's voice almost made her smile. Take that.

"I'm sorry." Her dad gasped shattered words. Jessica heard the loneliness and shame. His face collapsed, and his body crumpled with sobs.

"Dad, it's not your fault. Not this time."

At Jessica's words, her mother sank to her knees. "For god's sake Mom, get up. What do you have to say for yourself?"

Jessica waffled between wanting to hurt her mother the way she'd been hurt and wanting to pick the woman up, dust her off, and set her carefully back into the house like an antique doll. Jessica hadn't broken her mother into the shards she painted, but her mother had broken, nonetheless. "I'm not going to stand here all day. You owe me an apology."

"I'm so sorry," her mother said. "I don't know how to do this."

"I don't know either, Mom. I think the real question is, do you want to?"

"Yes," her father yelled.

"Okay, Dad. What about you Mom? I mean really, what the hell is going on?"

Her mom heaved herself up, using the wheelchair as a brace. She wiped her eyes on the sleeve of the god-awful yellow cardigan she wore. "Everything you said was true. I left you there. I could have tried harder. I should have come to see you. All these years I've been telling myself that you didn't want me. And you did. You needed your mother. What was wrong with me? Why didn't I go to you?" Her mother crumpled again, bent over like a much older woman.

"We all did things wrong." Jessica laid out the offering. "But we can decide to stop acting like idiots."

"Yes," her dad said. He stretched his good arm out wide. "Hug?"

His gesture demolished her. This all sucked so much. She wanted to hate them. And couldn't. She walked in the gate and hugged her dad with all her might. A lot of rocky ground lay between them, but they'd each taken a step forward. Jessica felt a hand on her back. She looked at her mother.

"I'm so sorry. I don't know what to say," her mother said through a tear-soaked face.

"Maybe don't say anything until you figure that out. When you're ready, I'll listen this time."

Her mother grabbed her in a savage hug. It wasn't enough, but it would have to do. Jessica had never thought of herself as someone who could heal things like relationships, she'd been better at avoiding them. But with her parents, she would have the grace to fix this as much as it could be fixed. For once, she had nothing to prove and didn't have to be tough. Didn't want to be.

"I'm going to go now, but you guys stay in touch. I love you." And it was true.

Chapter 22

She followed Angus's dumpy car all the way home. The Lexus drove like a sleek show horse stuck behind a donkey, but she had no reason to hurry. Other than wanting to see her dog, the rest of her life didn't excite her. After Doraliz, after her parents, she couldn't go backward and didn't yet see a way forward.

When they reached El Paso, Angus called her. "Can we stop by my place first? Before you take Alma's car back?" he asked.

"Isn't it kind of out of the way?"

"Yeah, but there's something I want to show you."

He'd driven all the way to Fort Davis to support her, and she didn't have any plans. She followed him into his apartment complex, decent, but not new.

"Your weird roommate won't be home, will he?" Jessica asked as they walked up the stairs to the second floor.

"He's probably still at work. Come on in."

Jessica had been in the apartment dozens of times, and it looked just as hideous today as usual. Two couches formed an L, one dirty chartreuse and the other maroon plaid. Her place wasn't much to look at, but at least it had a sense of peace instead of a psycho bachelor vibe.

"Sit," he said, suddenly nervous. "Do you want something to drink?"

"No thanks. What's going on?"

"I've got something I need to tell you. Something exciting." He sat beside her, but on the edge of the couch like he was about to drop to one knee.

"Wait a minute! What the hell is going on?" Nerves gripped her stomach like an iron fist. Surely, he wasn't stupid enough to propose to her, especially given the train wreck her life had become.

"I'm changing my business. Like, a lot."

It took a second for his words to catch up with her. Relief, or something a little less optimistic, flowed through her. "Tell me about it."

"You know how I told you last night I maybe had a plan? So, there's this guy who comes into the shop, Dr. Cabrera. He's a cyclist, but he likes looking through the records, and says he has a misspent youth as a bass player. He's also got three kids who want to play music. The oldest one is ten, and he's a little rocker. He probably knows as much about Judas Priest as I do."

The conversation surprised Jessica. The Angus beside her, filled with excitement, revealed an old familiar piece of her friend. He reminded her of the Angus from college who studied music theory at UTEP and had the most popular cover band in town. Before his dreams of a life on the road had been quashed by the reality of the music industry and a desire to stay near family in El Paso. She wanted to dig her fingers under his skin and draw some of his new energy into her tattered life.

"There's this chain of schools that teaches kids to play instruments and gets them performing in shows almost immediately. He wants to partner with me on a franchise here in El Paso."

"Why?" She wished she'd come up with a less offensive question. She'd meant to ask why Angus was changing. Why now, not why Angus.

"Well, for one thing, he can put his kids in the Saturday band practice and go on a bike ride. But he thinks it will do well here. His sister's kids are in the program in Los Angeles, and he says they love it." Angus took her hands in his. "I'm really excited about this."

"I can tell. I think it's great, but are you going to get rid of the record shop?"

"I'll transform it. Maybe I can keep a few rows of records to introduce the kids to interesting music. I've got some good stuff in there. I can still sell instruments, in fact, that part of the business will probably grow."

"And you think it's a good business deal?"

"He's even giving me the opportunity to buy him out down the line if things go well."

"Wow." Jessica saw the excitement in his eyes, felt the buzz in the room. He was moving into his future. And maybe leaving her behind. He deserved this.

"Yeah. Alma helped me with the contract. While you were gone." He reached for a manila folder on the table and handed it to her. "Would you look through this and let me know what you think? I know you review real estate contracts all the time."

"I'm happy to."

Angus looked at her expectantly.

"Right now?"

"Please." His puppy stare melted her heart.

"Okay, but you can't just sit there and stare at me. Go get me something to drink."

Angus brought her a glass of water while she reviewed the franchise agreement and the contract with Dr. Cabrera. Alma had done a great job with the contract, but Jessica wondered if Angus had thought through all the business implications. The numbers part of reviewing real estate deals kicked into gear.

"The franchise fees are pretty steep. Do you know how many kids you'll need per month to break even?" Jessica donned her work hat and helped him figure out a business plan with varying levels of sales projections.

Helping Angus build a solid plan only paid back a tiny portion of her debt to him. "Let me help you with the books each month. We can adjust the plan with the actual numbers throughout the year. It's great that you already have ten kids committed."

"Yep. We're ready to go as soon as we build a couple of soundproof rooms."

"It sounds like a done deal." She wished she could muster a little more excitement. But a niggling fear told her he'd turned a corner she had yet to reach.

"Are you okay?" Angus must have noticed her lack of enthusiasm.

She had to do better for him. "I think it's wonderful. I'm really excited for you." She threw her arms around him and relaxed into his warmth when he hugged her back. He always felt like home. So much more than Fort Davis and the blue house with its sad, sad people. More than her tiny home at Luz and Sarah's. Maybe not more than Tela. But maybe that much.

"I know you've always thought I didn't have a real job, you know, one with a future. But I think I do now. Or at least I will. I've got a lot of work to do to get there."

"It's great, really. You should have told me sooner. It's just a surprise. I never pictured you working with kids."

"That's the best part. I love helping Sarah with her autism therapy program. The kids are great. And with this, I still get to work with kids, but I get to teach them music, help them form bands, and put on concerts. Of course, I won't be doing most of the teaching. That's one thing Dr. Cabrera and I talked about. I need to focus on the business."

"Well, you certainly have plenty of washed-up wanna be rocker friends who can teach the kids."

"Totally. That's like a really long list." Angus's smile faded. "You know, with you visiting your parents and me starting a real business, it's kind of like we're growing up."

"Ha! I feel as far from grown up as I ever have."

"Well, you're not. It took balls to go see your parents. You'll see. This is going to change things."

"Thanks." It was a sweet thought, but saccharin when you didn't really believe it. She wanted so much more for her future.

"Well, you better get back to Alma's office before traffic gets too bad."

"Angus, thank you for driving to Fort Davis just to make sure I was okay. I really needed your help."

"I'm always going to be there for you. We're good for each other. I'm finally getting my shit together. You faced your past." He ran a finger along her jaw. "Do you ever think about us being together long term?"

Jessica's spine stiffened. She loved him like her favorite worn T-shirt but feared he desired a more constraining garment. Something in white.

"Oh, Ang. My shit is still scattered all over the place." It was too easy to lean forward, to plump her lips against his, press her body into his warmth. Why think about the dark void of the future when they could have immediate pleasure?

He pulled away from her. "Well, it was worth a shot. Let's get you back to Alma's."

Desperation crept into her as he stood and took Alma's keys from the counter. Last night he wouldn't sleep with her either. His life had moved forward while hers seemed stuck in a painful past and a shitty future. She blinked quickly to keep the tears at bay. She loved him. But she wasn't sure she loved herself enough to be with him. Life with him would be easy. Experience had taught her easy didn't exist.

Chapter 23

She drove away, heavy with all the change that had happened in such a short time. He'd figured his life out. She hadn't, but she had plenty to work on. Alma would still be at work, so she drove downtown. She valet-parked in the bank building that housed the law firm. Instead of going upstairs, she crossed the plaza and headed toward Tomás's office.

"Hola, Jessica. Tomás isn't here. Was he expecting you?" Soledad's professional greeting lacked some of its usual warmth.

"That's okay, I'll wait." She sat in one of the plush yellow chairs lining the wall.

"I think it might be a while. He just left to see his attorney, and I'm not sure he'll be back after that. I can tell him you stopped by."

"No worries, thanks." Jessica jumped out of the chair and left the office. She returned to the bank building and took a chair in the lower lobby where she could glimpse the elevator doors but was unlikely to be seen by someone exiting them. Twenty minutes later, Tomás emerged from the elevator.

She followed him, feeling like a real detective for the first time. He turned away from the plaza and strode down a side street that passed the main library. She tried to stay half a block away from him and only glanced at him occasionally. She feared he'd feel her eyes on his back if she stared at him.

He entered the lobby of one of the downtown hotels and turned into the passage that led to the elevators. She waited two seconds then slipped into the building and hid just outside the elevator nook. After she heard a ding, she peeked around the corner. She saw the last of his pant leg as he stepped inside. As soon as the doors slid closed, she went to the elevator and watched his ascent.

He'd probably head to the top floor, which had a restaurant and bar with an incredible view. Perhaps he would meet someone there. She didn't expect it to be Doraliz. Instead, the elevator stopped at the sixteenth floor, one below the top. She pressed the elevator button.

Her nerves grabbed hold of her when the elevator stopped on the sixteenth floor. What would he do if he saw her? What would she do if she didn't see him?

The doors slid open and a man she didn't recognize stood in front of her. She stepped out and he entered the elevator behind her. Creepy. The doors shut with a whisper, and she peered into the long, empty corridor. She walked down to the left, neither seeing anyone nor hearing anything unusual. She turned back and passed the elevator as she headed down the other side of the long hallway.

Voices. She immediately recognized Doraliz, yelling. "You can't keep me here. I'm not a pet. I can't believe you send a babysitter to watch me when you're gone."

"It doesn't have to be like this. You know exactly what it's going to take to get your freedom back."

"A life with you isn't freedom. It is worse than jail."

"You used to love me. You can again."

"You bastard. I was in high school. That was long before I understood you only wanted my father's money." Doraliz's voice was pure ice.

"I want the whole package. The wife, kids, a wonderful life." Tomás sounded bored.

"Let me go. Just let me go live on my own." Jessica heard a struggle and retreated down the hallway. The next door was the emergency exit. The shallow niche of the stairwell door gave her just enough space to hide. She pressed herself into it, then called the hotel.

"Would you check on room 1620? I think there's a problem," she whispered into the phone.

"Are you staying in the hotel?" the person on the other end of the line asked.

"I was just up there. I heard someone calling for help, but I had to leave. You should send someone right away." Jessica hung up the phone. She wasn't sure her plan would work, but she had to try something. Calling the police would ensure Doraliz ended up back in her father's clutches. Somehow, Jessica needed to get Tomás out of that room.

A landline rang. "Hello." Tomás's voice. "No, everything is fine."

"Help! Get me out of here!" She heard Doraliz's scream at the same time she heard a thud. Probably Tomás slamming down the receiver.

"You stupid bitch." Tomás said. "One wrong move, and I let your father know where you are. You are out of choices. You know you can't run. I'll find you every time. And I know you'll do anything to stay away from your parents."

She heard a grunt. Then silence. Had he hit her? Jessica wanted to find out, to try and save Doraliz. She took a step into the hallway, then heard Tomás's voice again.

"Carlos is on his way back up here. If you leave, I will hunt you down. You are already missing, making you disappear would be easy. We'll talk more when I get back. There's a perfectly reasonable way out of this."

A door opened and Jessica pushed back into the wall, praying she couldn't be seen. The door slammed shut, then footsteps walked away from her, toward the elevators. She peeked around the corner and saw Tomás striding down the corridor with a landline telephone hanging from his hand.

She waited for the ding of the elevator, then a few more seconds just to make sure. She rounded the corner, raising her hand to knock just as Doraliz barreled out of the hotel room door. For one quick second, they stared at each other in shock.

"Here. Emergency exit." Jessica pointed toward her hiding place. Doraliz sprang forward and rushed past her. They both started down the stairs.

"What are you doing here?" Doraliz asked.

"I saw you on the tarmac in Roatán. Then I found and followed Tomás today."

"Good job. You really are a detective."

"Yeah, well we've still got to make it down sixteen floors of this building and find a way to escape him and his goons."

"I'd run down a thousand stairs to get away from him. Do you have a car nearby?"

Jessica had left the Lexus at the bank building and had the garage tag in her pocket. "It's in the State Bank building, valet."

"Shit. Okay. We have to make it. Run faster."

"I'm trying," she huffed. Jessica had several inches on Doraliz, but the other woman sprinted down the stairs far faster. She was half a floor above Doraliz when a shaft of sunlight entered the stairwell. Doraliz had made it outside.

"Give me your phone," Doraliz said, holding the door open for her.

"What?"

"Fast. Give me your phone. That's how he's been tracking you."

Shit. The phone Tomás had given her after he broke hers. How could she be so stupid? She handed the device to Doraliz. The other woman heaved it down the street, opposite of where they needed to go. Jessica watched it bounce on the pavement, then Doraliz pulled her across the street.

They ran to the bank building, but it took several tense minutes for the valet to bring her car. Doraliz hid behind a column in the garage while Jessica stood there, panting and sweating, as people in suits walked by. Finally, the Lexus pulled up from the depths of the parking garage. Jessica slid into the driver's seat while Doraliz flung herself across the rear bench.

Jessica pulled out of the garage, glancing to the right in the direction of the hotel. She could see a man in the middle of the street several blocks down. She steered the car in the opposite direction and left downtown.

"Where to now?" she asked Doraliz.

"I need money. Go to an ATM. You'll have to lend it to me."

"How much?" She'd have to dip into her house fund after paying back Doraliz's father and shouldering the cost of her trips to Boston and Central America. Buying Doraliz another chance at freedom satisfied a more immediate desire.

"I need a thousand dollars."

"Holy shit. Really?"

"Jessica, please. I have money stashed away, but it would take time to get to it. I have to escape now. I need your help." Doraliz's voice broke.

Jessica caught a glimpse of the woman in the rearview mirror. She looked terrified. And young. Jessica drove to a branch of her bank outside of downtown.

"I'll have to go in to get that much. Do you want to come in or stay here?"

"I'll stay." Doraliz hunkered down in the seat, invisible to anyone in the other cars in the lot.

Fine. Jessica took the car keys with her. She wanted to help Doraliz, but there was no way she'd trust her with Alma's car.

When she returned, Doraliz hadn't moved. Jessica handed her an envelope. "There are nine hundreds and five twenties." Straight out of her savings.

"You need a new phone. Go get one now and get me a burner phone."

"Can I use some of the money I just gave you?"

"Use the money my dad paid you. That's what got us into this mess."

She wasn't wrong there. Jessica sorely wished she'd never taken this job. "I can't. I paid him back."

Doraliz shook her head. "You are the most ridiculous woman I've ever met."

"Yeah, it kind of feels that way." Jessica started the car and went to a nearby phone store, one she prayed had no association with Tomás or his company.

She returned with two phones, the cheapest version of the iPhone for her, and an even cheaper phone for Doraliz. "Now what?"

"I need you to drive me to the southern bus station in Juarez."

It would take almost an hour to drive down there, and who knows how long to get back. The wait on the bridge could take hours. But the plan made sense. It would probably be the last place anyone would look for her, and it would be easy for Doraliz to get lost in Mexico.

"You better get in the front seat then. Immigration might wonder if you're in the back."

Doraliz climbed into the front seat. "Thank you for helping me. Let's not talk. If you don't ask me questions, you won't know anything. I hope you understand now how badly I need to escape."

Jessica nodded but didn't let a word pass her lips. She didn't want to know the woman's next step. Jessica would have a lot to answer for, with Tomás, and perhaps with Doraliz's father at some point. But she'd deal with that when it came. For now, it was enough to help the woman she'd found twice escape one more time.

Quicker than Jessica expected, she pulled into a space at the bus station but left the engine idling. "Be safe. And good luck."

Doraliz nodded. "Thanks. I'll try to pay you back, someday."

"Don't worry about it. Good luck with your life. I mean it."

"My dad . . ." pain shot through Doraliz's gaze. "You can handle Tomás, he's just a bully. But my dad is something else entirely. Be careful."

"Yeah, I know. I'll deal with it. Take care of yourself."

Doraliz nodded again, then opened the door. Jessica steered away before she entered the building. After chasing her across the hemisphere, Jessica let her go.

———

By the time she crossed the border again, Jessica had arranged to pick Alma up and drive her to happy hour. As they settled into the car, Alma in the driver's seat, Jessica's thoughts turned to Ruben Velasco. Alma didn't need to know Jessica had seen Doraliz again, to help her escape this time. Despite the foreboding in her gut about his response, she had some hope Alma's idea to return the money had worked. It was time to find out.

Alma spoke first. "How was your visit with your parents?'

Jessica sighed. "It was a lot. I didn't know about my dad. I kind of wish I had gone earlier, but I'm relieved he's still alive. Although, I wish he and I could have a real conversation. My mother's a complete basket case."

"Yes, not to take anything away from how much you suffered, and you really did, but at least you got on with your life. Your mom has wallowed in her questionable decisions for so many years it's changed her. She used to be the most vivacious woman I knew."

The words struck Jessica with urgency. "I do not want that life. I've made a lot of poor decisions too, and I want something better." She looked out at the land around her. Plastered with houses, this corner of the vast desert suddenly felt lonely. "But I need help."

"I'm here for you. I've always been here for you." Alma looked over at her, her brown eyes soft. Jessica thought she saw a tear threatening to fall from the practical face.

Jessica's heart broke in two. She'd been so hurt by the people she thought didn't love her that she hadn't recognized the love surrounding her. She vowed never to let that happen again. After all, unlike Doraliz, she could make things better here.

"I want to be like you. I want to help women on the border. With Doraliz, hell, just living here all my life, I understand what can happen to women. I know how their choices are taken away. But I also know there are people like you, and the woman who runs the county, and Luz and Sarah. You are the women I look up to. You all spend your lives making this place better. I want to do the same. I want to help women with few choices figure out their best options the way you do. I want to be an attorney."

The words came unbidden, flowing like a river off her tongue. They surprised her, but her subconscious must have worked through the idea. Whether it had started in a professor's office in Boston, frightened on a boat far from land, or listening to a friend move forward, she had uncovered her direction. It burned in her like the afternoon sun.

"I've been waiting about ten years to hear that. I've always thought you'd be a fantastic attorney. I've told you that."

"Yeah, and I never listened. All because my dad was a lawyer, and I didn't want to follow in his footsteps. As if the only path for an attorney was to become a DA and break the law." She smiled at her ridiculous beliefs as they unfastened themselves from her and floated away. They'd been part of the armor that held her down.

"You know, this is a long road, and you have to be fully committed." Alma's legal counsel voice had returned.

"I don't even know where to start. I need to go to law school. But I know I can work my way through, just like I did in undergrad. I can take out student loans if I need to, and I do have some money saved." She'd looked into it before. Law school took three years. Maybe longer if she went part time. She'd done harder things, and she'd get paid back in work that meant something, work that made a difference.

"You'd use the money you've saved for a house?" Alma asked.

"Yes. I can put that off a few more years. Besides, I doubt Luz and Sarah are ready for me to leave." Jessica gave a weak smile at her attempt to lighten the mood.

"If you are committed to this, I have a proposal for you. My firm is looking for a paralegal. I'll recommend you for that job. But that means no more cross-border deals. You can't do anything that might negatively impact the firm."

Jessica sat ramrod straight. "I'll do anything for that opportunity." Had it always been this easy to move forward? She wanted to jump into the rest of her life without looking back.

Except that a few outstanding issues threatened the rest of her life. "Did you hear back from Velasco after you sent the contact cancellation?"

"No. Have you checked your bank account?"

"Yes. He hasn't cashed the check."

"If he tries to contact you again, let me know."

Jessica sunk back into the seat, and a sense of unease crept past her earlier high. What if she screwed everything up? She looked out at the desert. Velasco's men might be hiding behind the next boulder or tumbleweed.

She shook her head. Too much travel and not enough sleep triggered those thoughts. Next, she'd see fairies dancing among the cactus and rainbow unicorns shooting across the sky.

She pushed the anxiety away. She'd learned to ignore fear until she could find new demons to dance with. Although she'd cavorted with devils one too many times. That behavior would have to stop.

Alma dropped her at her house, leaving with a crunch of gravel under tires. Her front door had grown shabby in the time she'd been away. Or perhaps her perspective had changed.

She dropped her bags inside and trotted over to the main house, relieved at the dryness of the early evening heat. Tela's excitement at seeing Jessica swept everything else from her mind. The mottled orange dog bounced chest high, making it impossible to hug her.

Sarah laughed as she walked out of the barn, followed by three other dogs who ran over to join in the fuss. "I'd have said Tela was really happy here, but she clearly missed you."

"That goes both ways. It feels like forever since I've seen her."

Jessica kneeled. The ranch dogs joined Tela, jumping and bouncing as if Jessica were a fun new toy, not someone they'd known for years. Eventually, they tipped her into the dirt. Sarah laughed again, the sun shone, and the world seemed a happier place.

Yes, she had a nut-job family, but she still had some time to sort that out. Her friends had stood by her, even when she thought they hadn't. She lived in a place with over three hundred days of sunshine a year. She loved her dog, and whatever anger she'd felt toward Sarah and Luz for hiding their relationship with her parents had vanished.

Faint tendrils of root began anchoring her to the ground. Before today, she'd have struggled to untangle herself. Now, the support allowed her to look forward with permanence instead of mere survival.

"I'm so happy to be here." The words slipped out as Tela, too big for a lap dog, curled into Jessica's now crossed legs. She hugged the dog as the world spun and her place in it changed.

"Will you be at happy hour tonight?"

"Yeah, I'm just going to grab a quick shower. I had to come see Tela first thing." Jessica shielded her eyes against the lowering sun and looked up at Sarah. "I'm looking forward to hanging out with you."

"You want to talk about your mother?" Sarah asked. "You should stay for dinner."

"Yeah. I do. And I will." She hadn't known until Sarah mentioned it, but the need to understand her mom's perspective scraped at her heart.

Chapter 24

Jessica walked back to Luz and Sarah's as the sun set orange on the horizon. She carried a bottle of cabernet, a gift from a real estate deal that she'd been saving for a special celebration. She would no longer wait for a better day to appreciate the good things in her life.

Equal measures of dread and longing rippled through her as she anticipated learning more about her mother. The fury at the way her mom had abandoned her at the art show had faded, but its replacement lay somewhere between pity and disgust. How much could she learn about such a fickle woman? But the child in her still wanted her mother.

When she arrived at the house, she'd hoped to see Angus's car. A pang of regret shot through her. He'd witnessed her mother's behavior, fawning one moment, absent the next. Would the others understand how bad it had been, or would they blame her for the continuing rift?

She wanted Angus there for another reason. She missed him.

"No Angus tonight?" she asked as she entered the warm kitchen.

"He said he needed to meet with his new investment partner," Sarah said. "Have you heard about that? He's really excited."

"Yeah, he told me all about it. It seems like a great idea. Imagine, Angus with a real plan for the future."

"I think you've always been a little too hard on him," Sarah said. The kitchen filled with a heavenly aroma as she removed a brisket from the oven.

Jessica let the truth of the words sink in. "Yeah, I always thought I was the one who had my shit together. And look at us now."

"Don't be so hard on yourself. You've got it together. You've just got a lot more baggage than most people."

Luz walked into the kitchen, looking freshly scrubbed and with her hair still damp from a shower. "Time to set that luggage down."

Jessica found a corkscrew in a drawer and uncorked the wine. Unable to find a good comeback, she searched for wine glasses in the cupboard. She did need to lose those old hurt feelings that constantly dragged at her, but everyone made it sound so easy. Like you just got up one morning and decided nothing would bother you anymore. But that would be like waking up as a whole new person. Jessica found comfort in the old version of herself, the woman who took risks with her body and her career but never her heart.

Her hand trembled as she poured the wine, as if the tension swirling through her could barely stay beneath her skin. She took the glasses to the table, turning her back on Sarah and Luz and hoping to hide her sudden emotions. They meant well, but she didn't stand on solid ground just waiting to flip a switch to a better life. The path ahead had quicksand and crags and cactus.

Sarah and Luz followed her to the table, Sarah with plates of brisket and Luz holding a bowl of potato salad in one hand and a green salad in the other.

"You're not on trial here," Sarah said as they all sat. "We'll answer any questions you have about your mom, but we won't push you."

Jessica pressed into the stiff-backed chair, wondering what she wanted to know most about her mother. "Why is she like this? One minute she's crying and telling me she's sorry, and the next she's standing me up at her art show." The buried rage threatened to erupt as Jessica remembered waiting in the dinky storefront full of her mom's paintings as the minutes ticked by. Jessica had shown up in Fort Davis and then at the art show. Her mom hadn't. "I hate her."

"I'm pretty sure she hates herself as well," Sarah said. "She wasn't always like that."

"What, so I'm supposed to feel sorry for her? She made her choices." Jessica grabbed onto the theme, expanding it into the silent room. "You guys give me shit about the way I live my life, but at least I'm not hurting anyone else."

"That's debatable." Luz broke in, cutting off whatever Sarah had started to say. "You don't think it hurts us to see the way you treat yourself?"

Jessica jerked back at the jab, this new wound more painful than a black eye. This wasn't what she'd come for.

"Not helping." Sarah pressed her hand against Luz's arm and gave her a look of steel before turning back to Jessica.

"When I met your mom, she was like a brilliant ray of sunshine," Sarah said. "We were at a horse show, and she rode in on a gorgeous palomino, her own golden hair trailing down her back. I was starstruck, and that was before I heard her laugh."

"Oh, my god." Luz rolled her eyes, but a smile played at the corners of her lips. "Her laugh could be heard across three states."

"I remember." The sound of her mother's guffaw used to send Jessica running from her room to see what was so funny. Usually, her mom sat with a group of friends in the living room, or with her dad at the breakfast table. Sometimes she was alone in the kitchen, reading the newspaper or in her room with a book. She always shared what had sparked the laugh, bringing her daughter into the circle of humor. The memory warmed her like a campfire and stung her eyes with smoke.

It seemed like the moment Jessica became a teen, her mother's laugh had disappeared. That was also when her father's trouble first started. A glimpse of what could have been burrowed its way into her chest.

"I stalked her for two days," Sarah said, continuing her story. "I was afraid to introduce myself because she was so beautiful and confident and popular. But then she marched right up to me. Within minutes she'd convinced me to help her pull a prank on Jason Butler. Everyone expected him to win the grand prize at that year's rodeo. Your mother made a fake unicorn horn and attached it to Jason's prize quarter horse. She braided the ties into the horse's mane, making it tedious to remove."

"Oh, my god. That sounds like Clarissa," Luz said.

"What happened?" Jessica asked.

"He was furious. He started cussing like I've never heard, and he got even madder when he heard us laughing. But he eventually forgave us. No one could stay mad at your mom."

"Did he win the grand prize?" Jessica had never thought of her mom as a prankster.

"No, actually. I did. But the biggest prize was becoming friends with your mom."

"I don't think there's any of that girl left in her," Jessica said.

"She didn't change until your dad got in trouble," Luz said.

"No." Sarah interrupted, her eyes landing gently on Jessica. "She changed when you were born."

Jessica waited for Sarah's next words on the edge of Pandora's box. Her mother's true reaction to her about to be released into the world.

"The very first day you were born, I visited you in the hospital. The way she held you in her arms and couldn't take her eyes off you, it was like a cloud of love had formed around you two. Her whole focus changed. She still cared about everything else in her life, but you were the center. You anchored her in a way I still don't understand. She transformed from popular girl to mother the instant she looked into your eyes."

Jessica blinked back tears, as vestiges of the woman Sarah described floated through her memories. But her mother had changed. The woman Sarah drew with pretty words wouldn't have left her daughter on her own at sixteen.

"She didn't always have it easy," Sarah said, as if reading Jessica's mind. "Just a few years after you were born, her parents died."

"Do you remember your grandmother at all?" Luz asked.

"No, only the stories."

"Your grandmother was an interesting person." Sarah's voice hovered on the word interesting.

Luz snorted. "That woman was a stone-cold bitch."

"Why?" Jessica asked, shocked at the reaction.

"She was," Sarah paused, as if searching for the right word. "Demanding. And cold. I think your mom spent a lot of time and effort trying to be the opposite of her mother. Clarice opened her arms to everyone and spread joy wherever she could. At the same time, she tried to live up to her mother's expectations: marry well, be involved in the right organizations, have the right connections."

"They used to go to parties. I remember a sparkly gold and silver gown she wore one night. She looked like a princess." Her mom had swung around for her, the silk billowing like clouds, then falling gently to her curves. Then she'd bent down and hugged Jessica tight, her kiss leaving a pink mark Jessica refused to wipe off. She longed to be a child again, just for a moment.

"Those people, at whatever gala she went to that night, they were the right kind of people. We certainly weren't." Luz's words cut with bruised anger.

"Honey, really. Do you have to bring that up?"

"What happened?" Jessica asked.

"Well," said Luz. "When your grandmother found out we were a couple, she wrote a letter to the editor in the *El Paso Times* about the dangerous influence of homosexuals in our community."

Jessica took a long, deep breath. "Fuck. I'm so sorry that happened." El Paso tended to be a liberal bastion in an extremely conservative state, but it had its own pockets of outdated morals.

"You didn't have anything to do with it, no need to apologize," Sarah said. "But the timing wasn't good. Your mom was so angry she stopped talking to her parents. And just a few weeks later, they died in a car wreck."

"Wow. That sucks." Jessica was proud of her mom for standing up for Sarah and Luz. She also understood how not getting to address a wrong stayed with a person.

"Yeah," Sarah said. "I think your mom always felt guilty about not fixing things with her mother. Your grandmother's views were hurtful and old-fashioned, but I think she tried to be a good mother. Her death was an enormous loss for Clarissa."

Luz snorted again and rolled her eyes. She looked like she wanted to say something, but Sarah stopped her with a hand on her arm. "Clarissa's mom might not have liked us, but she did a lot of good in the community."

Sarah turned to Jessica. "Your grandmother raised money for women's shelters and childcare centers throughout El Paso, and your mom continued that work."

"She used to take me to them," said Jessica. "We'd take blankets, clothes, and toys, and I'd get to play with the kids."

"Yep," said Sarah. "That was Clarissa. She moved from rodeo queen to fundraiser extraordinaire. She helped a lot of people."

"So, while I'm still totally pissed that she abandoned me, why would she leave her philanthropy behind if it meant so much to her?" Jessica couldn't reconcile these seemingly different parts of her mother. Did she only care about things when it was convenient? That might fit the pattern. Jessica had become an inconvenience.

"Did you know they arrested your dad the year your mom became president of the Junior League, the year after she'd been chairwoman of the YWCA?" Sarah asked.

"She was a force to be reckoned with back then," Luz added.

"No," Jessica answered. "But isn't the Junior League just a social organization? I always thought it was a 'ladies who lunch' kind of thing."

"That's what I thought too," Luz said. "But your mom convinced them to fund a shelter for homeless women that year. We worked with them on locating it on unused city land. Unfortunately, it never happened."

"Why?" Jessica asked.

"Because after they arrested your dad, your mom's friends kicked her out of the Junior League." Anger threaded through Sarah's voice. "She was also removed from her position on the board of the YWCA."

"But it wasn't her fault." Her dad had broken the law. Her mom had nothing to do with it.

"There were plenty of women happy to see your mother fall off the social ladder," Luz said. "More than a few yanked on her skirt."

"That's true," Sarah said. "Your mom was everything those women wanted to be, kind, beautiful, generous. Some of the women she thought of as friends were almost gleeful about what happened. It was ugly. I'm not sure she ever recovered from the shame of being ostracized by the only community she knew."

"It was pretty awful," Luz said quietly.

"Why did she care so much about a bunch of socialites? That hardly seems important."

"They were friends. She'd grown up with these women. They'd been her parents' friends. El Paso is kind of insular that way. Being cast out devastated her. Your mom's family had been El Paso elite, and they did a lot to help this city. Clarice carried on that tradition, and I'm sure she thought you would too. Then it was all ripped away from her."

"Hmm. I never really thought about it before, but my mom's old friends never came around after she left. Only you guys did. Some of the girls I used to hang out with I hardly talked to after my parents went to Fort Davis. But I always blamed myself. I was just trying to survive back then. Besides, I'm not exactly debutante material."

"You're a very different person than your mom," Sarah said. "I can't tell you what to do, whether to forgive her or not, but you need to understand what she went through. In a few short years, she went from having everything to losing everything, even you."

"She didn't lose my dad. She chose him over me."

The room grew quiet, and Sarah slumped back against her chair. "She didn't mean for that to happen. Your dad wanted to leave because he was afraid of those he'd double-crossed when he confessed. But your mom, she ran from the shame. She couldn't function in a world of gossip and hate. But you wouldn't go with her."

Jessica twirled a spoon in her hand, watching it catch the light with each rotation. Words and stories. They never made anything better. And somehow, they always seemed to land on what Jessica had done wrong. "I'm glad I didn't go with them."

"I think I am too," Alma said, joining the conversation. "All that stuff she went through, it broke your mom. I know it's not the same as family, but we tried to be there for you."

A lump of tears and shame welled in Jessica's chest. "You are my family. You call me on my BS. You've given me a home. I may not always seem grateful, but I am. Thank you."

"Aw, we love you." Sarah left her chair and embraced Jessica. "I'm so sorry about what happened with your mom. She shouldn't have left you at the gallery, but we are always here for you."

"I know, thanks."

"Me too," Alma said.

"Yeah, about that. I want that job."

"You got it." Alma grabbed her hand and squeezed. Jessica had a lot to be grateful for.

A harsh pounding on the door surprised them all. Luz rose to answer it, then Jessica overhead Tomás asking for her.

Jessica's gut dropped. In seconds, Tomás burst into the room.

"We need to talk," Tomás said when he saw her. His authoritative voice didn't match his zealot look. Tense red eyes darted around the room and his usually perfect, slicked-back hair spiked in unruly chunks around his face.

"Anything you have to say to me, you can say here." Bolstered by the women around her, Jessica also feared for them. She couldn't judge his level of desperation.

He looked at each of the women, then focused on Jessica. He radiated anger. "Come on. Let's go for a drive."

"I'm not going anywhere with you. Ever." She crossed her arms. Impasse.

"Damn it!" His fist crashed down on the table, fast as a cat. "Where is she? We found your phone. I know you took her."

"Hey," Luz barked, stepping toward Tomás in anger. "This is my house."

"She took something of mine." He jabbed his finger toward Jessica, spittle flying across the room.

"No. You took something that didn't belong to you. You can't own people, and you can't steal them. It's becoming clearer to me how so many women have disappeared in Juarez."

"You don't know what the hell you're talking about. This is a very dangerous game."

"Yeah. You're probably in a lot of danger for not telling Ruben Velasco you kidnapped his daughter and held her against her will in an El Paso hotel room."

"That's it. We're leaving." Tomás darted around the table toward her, but Alma stepped in front of him.

"You are the only one who needs to leave," Alma said.

"Yeah. And I'm calling the police chief," Luz said, waving her phone. She pulled the device to her ear. "Chief Valdez, this is Luz Rey. I've got a problem here at my house."

"I fucking own the police," Tomás said, pushing Alma aside and grabbing for Jessica.

"You heard that?" Luz asked.

"I've got a unit headed your way." The chief's voice, now on speaker, boomed through the room. "What's your visitor's name?"

"Tomás Garcia," Jessica said. "He owns a local cellular franchise. He did something to my phone so he could follow me."

"That sounds like stalking. At a minimum. And he just assaulted me. Chief, this is attorney Alma Rey."

Tomás spun and sprinted out of the house. The women seemed to heave a unified sigh of relief.

Jessica collapsed into a chair. "This has been the longest fucking day in history. I'm so sorry he came here."

"Hang on," Luz said into the phone before leaving the room. They heard her speaking to the chief in the other room.

"What's going on?" Alma asked.

"It's about Doraliz, and I'd rather not say. She needs a chance to get away. If the police get involved, then her father will find out."

"The police are already involved," Sarah said.

Jessica looked around the room. "I'm scared for her." The words hung in the air.

Alma finally broke the silence. "The three of us can talk to the police. You don't need to be here. That way you can't reveal anything."

"Thank you."

"We'll take care of it," Alma said. "But no more Juarez. No more crazy deals. No more danger."

"No problem. Luckily, a lawyer I know just offered me the perfect job." She grinned at Alma.

Luz's phone rang. "Hey Chief," she said, then listened. Soon she thanked him and hung up. "They've already stopped him. The chief sent a car out as soon as I called, and that jerk almost hit their cruiser as he sped around a corner."

"That's amazing." Relief flooded through Jessica. Although with his money, he'll probably be back out soon. "Oh," she turned toward Alma. "He uses your law firm."

"Well, that's going to change immediately." Alma turned her attention to Luz. "I assume the police want us to give a statement?"

"Yep. I'll drive," Luz said.

The women looked around the table at each other, then came together and locked hands. The closing of the ranks was a solid thing. These women would protect their own.

"Let's go," Luz said. "Otherwise, this is going to be a long night."

———

Once they'd left, Jessica returned home, her dog at her side. She trudged through the front door, tired from the long weeks and too much emotion. Her rumpled bed invited her to spend hours catching up on desperately needed sleep.

She heard tires on gravel outside the front door. A smile came to her lips. Perhaps Angus had come to visit. In that case, sleep could wait.

A low growl from Tela quickly followed the thunk of a car door closing. A sharp knock on the front door reverberated in the pit of her stomach. Not Angus. She grabbed her phone from her pocket, ready to dial 911.

"It's late. Go away." Jessica stepped away from the door as she yelled the words.

"Abre la puerta."

She would not open the door. Her gut wrenched when she saw the handle turn. She'd just come home and hadn't locked it yet. Velasco's ugly, gun-toting henchman flew into the room faster than she'd thought he could move. Another man slid in behind him, gun raised.

Jessica backed into the tiny kitchen, but there was no place to run. Ugly grabbed her phone and threw it to the floor, shattering the screen. Then he ground his boot heel into the device. Her brand new phone, destroyed. Although, that was the least of her problems.

Crazy with the violent movement, Tela growled, barked, and bounced, unsure of which man to focus on.

"Cállate! Shut up!" the second man yelled, pointing his gun at the dog.

"If you fucking shoot my dog, I'm taking you straight to hell." Fear and anger fueled her shriek.

"If you stay quiet, the dog lives," Ugly said.

"Tela, hush."

The dog grumbled deep in her chest but stopped barking. Jessica scanned the counter for any type of weapon, but a paring knife wouldn't stop a bullet. Nor would her giant bottle of Tylenol, the only other object within reach.

He grabbed her wrist and pulled her toward the door. She held on to the counter for a second, resisting, but this set Tela off again. The dog lunged.

"Tela, down," Jessica shouted, relieved when the dog listened again. She'd been about to sink her teeth into Ugly and that would not have ended well.

Ugly dragged Jessica out the door. "Cierra la puerta," he yelled to the second man.

The minute the door closed, Tela resumed her frantic yowling. But the house was too isolated for anyone else to hear. Jessica pulled hard against Ugly thinking she could run for it, but his iron grip held her tight. Then, in a swift, practiced move, he spun her around, grabbed her other wrist, and zip tied them together before she knew what had happened.

He hustled her toward the back of the SUV and shoved her in. At least her dog was safe. That was the only sliver of relief. The rest of her future bled into darkness. This was likely her last night, but instead of being frightened, anger consumed her. Just when she'd figured out a path forward, the past roared back to defeat her.

Ugly sat beside her, and the second man took the driver's seat and backed the car out of the driveway. She had to talk her way out of this.

"Do you really think kidnapping an American on US soil is a smart move?" she asked.

"Save your words for Sr. Velasco," Ugly said in a voice as unattractive as his face.

"But you're the one doing this. He won't take the fall for it, you will."

"Cállate. Shut up." Ugly fumbled around in the side door and pulled out a roll of duct tape. "One more word and I tape your mouth closed."

Jessica settled. The claustrophobic tape would take away what little remaining power she held. The vehicle cut through silent streets. She peered out the window, hoping to use whatever magic in her eyes normally attracted others. Surely, blue eyes could plead her cause to someone in a passing vehicle. Even though she knew the window tint of the Cadillac was too dark. Even though they took back roads to the downtown bridge through empty streets.

Jessica remained strangely calm, despite the certainty of the night ending badly. She'd take advantage of every opportunity she could find, but she didn't think it'd be enough. Her life had always hurtled toward a disastrous end. That's what happened when you played with fire. It could have been a man she picked up at a bar. Instead, her work would be her downfall. Just when she'd decided to change jobs.

Perhaps she deserved this ending. She'd lived her life setting things ablaze. Relationships, career, morals, happiness. No wonder she was afraid of the water.

As they approached the bridge, she had a moment of hope. They'd have to pass through the border guard station at the entry to Mexico. Maybe the guards would think there was something strange about a handcuffed woman in the back seat of a dark vehicle. Maybe she could scream.

She turned her attention to the windshield and the narrow lane they had to pass through where the Mexican border guards usually asked about citizenship. In the hundreds of times she'd driven across the border, they'd peered at her, asked her to roll down her window, questioned her, made passes. She'd bought the fake engagement ring because of them. It cut down on the questions and flirting. Now, she longed for that attention.

The driver flashed the high beams, briefly flooding the area ahead with light. Then, they drove through the checkpoint without stopping. A guard stood at attention, his back to them.

Well, this was it. Velasco wouldn't let her go. He'd never risk her going to the cops. She'd become one of the disappeared. Just one more in a mass of women destined for a desert grave and perhaps a mention in a dissertation.

Her calm surprised her. All that worry about drowning on Doraliz's boat, and now that she faced a more arid demise, she stayed largely unruffled. She'd had a good run of it. She thought again about how this felt like destiny, something she'd been heading toward all along. If she'd wanted to live to old age, she would have led a different life.

She promised herself not to give up Doraliz. Jessica wouldn't make it through the night, but if she kept her mouth closed, Doraliz had a chance to start over.

Chapter 25

They pulled up to a high white wall in a neighborhood near the country club. Arched metal gates rose to seal an opening in the wall. The driver pressed the button on a speaker and said a few words. The gates slowly creaked open.

Jessica waited to pass through the gates of hell with blunted emotions. A normal person would have quaked in terror. Instead, her capacity for fear had seemingly transformed into the bravery of not giving a fuck. She'd die like she lived, stupidly hanging on to the badass version of herself that just didn't care.

One small piece of her mind hoped they wouldn't torture her. Mostly, she was just pissed off. Each mile they'd traveled in the huge vehicle fed her anger. She'd finally figured out what she wanted in life, and now this asshole would rip it all away. But that didn't mean she liked pain.

Ugly came around and opened the car door. She slid out of the vehicle and onto a cobblestone drive. An enormous house loomed over her. Who the hell was stupid enough to bring someone to their home for an interrogation? She answered her own question. Only someone with no fear of repercussions.

Would they kill her here? She assumed they'd shoot her, but that would be messy. Maybe that part wouldn't happen here. She would save her fear until they drove away. Now, she could channel her anger into the demon behind the door.

Forming a tall arc, the double doors opened wide before her. Jessica shuffled forward, braced by goons on either side. An executioner's song should have been playing. Something in heavy metal.

They walked her down a hallway and into a wood paneled room with oriental rugs covering Saltillo tile floors. Exotic animal heads filled the walls. Antelopes peered at her, adorned with every type of horn: curly, grooved, straight as spears. A boulder used as a pedestal displayed a stuffed cheetah. She saw a wild boar with curved tusks and a massive black animal with bony horns sitting atop its head like a wig. Water buffalo? Wildebeest? She had no idea. The death on exhibit seemed highly appropriate to tonight's task. Velasco had planned it this way.

Past the lair of dead animals, a large desk faced her. Empty now, Jessica imagined Velasco sitting there surveying his destruction and taking joy in each animal he'd killed.

Ugly led her to a chair in front of the desk. "Sit."

"Can you release my hands? I won't be able to sit with them behind my back."

"Sit," he commanded, his face growing even more grotesque.

Jessica perched on the edge of the chair, trying to relieve her arms from the awkward pain. She glanced over her shoulder and saw Ugly standing like a sentry behind her. Creepy, but everything about this room creeped her out.

Footsteps walked away from her, and the door behind her closed. Goon number two must be on his way to retrieve his highness. Silence followed, broken only by Ugly's heavy breathing and her own heartbeat. She searched herself for terror, but numbness and apathy prevailed.

The moments dragged on until she heard steps outside the room. The click of high heels slowed briefly near the door, then faded away at a fast clip.

Finally, voices and footfalls approached. The swish of the opening door reached her overly sensitive ears. Then, Ruben Velasco entered her field of vision.

He ambled leisurely around the desk and took a seat and steepled his fingers. "Miss Watts. Where is my daughter?"

Jessica glimpsed anger running under his skin like kerosene, threatening to ignite them all. His question had been neither tender nor caring.

"I have no idea. And I am no longer working for you. I assume you received the paperwork and money from my attorney?"

"Where is my daughter?" he repeated. This time, the underlying fury punctuated each syllable.

Jessica stood. Fuck this. She had no way out of this room, so why should she put up with one more second of his bullshit? She'd moved beyond numbness into the land of last stands. All she wanted now was for him to take her words to his grave.

"Sit down!" Velasco barked.

"Why? Are you going to threaten to kill me? Seems like the kidnapping did that for you."

"You have no idea how bad things can get for you." He sneered and tried to stare her down. "Tell me where she is. I know you found her. My wife received a call from her. Doraliz told her mother she would kill herself if we sent anyone else after her. Do you know how hard that is for a mother to hear?"

Jessica remained silent. Why had Doraliz called her mother? Perhaps to warn her to stay away. Or to let her know she was alive.

"You are going to tell me where she is." Velasco's palm slammed the wood of his desk.

"Fuck off."

Velasco jerked to his feet. "You will not talk to me like that." Rage-fueled spittle flew from his mouth. Then his eyes moved behind her. "Make her sit."

Strong arms grabbed her shoulders, pushing her back and down. The hands continued pressing after her butt hit the chair, fingers digging painfully into sore muscles. She refused to wince.

Velasco walked around to the front of the desk and slapped her. "You need to learn respect."

The side of her face stung, and she tasted blood. Elation zinged through her with the knowledge she'd struck him where it hurt. Ruben Velasco was worthless, a terrible father. Doraliz was right.

Jessica smiled slowly, letting the satisfaction ooze out of her. Maybe she'd lost her mind, but the chance to let loose fourteen years of pent-up vitriol filled her with joy. She chose her words carefully, hoping to land each blow. "Doraliz is lucky. She escaped and you'll never find her."

He raised his hand again.

"Do it, you filthy piece of shit," she yelled. "I have a father just as disappointing as you. You want to kill me, torture me, fine. All daughters of men like you are tortured every day of their painful lives. It would be a mercy not to deal with this shit anymore. Do whatever you want to me."

Releasing those words satisfied her more than a night of mind-blowing anonymous sex. The high surpassed three bottles of good tequila. She poured every scrap of hate she owned into her stare. And then she heard sirens.

Someone pounded on a door far away. A garbled voice came through a loudspeaker.

Velasco nodded at one of his men. When he opened the door, Jessica heard a woman's shriek. "La casa está en fuego!"

A fire in the house. Jessica turned in the chair, expecting to see flames. Perhaps the devil himself had arrived to burn this atrocity to the ground.

"Los bomberos estan adentro de la casa," the henchman at the door said.

Firemen. In the house. They'd find her. Good luck to Velasco trying to explain a zip-tied American in his trophy room. Although, he probably had the funds to buy them all off.

"Todos tienen que evacuar la casa inmediatamente." A voice from the loudspeaker ordered them to leave the house immediately.

"Get out now, before they find us." Velasco's voice rang with urgency.

"What about her?" Ugly seemed to be the only one still aware of Jessica's presence.

"Leave her," Velasco said. "Maybe she'll burn."

Stunned to silence, she watched them go. After the door closed, she heard the click of two locks turning. How ironic. Days ago, she'd been afraid of drowning in an ocean. Now it looked like fire would be her demise. There were definitely better ways to go.

A locked door, hands zip-tied behind her. Jessica stood and surveyed the room, searching for a way to escape. The marbled eyes of dead animals met her gaze. The only door remained double locked. This room was a cemetery. She shuddered, unable to push away the thought that she'd be cremated here with half the species of Africa.

Commotion outside the door continued. Mostly male voices, and none of them close. The room smelled of polished wood, dead animals, and her own sweat. No smoke. In this massive house, surely the firemen would contain the blaze before it reached her. Then what? Would Velasco continue his interrogation, or had he finished with her? She imagined a drive far into the desert that ended with a bullet. Escape loomed as deadly as the fire.

What would she be most sorry for? What was she afraid to leave behind? Angus. Tela. Her mother's tired face flitted before her. That couldn't be right.

The distinct sound of a key sliding into a lock came from the closed door. The lock turned. The sound repeated a second time. Then, the door swung open to an apparition in black. Yoga pants and a hoodie covered a svelte frame, and smooth pale skin shone beneath the drawn hood.

"Come quickly." Sra. Velasco's voice barely reached her.

Shocked by the strange twist, Jessica froze for a moment. Had Velasco decided he hadn't finished with her after all and sent his wife to retrieve his prey? Maybe, but it was a chance to survive at least a little longer.

"My hands." She turned her back to the woman, exposing her tied wrists.

Sra. Velasco dashed across the room, opened a desk drawer, and pulled out scissors. "Come here."

Jessica obeyed, and the woman cut through the plastic before returning the scissors to the drawer.

"You must come with me," Sra. Velasco said, dipping to grab the cut zip tie and stuffing it into a pocket.

"Where are you taking me?"

"I will help you escape."

The possibility seemed too much to hope for. "Why should I trust you?"

"I set the fire." Sra. Velasco stared into Jessica's eyes for a heartbeat, then strode toward the open door.

Jessica followed.

They turned down a long hallway, heading away from the front door. Shouts and bootsteps from the opposite direction gradually faded as they entered the labyrinth of the mansion. How far away could the fire have been set? She briefly wondered whether the home predated fire sprinkler codes or if those codes even existed in Mexico.

Her focus returned when Sra. Velasco opened a door to the right and entered a smaller hallway. Gone were the grand paintings on the walls. The carved and polished doorframes and baseboards had gone missing as well. This passage had simple white walls with plain wooden doors on either side every twelve feet or so. Sra. Velasco used a key to enter the last door on the right.

Inside, the room held a single bed and a small bookshelf. A crucifix with an eerily lifelike carving of Jesus hung on the wall. On the far side was another door. When Sra. Velasco pushed it open, the room filled with fresh, outside air.

Smoke stung Jessica's eyes as she followed Sra. Velasco onto a patio. A single light illuminated the blue water of a swimming pool on her right, while a long stretch of lawn lay to her left. At the far end, many yards away, several firefighters aimed a hose at the second floor of the home. Smoke billowed out the windows in a greater volume than the water shooting in. She couldn't see flames but a shifting yellow glow lit the far roofline.

"Quickly," Sra. Velasco said as she stepped toward a building on the far side of the patio.

Jessica paused, wondering if she should run toward the firemen and beg them to protect her. Could she possibly escape this nightmare?

As if he'd heard her thoughts, one of the firemen looked up and yelled at her. "Salgan de la casa! Es muy peligroso."

Yes, she wanted to get away from the house. She understood how excruciatingly dangerous it was, and it had nothing to do with fire.

"Nos vamos! We are leaving!" Sra. Velasco yelled toward the firemen with a quick wave.

Jessica's feet remained planted on the pool deck. Driven to save herself, she didn't know which way to run.

Sra. Velasco turned to Jessica. "I can't promise you safety with them." She nodded toward the firemen. "I will do my best to protect you if you come with me. But you must hurry."

"Why? Why did you do this? Why would you save me?"

"Because you are a daughter. And I failed with my own." Sra. Velasco turned and jogged toward the building at the far end of the patio. Instead of heading for the door, she slipped around back and disappeared.

"Oye," the fireman yelled, trying to get her attention.

Jessica glanced at him, then ran after Sra. Velasco.

She had to turn sideways to fit in the narrow space between the building and the high stucco wall. Two yards away, Sra. Velasco struggled to open a metal gate in the wall. Finally, the lock clicked open, and the hinges creaked as the door pushed outward.

Jessica followed her through the opening and stepped onto the lush grass of the Campestre golf course. As Sra. Velasco closed the gate behind her, the world seemed to fall silent, the noise of the firemen and their equipment muted by the wall between them. In the distance, more sirens approached.

"Come. And stay against the wall in case anyone is looking." Harsh and demanding, Sra. Velasco's voice pulled Jessica forward.

She tramped after the woman. The night hardly seemed real. First the panic of being stolen, then the odd lack of fear she'd had in front of Velasco. Even now, her body seemed to function unattached to her brain. Just take another step. Maybe the nightmare would end, and maybe she'd be thrust back into the worst part of it.

She could try running across the golf course, hoping to find safety, but Velasco would probably buy off anyone who found her. The woman in front of her had the only motivation that might save her. Family, that most treacherous of heartstrings.

They walked for what must have been a quarter of a mile. Sometimes the high walls of the monied elite gave them cover. Occasionally, they passed an empty lot, divided from the green golf course by a razor-wire-topped chain link fence. At one corner where fence and wall met, Sra. Velasco slipped into a gap where half the chain link curled away from the pole it should have attached to.

Jessica clawed her way after her. Her height made it difficult to squeeze through the low opening. Finally, she crawled through on her knees, dusting herself off once she'd made it.

"Are you okay?" Sra. Velasco asked, her voice low.

"Fine. How did you find this place?" Watching this bougie woman slinking around dirt fields and chain link fences definitely added personality to the picture Jessica had painted of the matriarch.

"Doraliz showed me."

Wow. On the boat, Doraliz hadn't had anything good to say about her mother, but clearly, she had tried, at least once, to help her mother escape.

They crossed the empty lot and arrived at an outcropping of brush and salt cedar, a many-trunked tree that resembled a hugely overgrown shrub. Sra. Velasco wound through the trunks, finally stepping onto one that shot out at a forty-five-degree angle, crushing the chain link fence beneath it. She dropped to the ground on the opposite side without making a sound.

Sra. Velasco should be the detective, Jessica thought as she clambered up the trunk, snagging her shirt on a branch that seemed to reach out and grab her. Once she untangled herself, she half jumped, half fell to the ground. Her palms smelled of bark and creosote.

Jessica turned at the sound of a vehicle on the road. A car without headlights approached. Just when they'd come so close.

Sra. Velasco waved the vehicle over.

Fear plunged through Jessica's stomach, shoving aside the fatalism that had accompanied her through the long night. She'd come so close to escaping, but this ratty old car came from the direction of the Velasco mansion. She pictured Ugly behind the wheel, and the cold black gun he kept in his waistband.

The car pulled beside them, and Sra. Velasco opened the back door and motioned Jessica inside. Jessica stooped to look through the driver's side window. The lined face of a Mexican grandmother, eyes tense with worry, greeted her. Relief and hope almost dropped her to the roadside. She still had a chance to make it through the night.

For a second, she wondered whether she should make a run for it, but Sra. Velasco's intentions seemed true. But why would she put herself at risk to help?

"You set the fire?" Jessica asked once she'd settled into the car that now trundled down the road.

"Please, do not speak of this," Sra. Velasco replied.

Jessica almost laughed at the woman's sudden return to formality. Each minute of this night seemed more absurd than the last. "Why? And where are we going?"

"We will take you to the border. You'll have to walk from there."

"Why are you helping me? I can't imagine your husband is going to be happy about this."

Sra. Velasco looked at Jessica for a long moment. She dropped a hand to Jessica's knee and her impenetrable mask dropped with it. The cold from the woman's fingers seeped through the denim of Jessica's jeans, making her want to pull away.

Sra. Velasco removed her hand, glaring at it as if it had betrayed her. Her face closed. The awkward moment passed. Jessica recognized herself in the woman's inability to use intimate gestures with the ease of most people. They traveled the dark road in silence.

"To be a mother is to fail," Sra. Velasco said, throwing the words into the silent car. "I hear my friends talk, and they all carry guilt about their children. But none of them have failed as I have. I deserved to lose my daughter. She asked for my help over and over. Instead of listening, I tried to force her to become someone she would have hated. Someone like me."

The words bore resignation, not the anguish Jessica expected underneath the polished veneer. She stared at the woman with her fully made-up face and every hair in place under her hoodie. Only her eyes, vast pools of regret, betrayed her emotions.

"You're not the only bad mother out there." The words slipped out before Jessica could stop them. Before she realized this was a hand she ought not bite.

Sra. Velasco's eyes narrowed. "I know Clarice Watts. Yes, she is another spectacularly bad mother."

Jessica started at her mother's name. "How?" She stopped. She couldn't fathom what question could possibly explain this situation.

"We knew each other socially. I know what she did to you, it was quite the scandal back in the day. Everyone talked about it. I like to think I would have never left my daughter. Of course, I was such a bad mother that my daughter left me instead."

Jessica hoped she wouldn't ask about Doraliz. She would never share information about her that could get back to Velasco. Tonight, she finally understood how horrible the man truly was, how driven to control the people around him.

"I don't know what Doraliz thought of you as a mother," she lied. "But your husband is true evil."

"Yes. But I lay in that bed long ago."

Jessica almost smiled at the appropriate turn of phrase. But the reality of her world, now that she had presumably survived the night, didn't allow for smiles. Velasco would keep coming after her until she told him about Doraliz. Or died. Of course, if he ever did get the truth out of her, he'd likely kill her anyway.

She'd have to disappear. The way Doraliz had.

A wave of regret spilled through her body as she realized all she'd give up. Angus. Any hope of a career helping others. Her friends. Whatever tenuous relationship she'd started to rebuild with her parents. Tears slid down her cheeks, the loss too great to contain. She wouldn't have missed them if she'd died, but to go on living and lose them still was too much.

"He'll never stop harassing me."

"He will." Sra. Velasco's voice was firm.

"He won't." The calmness that had kept her sane early in the night departed, and Jessica struggled to keep from sobbing.

"Jessica, listen to me. I have planned for this. He will not bother you again, as long as you do not come back to Juarez."

"But—" Jessica started to protest, then closed her mouth. She needed to give this woman a chance to explain.

"You cannot be married to a man like that for thirty years without learning his ways. I know too much. I've spent years, decades, gathering damning information on my husband. I have plans in place to distribute it if something happens to me. You are now covered by this insurance policy."

"What?" Such a strange way to live, but if it worked . . . Jessica wondered if the information went back to her father's time. His crime. Too many thoughts flew through her head, and she could only stare at Sra. Velasco in wonder.

"If anything happens to you, or to me, the world will learn how truly evil my husband is. And, more important than that, the information will go to the right people in the US government. They would have enough to extradite him, and he will never let that happen."

Jessica let her words sink in. Doraliz's mother had thought of everything. "Wow. You're kind of a badass."

"No. I am no better than he is. I've just learned to play his game."

Jessica had seriously underestimated this woman. And she knew exactly how she could help. "There's one more thing. Tomás Garcia."

"Doraliz told me. There are many ways to take care of someone like that. I could tell my husband. I could have him married off. I will deal with it, and I promise he will never bother Doraliz again."

They rode in silence until the car pulled up to a street corner near the downtown bridge to El Paso. Sra. Velasco had turned to stone, and Jessica practically held her breath waiting for the plan to come undone.

"Go. You're on your own from here," Sra. Velasco said as soon as the car came to a complete stop. "And remember, you cannot come back to

Juarez. The city's reputation as a place where women go missing covers all kinds of crimes. I cannot protect you here."

"Thank you, I—"

"Go. I should have taken a risk like this for my own daughter. It is too late for that." For the first time, Sra. Velasco's voice cracked.

"You can come with me. You can disappear." It had worked once.

"Go!" Sra. Velasco waved Jessica out of the car as her tears began to fall. Jessica heard the muffled wail of a broken woman as the vehicle drove away.

Chapter 26

Jessica stood on a street corner, unceremoniously dumped into a crisp night and the rest of her life. She could turn south, toward oblivion and the dangers of the past. To the east and west lay the unknown, adventures she couldn't foresee. But she turned north, toward home.

Too much had happened in one night. The certainty of death, the driving urge to wound Velasco with her words, and finally, an absurd rescue by a woman she hadn't considered an ally. And now, what?

She trudged up the bridge that spanned a dry riverbed. Decimated by drought, the mighty Rio Grande of lore and song had disappeared here, its remnants stashed hundreds of miles away in a New Mexico reservoir. She longed for it to flow again, to wash away years of grime and bring new life.

At the apex of the bridge, she stopped. The soft, glittering lights of civilization stretched along the bends of the riverbed and climbed the hills to the mountains. The herby scent of the desert at night filled her lungs with piñon, creosote, and sage. She belonged here.

This place had made her, forged her from the heat of hot summer days and the fire of a burning mansion. But she'd been tempered by the water of the blue Caribbean Sea, and the tendrils of love that she'd discovered made people both stronger and weaker than she'd ever imagined.

She let the night fill her with its quiet light. This was her origin story. Not the emotional teenager angry at life and parents, or the woman who survived on tequila and strangers. She could discard them on this bridge. She was someone different now.

Jessica lifted her arms to the sky and the power of who she'd become. She could be both steel and water. She'd use her sharp edges and cutting knowledge to help women like herself and Doraliz. She'd collect their stories and guide them through their own fires.

But she could also become more liquid and fill herself and others with the love they deserved. She'd always thought love was a risk, something one gave for the purpose of ripping it away. Instead, it grew and spread. Love, like water, resided deep underground, feeding the desert. It surrounded her in the air, sometimes falling as tears, other times as rain. She only had to open herself to it and drink.

She took a solemn step forward down the slope of the bridge. Much needed to change. Today she would apply to law school, after a shower and sleep. The slope plunged steeper as she walked, bringing her future closer. She would call Alma today and start working as soon as possible, tomorrow if she could. The steel in her brightened with the desire to learn the stories of the women she'd help, women like Doraliz, like herself, but with fewer means and bigger obstacles. She'd master new skills and make their lives better, make her home better. She'd remake herself into someone she could be proud of.

She'd show up for her friends with more than a six-pack and a bag of chips. She would connect to people in new and more responsible ways. Knitting herself into a community wouldn't weaken her. She was steel and water and nothing would take that away.

Jessica stopped. Her chest crushed with understanding. Life had stripped her mother of the things she'd loved most, not just people but her identity and power. That could break a person.

Filling her lungs with air, Jessica straightened her spine and took another step toward life. She would mend this relationship. She'd visit her parents again, this time not to seek retribution or relive the wrongs of the past, but just to get to know them and help where she could. They weren't a weakness; they'd made her strong.

She neared the border station which glowed bright with fluorescent lights. Her step quickened, a better life drew her forward. But as much as she wanted to run into the future, she couldn't leave the past entirely behind. She paused just before the arc of the bridge flattened to solid ground and looked back at Juarez. It had been a bright, shining world of opportunity once, and Jessica had seized it. She regretted having it cut from her life, but she would not go back, at least not until Velasco had died from old age or treachery. Juarez hadn't failed her. She had lost her way, always pressing forward, all attitude and no map. It would have happened anywhere.

She turned back to El Paso. She had one more item to add to her list, and she could accomplish it tonight. There was no future without Angus.

She opened the glass door to the station, empty except for one lone agent. He stared at her with unfriendly eyes. Short, with thick muscles and close-cropped hair, he wore his uniform with military conceit.

Jessica had planned on asking if she could use his cell phone, but this guy looked like he'd have more questions than she wanted to answer. She'd hate to end up in a police station explaining a kidnapping. The urge to protect Sra. Velasco kept her lips sealed tight. That woman would pay enough for what she'd done.

A few more steps through a turnstile and metal detector, and she would leave a part of herself behind. She had liked that woman, the tough girl who'd created a job out of relationships and bravado. She'd paused halfway to the border guard, stretched between the past and the future. He stared at her, suspicion etched across his face.

"Is there a problem here?" he asked when she finally approached. He crossed his arms in front of his chest.

Jessica shook her head. "No, no problem." She slunk forward, making her way through the metal detector.

"Citizenship?"

"US." She pulled her passport card from her wallet. She'd been lucky. If they'd kidnapped her just a few minutes later, she'd probably have already taken her wallet out of her pocket. God knows how long she'd have been stuck here with this guy.

"What were you doing in Mexico?"

"Visiting downtown." She tried to keep the frustration from her voice. Questions were unusual when you looked and sounded American.

"It's kind of late to be coming back alone."

Jessica stared at him. What was she supposed to do? Turn back time to a more appropriate hour?

"Have you been drinking? Doing drugs?" he asked.

"You aren't allowed to ask me questions like that." She kept herself from adding 'asshole' to the end of the statement.

"I am allowed to search you."

"Go for it," she said, spreading her arms wide. She had nothing on her but a wallet, and her tank top and blue jeans were form-fitting enough to leave little to the imagination.

"Get out of here." He sneered and nodded toward the exit.

Man, there were jerks everywhere. One more hurdle crossed. It had been an easy one for her, but as she looked to the future, she realized she'd cross his type again. Next time, she'd be helping someone who couldn't easily mouth off to the authorities without dire consequences.

She glanced at a clock on the wall as she left. Midnight. Now she just had to figure out how to get home.

A vestige of her earlier self wanted to walk to her favorite downtown hole-in-the-wall bar and wrap her fingers around the familiar comfort of a shot glass. But the relief of the bottle only helped short term. No more postponing the future.

She walked instead to the closest downtown hotel. Plodding down four blocks of closed storefronts, she passed metal grates that protected plate glass windows but didn't conceal the voluminous quinciñera dresses, rows of blue jeans, and spectacular variety of cowboy boots on display. She loved this part of El Paso, where during the day, the streets brimmed with shoppers from Mexico. Tonight, she was alone, save for two homeless men, one lying under a flat piece of cardboard, the other asleep in a blanket. She had so much to be thankful for.

She crossed the street to enter the Paso del Norte Hotel, its hundred-year-old brick façade frosted with concrete scrollwork. The poshest hotel in town, the lobby soared two stories with salmon-colored granite walls and white marble floors. Even in the middle of the night, two receptionists sat behind the high check-in counter.

Jessica approached the friendlier of the two, a Hispanic man about her age who smiled when he saw her. The middle-aged woman next to him couldn't keep the judgment out of her eyes, despite her closed-lipped smile.

"Hi, would it be possible for me to borrow a cell phone? I need to call someone to come pick me up."

The man looked at her quizzically for a moment but reached for his pocket. The woman next to him, Miranda, according to her badge, spoke up. "Are you a guest of the hotel?"

"Well, if I were, I probably wouldn't need a ride home." Screw her and her disapproval.

"This hotel is for guests." Miranda glared at her counterpart, whose hand held a cell phone suspended between the two women.

"Honey, I've dropped more cash in your bar," Jessica tipped her head to the ornate lounge capped with a Tiffany dome, "than you probably make in a month."

Miranda harrumphed, then pursed her lips and looked away.

Jessica turned back to the guy. "Jesus," she said, reading his nametag. Fitting, she needed a little help from Jesus right now. "I've had a terrible night, and an ugly brute from Juarez destroyed my phone. Please help me. I just want to go home."

Jesus frowned but placed his phone on the counter. "Thank you," she said. Then she thanked god that Angus hadn't changed his phone number in over a decade. She pressed the keypad from memory.

"Hello?" Angus asked, his voice sleepy.

"It's me."

"Hey, how's it going?"

She smiled into the phone even though he couldn't see her. There was no rebuke in his tone, no annoyance, no blame, despite the late hour and strange phone number. He just wanted to know how she was.

"Well, I can pretty much promise you this will be the last time I call you needing something in the middle of the night. I'm at the Paso del Norte Hotel. I need a ride home."

"No car? Have you been drinking?"

Fair question given her history. "No, not since dinner with Sarah and Luz. Velasco's men got me and took me to Juarez, but I'm free now."

"Free?"

She could tell her story confused him. It likely would have confused anyone, even if they hadn't just woken up from a dead sleep. "Yeah, I'll tell you all about it. Can you come get me?"

"Sure. I'll be there in fifteen minutes."

"Thanks." Jessica pushed the button to end the call. A wave of emotion buffeted her, threatening a breakdown. She hadn't slept since she'd left her parent's house, and that seemed like a lifetime ago. She had to hold it together just a little longer.

"Thanks," she whispered in a husky voice as she set the phone back on the counter.

She made her way to a leather wingback chair that faced the circular drive. Each second took a minute to pass as she attempted to contain her thoughts. A flash of blue ocean linked to a blue house and her mother's blue eyes. Shut it down. No thoughts, just breathing. The golden grass on the drive to Fort Davis, Angus traveling the same path to find her, then heading in a new direction without her. She steered her mind away from the sense of loss. Inhale. The smell of smoke then cedar on a strange Juarez night. The desolation of Sra. Velasco's cry as she drove away. Exhale.

Each tortured thought tried to bury her, but she pushed them away. From this moment on, things would get better. She couldn't help Doraliz or repay Sra. Velasco for her unexpected bravery. But she could still save herself. And she would learn to help others as well.

Twin lights shone in the black night, drawing nearer. Angus's dumpy car pulled into the posh drive and emotion billowed through her. This was everything. Why had she never seen that? Like Shaggy pulling up in the Mystery Machine, he always arrived to save her right on time.

Knights in shining armor dimmed by comparison, and she even had her own little Scooby sidekick.

These were the good times. She just hadn't chosen to see it that way.

She threw herself into the car and squeezed Angus tight. "Thank you for picking me up. I love you."

Angus pulled back from the awkward embrace. "Hey, are you okay?"

"Beyond okay. Things got crazy, and I was afraid I was going to die, that Velasco would have his henchmen kill me. But I wasn't really afraid, I was just pissed off. I don't know how to explain it. But then Sra. Velasco lit the house on fire and saved me. And now you're here. You saved me." The words tore out of her in a single breath.

"Slow down. They kidnapped you, and then someone lit a house on fire?" Angus put the car in park and turned the engine off before shifting to face her.

"Yes, but none of that matters. I want a better life. I want a life with you, and I want to do the hard good things that will help others deal with crappy situations." She babbled mindlessly like a drunk, pure conviction pushing her on. "I don't really have to change. I can still be a bitch when I need to be, and I'll have to work hard and won't make any money for a while, but I can help people. There are lots of Velascos out there, lots of women who get abandoned or escape. I can help them."

"So, you're going to use your powers for good?" Angus's brows lifted at the question, but a smile played at the corners of his lips.

She chuckled. "Yes, I'm going to use my evil powers for good. But it only works if you're there to help me."

She sighed, the rest of the world falling away. Angus was the missing piece of her puzzle. He'd been there all along, and she'd picked him up over and over again. Toyed with him, then put him aside.

How had she been so cruel? The thought plunged into her heart. No wonder he'd pushed away her latest advances. He deserved better. "I'm so sorry for how I treated you. Please tell me it's not too late for us."

His smile faded. "I'm done with games. And I'm not sure exactly what you're asking for. We'll always be friends, but if you want more than that, you're going to have to spell it out."

Shit. It was one thing to talk about the future or to take small steps like a new job or a grad school application. But he was right, a better life required commitment. She'd made promises to herself on that bridge. It was time to see them through.

She took his hands in hers, kissed one set of knuckles and then the other. Her love flowed through her fingers into him and then seemed to swirl around them. When she looked into his eyes, her love lit the air between them. All this time she'd kept it bottled up inside, denying them both happiness. No more. "Angus, will you marry me?"

His eyes grew big, but the rest of him stayed stock still. "What?" he finally blurted.

"Angus Delgado, will you marry me? Just you and me, forever. Or as long as we both shall live." Ironic to say that on a night when she'd been so sure of dying. Her stomach squeezed as the moments passed. She had earned his delayed reaction.

His face lost any hint of a smile. "If I say yes, that means no more bars, no more men. That would kill me." The last sentence came out in a whisper.

"Angus, I don't want to be with anyone else. I'm not sure I ever did. I just had to keep torturing myself for some reason." She stopped. If she was going to change, she needed to start by being honest. "I've been so afraid. Afraid of recreating something bad that would hurt other people, the way my parents hurt me. So, I hurt myself instead. I had a gaping hole that I tried to fill with tequila and sex. I know so much more now."

Understanding came to her in a flash. "Family created that hole, and family is the only thing that can fill it. It's a fucked-up world out there. As bad as my dad is, he's nothing like Velasco. And my mom. Sra. Velasco told me that mothers always fail their children. But I think most of the time they love them the best they can. I don't know. I'm sure I won't get the future perfectly right, but I know it will be better with you than without you."

She looked into his eyes, trying to shape her jumbled thoughts into something he could recognize and latch on to. Something that would last forever.

"You are the best thing in my life. You are my home, my family. I see that now. I don't know if you can make it past all the times I hurt you, and I can't promise I won't hurt you again. But I can promise I'll never cheat on you. And I can promise that I will love you until they bury me. That would have happened anyway, I just finally realized how to take care of that love."

There it was, her heart cracked open in front of him, waiting for his decision. She'd survive either way, but she had never let herself want anything this much before.

"How about this Friday at happy hour?" he asked, a grin returning to his lips.

"Or maybe we could do it in Fort Davis so my parents could be there."

"Wow," he reached out and stroked her cheek. "You really are ready."

And she was.

THE END

———

To join Kathryn Dodson for updates, events, book info, and more, visit www.KathrynDodson.com.

Other novels by Kathryn Dodson
The Jessica Watts Southwest Suspense Series
She's not a cop. She's not a PI. She's the woman who won't walk away.

Jessica Watts is haunted, reckless, and relentless when it comes to uncovering the truth. From missing women to buried bodies, every case drags her deeper into secrets that could destroy her. And some secrets are deadlier than the truth.

———

Unfinished Business: Stories of Bold Women
Midlife isn't the end of your story—it's the plot twist.
Meet a series of extraordinary women who prove that life's most powerful chapters are written after 50. In this compelling collection, discover what happens when women stop asking permission and start taking action. Three novels about what comes next.

Portrait of Deception
A photographer on the brink of fame. A dictator with a fatal agenda. A terrifying trap she may not escape.

About the Author

Kathryn Dodson grew up writing and riding horses in far West Texas. She graduated from SMU in English/Creative Writing and went on to get an MBA from Thunderbird and a PhD from Clemson.

She has worked on both sides of the US/Mexico border and has held jobs with governments, chambers of commerce, and other businesses. Now she spends her days writing about interesting women in fascinating places.

Join Kathryn for updates and extras at www.KathrynDodson.com.

NOVELS
Tequila Midnight
The Podcast Chronicles
Portrait of Deception

Acknowledgements

First and foremost, thank you for finding and reading this novel. Readers give my words meaning, and I hope you enjoyed Jessica's journey.

You'd think writing would be lonely, with an author holed up somewhere with only a laptop and an endless supply of coffee. Fortunately, that hasn't been my experience. I'm online writing with friends almost every day. This includes the Same Story Different Year crew (Maggie, Barb, Sarah, Sarah, Lynn, Sandy, Beth, Renita, Tara, and Julia). I also write with my early morning NaNoWriMo group (thanks Michelle) and am a Tuesday regular at WFWA (thanks Michele).

Christine Adler, Orly Konig Lopez, and Nancy Yeager have been generous with their time and moral support. I have the world's most amazing critique partners, Claudia Armann and Sydney Clark. And this book wouldn't have made it into the world without weekly check-ins with Jocelyn Lindsay.

Finally, I'd like to thank my family who have supported me in ways too numerous to count. Mom and Dad, sorry about all the sex and drinking in this novel. Tom, your love makes me strong, and you are the opposite of Tomás. Jack, you believed in me more than anyone else, thank you.